PREFACE

FREE DOWNLOAD

Sign up for my newsletter and receive a free Jamie McFarlane starter library.

To get started, please visit:

http://www.fickledragon.com

1 / MASK

Vᴜᴋ Sᴇʀᴠʏ ᴀᴅᴊᴜsᴛᴇᴅ his baseball cap and kept his eyes downcast, avoiding the security camera mounted high on the wall.

"Can I help you find something?"

Servy scanned the soft face of an older man, still careful not to look up at the camera. The employee wore a red apron with the name *Hank* scrawled in sharpie on the front.

"Raccoon traps?" Servy asked, giving Hank his best smile and adopting a slight southern accent. "Missus is having trouble with them digging up her garden."

"Are you sure it's raccoons?" Hank asked. "They're not really known for poaching gardens. And 'coon season is done end of February. I'm afraid you're out of luck for this year."

Servy's smile faded as Hank rambled on. Scanning the store, he slipped a hand into his pocket. His fingers closed around the smooth metal of his knife. They were alone. It would take no effort to flip the blade out, slide it under Hank's chin and stop the man's incessant chirping.

He broke from his reverie as a lanky young girl, probably ten or so, appeared from around the end of the farthest aisle. Under her cowboy hat he could see she was pretty, with long sandy-blonde hair and a ruddy face that suggested she wasn't a stranger to working outside. Of course, why would she be? He was in ranch country. His mind drifted to what she might look like without quite so much ...

"Can you add this to our tab, Mr. Billings? Mom's in a hurry," the girl said, holding up a bundle of braided rope. "It's the fifty-footer."

"Sure thing, April," Hank said. "Give her my best."

The girl looked innocently at Servy, but when her eyes met his, she took a step back. "Uh, sure," she said and skipped toward the door.

"Who's that?" Servy asked.

"Uh, April Hudson," Hank answered, obviously uncomfortable with the question. "Family runs Hootskill bar on the edge of town."

"Pretty little girl," Servy said.

"I suppose. She's only ten, though." The bell above the door rang again and Hank turned to the front. "Be just a minute," he called loudly. "Where were we?"

Irritation soured Servy's stomach. The old man could barely keep a thought in his head. How easy it would be to put him out of his misery.

"Traps," he said, forcing a thin smile onto his face.

"Bottom of the stairs, at the end of aisle five," Hank said, frowning. "Hunting section is the whole back wall."

Servy replayed the conversation in his head as he walked away from the man. What had he said? He was normally so good at fooling the simpletons of the world. Was it his comment about the girl? How could an old troll like Hank not see what a sweet thing she was? Of course, he probably did see it. That was the problem with people these days, they were always so damn politically correct. It wasn't like he'd told Hank what he really wanted to do to her. He grinned, imagining the look on Hank's face.

In the hunting section, Servy found Hank's thin supply of traps. On the highest shelf was exactly what he was looking for: a big wire cage. Stepping on the lowest shelf, he jumped up and dragged it off, showering himself with dust. The tattered price tag read forty-two dollars and the description on the faded paper stapled to the mesh suggested the trap was good for a variety of small to medium-size animals.

"Find what you're looking for?" Hank asked as Servy set the cage on the front counter.

He forced a smile back onto his face and nodded. Seriously? He'd brought the cage up and put it in front of the man. What did Hank expect him to say? *No? I didn't find what I was looking for, but I decided to buy this anyway?* Through gritted teeth he finally managed, "I was thinking about it. You're probably right. It's not a raccoon. Maybe rabbits."

"Well, this trap is a bit big for rabbits," Hank said, starting to remove the trap as he walked from behind the counter.

Servy slammed his hand on top of the trap. "No. This is what I want."

"Okay." Hank tipped his head back to position his reading glasses so he could read the price.

"Hootskill Bar, you said?" Servy asked as Hank counted back change from the fifty he'd provided.

"The Hudsons?"

Servy pushed down the anger at Hank's question. Every idea that entered the doddering old man's head slipped away as quickly as it arrived. With disgust, he pulled the cage from the counter and stalked out, no longer caring if he got an answer.

A brisk wind caught the trap as Servy exited the hardware store, swinging him around. He smiled, believing the force to be the same unseen hand that had awakened him so many years ago. Once again, he was being pushed down the right path. He looked up and caught sight of a small pen of wire fencing set up in front of the drugstore. Hay spilled from the enclosure and the chubby leg of a puppy poked out onto the walk.

He strode forward with purpose, whistling happily to himself. Hank had nearly pushed him over the edge, but he'd remained strong. Now his discipline was being rewarded. A young mother in coveralls, smelling of cow shit, looked up and spoke. He was unable to hear her words over the equally bad smelling child whimpering in the cold. A cardboard sign hung from the cage – *Lab / Border Collie*, $200. There was only one puppy left in the makeshift kennel.

Servy pushed his friendliest smile onto his face. "Sorry. I only have a hundred-fifty," he said to her, yelling over the child.

He could tell he'd won before she even spoke. "No papers. She's not pure-bred and she's not spayed neither."

The sign clearly said *Lab / Border Collie*. Shit, how he hated simple people. Their stink, their grammar and worst of all, how they overstated the obvious. "I just need to put this in my car." He lifted the cage to show her.

"I was just about to give up for the day," she said.

"Little guy is probably getting cold. Why don't you start your car and get it warmed up?" he said. "I'll load up the pup. That way I can help you tear down."

The woman gave him a relieved look. "That would be super. I'm parked around the corner in the alley."

Servy set the cage on the sidewalk and reached for the sleeping puppy. "Now, what should we name you?" he asked, noticing the woman giving him a suspicious look.

"You're not going to keep him in that cage, are you?" she asked.

"Just to help me get him home," Servy said. "It's actually a trap. We have rabbit problems. The trap helps me keep 'em alive until I move them somewhere else."

"Oh, like a park or something?" she asked.

"Exactly." Kneeling, he gently slid the puppy into the trap.

The woman smiled, her concern dissipating. "I'll be right back. I'm so glad you came along."

"My pleasure," he reached into his pocket and pulled out his wallet. "I'll get your money ready."

At the last moment, as the woman turned the corner into the alley, she looked back questioningly. Servy smiled and waved, his hands clasped behind his back. Satisfied, she disappeared into the alley. He counted to five, picked up the cage, and walked off.

"THE CORRAL IS JUST another mile over the next ridge." Faith Hudson sat tall in the saddle, urging her Paint, Vegas, forward as the trail narrowed. Between her broad-brimmed cowboy hat and the long-tailed leather coat which flared out over the horse's rear quarter, she could have easily been from a different century.

"I can't believe you're making us go camping in March." April, Faith's ten-year-old daughter, scooted her small chestnut Appaloosa around us, taking the lead. Like Faith, April was tall for her age, thin and full of attitude.

"Forty-five degrees, nothing but blue sky and a thousand square miles of virgin forest," I called after April's back. "This is living, kid."

El Chubby snorted in derision at being passed but settled as the hill steepened. I loosened my grip on the reins to give him his head as he muscled his way up. April was right. We were pushing camping season a little, but I could think of no place I'd rather be than in the pristine hills of Sage Creek National Forest.

"You were a lot cooler when your leg was shot and you liked watching TV," April lobbed back.

Diva, my German Shephard, took that moment to join the conversation and barked, running next to the path to catch up with

April. I smiled. There was just something about kids and dogs. Ever since I'd met Faith and introduced Diva to April, they'd become best friends. It'd taken some work to get the horses comfortable with Diva but then, according to Faith, that's what owning horses is all about.

The radio on my belt crackled. I promised Acting Sheriff Gene Ellis that I'd carry a radio, even though I was supposed to be off-duty for the weekend. I twisted the fine-tuning knob and caught the end. "... Butte-Base. Over."

We'd agreed on a frequency for contact and while I was disappointed, I wasn't particularly surprised. Ellis was a good man, but he wasn't a leader and needed help when things turned sideways. Faith looked over her shoulder. She must have heard the radio and I smiled apologetically. She gave me a reassuring look and turned back to the trail.

"Butte-Base, this is Butte-2. Over," I called.

"Biggs, can you hear me okay?" Gene sounded like he was yelling into the radio, but it was good because he was breaking up.

"Go ahead, Gene," I said. "I've got you five-by-five. Over."

"Biggs, I got a call from Ranger White," he said. "He's not far from your location. Maybe a few miles. They've run into something and need us to take a look. Are you in any position to take a run over to the old Gold Camp?"

National forest land was the purview of the U.S. Forest Service, which was federal. Ranger Jasper White worked for the state. In and of itself, the crossover wasn't uncommon and sometimes the poorly funded federal rangers would bring in State Game and Fish. When Game and Fish called the sheriff's department, however, that typically meant someone had discovered the one thing strictly under the control of the local sheriff – a dead body.

"I'm not sure where that's at," I said, "but I have a map. We've only got a couple hours of daylight left. Does he want to meet tonight? Over."

"That's affirmative," Ellis answered. "Something's got Jasper pretty worked up."

"Understood," I said. "Butte-2, out."

"What was that all about?" Faith asked, slowing so I could catch up with her.

"You ever hear of a place called Gold Camp?"

"Sure. It's a few miles over on Bald Ridge," she said. "I used to camp there with dad when I was younger. Why?"

"Game and Fish have something going on over there. Ellis needs me to meet them. We can set up camp and then I'll head over."

"Hold up, April," Faith pulled her Paint to a halt. She flung a long leg around the rear of the horse, slid to the ground, plucking a battered map from her saddlebags.

I jumped down, grabbed Vegas' reins and held them with mine. "What's up?"

"It's going to be dark in three hours," she said. "We should change our plans and go directly to Gold Camp. You'd never make it back and I don't like you being on trail in the dark."

I nodded. "I'm sorry, Faith. I don't think Gene would call if it wasn't important."

Faith smiled, her weathered face beautiful in the brilliant afternoon sun. "Camping's all about adventure. What's a couple more miles?"

"Aww, are you serious?" April complained, having joined us. "My butt's starting to hurt."

"I'm sorry, April. Ranger White has something going on over near Gold Camp," I said.

She lifted her eyebrows as if she knew she had me. "You're gonna owe me."

"What's the bill, boss?" I asked.

"You and me. *Ranchers* and pizza," she said, grinning. "Next Friday after 4-H."

"That show is so bad," Faith said. "I can't see why you guys like it so much."

"It'll have to be Saturday. I've got the basketball game in Hemingford on Friday," I said.

"Then you better bring ice cream," she called over her shoulder as she sashayed back to her horse.

"She's so sassy," Faith said. "I was never that bad."

"I'll bet," I said, loading back onto El Chubby.

After half a mile, the hill we'd been climbing for much of the day eased and we reached what had been our destination, simply denoted as Corral-2E on the National Forest map. While very rustic, the campground provided a well-maintained wood-planked horse corral with a hand pump for water.

"We should stop and let the horses rest." Faith turned off and approached the corral. "We might not have good access to water over at Gold Camp."

I'd been distracted for the last part of the ride, busy mulling over different reasons Ranger White might need my help. Most likely, a hiker had gotten lost and died of exposure. The thing was, if there were no suspicious circumstances, White would have already taken pictures and arranged to bring the body down. He wouldn't need me. I sighed. I felt the urge to keep going, but I also knew better than to push. Faith was putting the horses first and I couldn't fault her.

"Last one there has to pump," April said, giggling as she ran through the hardened snowpack. Where the sun hadn't been able to penetrate the thick pines, several inches of crusted snow remained.

Her exuberance pulled me from my thoughts and I chased after her. "You forgot the bucket," I taunted, touching the pump well after she did.

She tugged at a nearby wooden trough, attempting to free it from the ice around its base. "Don't need one, silly."

"You were saying?"

"Just help me," she implored.

I did as she commanded, but it was clear the heavy piece wasn't going anywhere.

"You might want to start pumping," Faith said, setting a large rubber bucket under the spout. "These wells are deep."

After twenty strokes I made no progress. "Are you sure this works?"

Faith poured water from a bottle into an opening next to the handle. "Sometimes we have to prime it. Keep pumping."

I felt resistance when the water finally made it to the pipe. Another thirty strokes later a thin stream finally trickled down the spout.

"You're getting it." April sat on the frozen trough, her voice playful and mocking. Diva had found her and the two were tussling.

I felt a sense of accomplishment when the next stroke brought a large splash of water.

Faith leaned against the corral, watching me work. "Thinking about that call?"

"Probably not something you want April to see," I said. "I hope whatever happened was not right at the camp."

"There are some cabins half a mile down," she said. "We could hole up there."

"What can't I see?" April asked.

"Cop things." Faith gave her daughter a look.

"I've seen dead stuff before." April was right. Death was just another part of life for those who chose a rural lifestyle, especially when it came to animals.

"I don't really know what's going on." I said, straightening.

"I haven't heard any helicopters or seen any ATVs behind us on the open parts of the trail," Faith said. "If you don't come up the back way like we did, the closest trailhead is at least ten miles from the camp. Can't be anything too big, can it?"

I knew better than to speculate. I'd seen horrific things as a ranger in the Army and then as the first on the scene at accidents. Anticipation only made it worse.

"Closest Fed helicopter is up in Rapid City," I said, focusing on El Chubby as he pulled water from the bucket.

Next thing I knew, a hand grabbed my waist. Faith had come up next to me. "Where'd you go just then?" she asked.

I shrugged, looking past her to where April and Diva were playing in the snow. Somedays I wished I were a dog. Diva had seen as much action as I had, but it never seemed to weigh on her.

"They're having a good time," I said, nodding at the source of laughter and barking up ahead.

"You're changing the subject."

"I guess."

Faith placed a hand on my cheek so I couldn't look away. "What do you see when you look at April?"

I didn't love talking about my feelings, but Faith had a way of pulling them out of me. "She's so happy. I hope that never changes."

Faith pulled her hat off, leaned in and kissed me lightly. It felt like sunshine. We'd been taking the relationship slowly and the kiss was welcome, if unexpected. Having come from an abusive past, Faith wasn't quick to trust and I had no issues with her in the driver's seat.

"Ewww," April said, running up next to us. "I hope you guys aren't going to be doing *that* the whole time!"

I chuckled and pulled away from Faith to fill the bucket again.

"Load up, April," Faith said a few minutes later.

With a lighter heart, I loaded up and fell in behind, watching as the two women who had somehow become the most important people in my life pushed down the trail.

＝

"Camp looks empty," Faith said, standing up in her stirrups.

We'd been on a slow descent for the last mile and the sun was getting low in the late afternoon sky. Sunshine had given way to clouds and it felt like we might be in for some snow, although weather reports suggested it wouldn't add up to much.

I urged El Chubby forward, bringing me even with Faith. Standing just off the trail, a weathered brown sign read Corral-3E on one line and Gold Camp on the second.

"Four-wheeler tracks up here." April wheeled around and urging her Appaloosa onto a trail that disappeared into the forest. I wasn't surprised at her curiosity, but my gut told me I didn't want her anywhere near whatever was going on. Fortunately, Faith must have felt the same way.

I swung a leg off and landed with a soft thud on the dirt trail. For a moment, I watched in admiration as Faith gave chase. Where riding was effort for me, Faith and her horse moved as one, seeming to float across the trail.

El Chubby nickered and pawed at the dirt. I didn't read horse that well, but I assumed he was chastising me for not seeing to his needs as efficiently as he'd have liked. I walked him to the wood fence of the corral and led him through the gate, pulling the packhorse I'd been leading for most of the trip close behind.

I stretched and looked at the sky that was turning grayer by the minute. We were in for bad weather and my senses suggested we'd get more snow than the weather service had suggested. I even thought I could see small flakes falling, although the wind could have been carrying old bits from nearby trees.

I unloaded El Chubby first and set my saddle on the fence. Most of our gear was strapped to the packhorse and it took several minutes to transfer the items to a pile outside the fence. Once done, I drew water and set to rubbing both horses down. I was just becoming concerned about April and Faith when I heard the rhythmic clatter of hooves on the trail.

I set the brush on my saddle and opened the corral gate. Something was bothering Faith as she slid from Vegas and led him into the corral. I raised an eyebrow as she passed in front of me.

"We found the game wardens," April said. "There's a group down at the cabins, just like I thought."

I glanced at Faith. Her pinched look suggested there was more to the story.

Faith glared wearily at her daughter. "You shouldn't have run down there."

"I didn't see anything," April shot back.

For a cop, her statement was akin to an admission of guilt. "What'd you see, April?"

"Nothing." The look on her face contradicted the statement. I continued to stare at her until she continued. "Just some dead animals."

"Where?" I asked.

"In the cabin. But the cops made me go back."

I pulled at the cinch buckles and helped April lift the saddle off.

"I told you to stop," Faith said, obviously not done with the conversation.

"It's no big deal, Mom," April said.

There was a weird tension between them and I knew better than to get in the middle of it. Instead, I redirected the conversation. "Did you see Jasper White?" I asked. Faith had been around White often enough to recognize him.

"I think that's him now." The sound of a four-wheeler's motor wafted along with the shifting wind. "He said he'd come up and get you."

"We're going to get snow," I said. "Let's set up the tent before I go."

Faith nodded. We'd brought one of her late father's outfitter tents along. At ten feet by twelve, it wasn't large, but it had the advantage of a small wood-fired stove for heat. I'd spent the previous weekend learning how to set it up in the barn and was anxious to get started.

Diva barked as White pulled up on a large forest service four-wheeler. I grinned. The government couldn't properly staff the forest with rangers, but they certainly didn't lack for equipment.

"Heel," I ordered, setting down a bundle of poles near a flattened piece of ground.

"Fancy running into you up here," Jasper said, wearing a broad grin as he dismounted the four-wheeler. "Sorry about the mix-up at the cabin. Wasn't expecting the young one to show up like that."

I glanced back at April who gave me a guilty look in return.

"What's going on?" I pulled off my glove and shook Jasper's hand. On the occasions I'd had to work with him, I'd found him to be a straight-shooter.

"It's a pretty grizzly scene. I hope the girl didn't get too much of an eyeful." His grin faded as he switched from greeting to business. "Probably best if you see it for yourself."

"That bad?"

He gave a quick nod of his head and looked down at Diva who'd worked her way over so her muzzle was beneath his hand. Her antics brought the smile back to his face. "It is. Glad you brought your tracker along, though. Maybe she could pick up on something." He rubbed Diva behind her ears and her tail thumped with joy at the attention.

"Give me thirty minutes?" I said. "I'd like to get the tent set up and a fire going."

"I'll give you a hand," he said and nodded to Faith as she approached.

"Sorry about April, Jasper," Faith said, joining us.

"Kids are curious. I hope she didn't see too much." Jasper was a single man and I wondered what his experience with kids was. "Is that an old Herter's panel tent?"

"It was Dad's," Faith said.

"I haven't seen one of these in ages," he said. I had started to unroll the heavy canvas material and realized I'd placed the door on the uphill side. Jasper grabbed one side and joined me as we rotated the tent.

It soon became evident that Jasper had set up his fair share of panel tents. The job that had taken me almost two hours in the barn, we completed in half an hour. Small flakes of snow were falling, but with a fire started in the tent's stove and the bedding laid out, I could finally feel like I wasn't leaving Faith and April in a bad spot.

"Do you really have to take Diva?" April complained.

"Sorry, kiddo. Diva's gotta go to work," I said.

"You'll keep that .30-30 in the tent then?" Jasper said, conversationally as I shrugged on my backpack.

At first, I thought he'd been talking to me. As I looked up, I discovered he was looking at Faith. The rifle was already in the tent, lying in its sheath next to the front entrance. Faith raised an eyebrow as she looked between us. Jasper's tone had been matter-of-fact so as not to alarm April, but his statement caused my stomach to flop.

"Sure will," Faith answered.

I unclipped my radio and handed it to her. "This is already set to the sheriff's department. This button toggles to Game and Fish."

She nodded somberly and stepped out of the tent with us. "What's going on, Jasper?"

"Hopefully nothing." His voice was raised as the wind attempted to steal the conversation. "We have six officers on the mountain. Counting Biggs, that makes seven. Whoever we're looking for is long gone. Just keep an eye out. You'll be fine. We're only a mile down the hill."

"I'll leave Diva," I said.

"No, don't. We'll be fine," Faith said. "Just go do what you need to and come back. I'll save some dinner for you." My stomach grumbled at the mention of food, but I pushed the thought away.

"You sure?" I asked, holding my hat on against a gust.

She leaned in for a kiss. "Yeah. Go." For a moment the world slowed and I enjoyed the comfort of being close to her. Unfortunately, since it was cold, she didn't linger and she slid back into the tent.

I followed Jasper to his four-wheeler and jumped on behind him, motioning for Diva to climb onto my lap. She'd been running most of the day and would be sore tomorrow. She didn't hesitate and piled in between the two of us.

The wind intensified as Jasper wound his way down the trail. Bright lights illuminated the interior of a simple timber cabin as we parked next to two ATVs. I saw figures working inside, so I snapped a six-foot lead onto Diva before dismounting.

As we approached, I could see through the front window that only two people were in the cabin. One of the officers looked up at us and came out the front door to meet us. "Where's everyone else?" I asked.

"With that snow coming, we sent the others home. They'll be back in the morning if we don't get too much." I didn't recognize the woman who spoke. She wore a State Forestry Service uniform and had just stepped out, closing the door behind her. She had a strained look on her face. "Bess Dawdry." She held her hand out and I accepted it. She was a solid-looking woman, although with a vest and winter gear, just about everyone could be described that way. I put her at five-five and maybe a hundred sixty pounds. Her handshake was firm.

"Henry Biggston, Butte County," I said. A look of concern crossed her face. I'd seen it before. The reputation of our department had been sullied by our previous sheriff.

"He's the one who took down Sheriff Leonard," Jasper said.

"I thought you had a different name," she said.

"Most people call me Biggs," I said.

"Right," she said. "Well, Biggs, I hope you have a strong stomach because this is a real shit-show."

3 / EYES IN THE HILLS

Vuk Servy pulled a pair of cross-country skis from the trunk of the ancient Buick Century and strapped them to his pack. He'd chanced upon an abandoned barn near the forest trailhead. It was the perfect spot to hide the car and for the last six months, it hadn't been discovered. Having spent the night curled up in the back seat, he was ready to get moving.

Servy relished the back-country challenge ahead, knowing that few were up to a full-day climb in such adverse conditions. While the snow had disappeared from the parking lot, plenty remained on the north facing trails. It was the toughest time of year for what had become a common trip. Where snow remained, hiking was difficult and in the sections the sun had cleared, it was impossible to ski.

A whimper came from his pack and Servy crouched next to it, laying back the flap to look inside. The smell of urine and feces greeted him. Puppies nicely represented everything he despised in his fellow man. They were dumb and if given the chance, would shit all over themselves, hoping someone else would clean it up. He'd read that dogs, bitches really, would nip badly behaved pups on the nose for discipline. He wasn't about to put his mouth on the unclean little beast, but he did flick the wiggling nose with his finger. Cowed, the puppy withdrew, pissing itself again.

"It'll be a long day. You might as well sleep," he said, pulling a zipper bag from his pocket. He carefully extracted two cotton balls and dropped them into the pack. Servy had become something of an expert at the use of chloroform. Too much would kill and too little was ineffective. The puppy continued to squirm as he lifted the pack onto his back, but before he'd reached the edge of the parking lot, all was still inside.

The sun was shining brightly as Servy set out, something he took as a good sign. The puppy added extra weight and his shoulders complained as the straps dug in. However, the condition was only temporary. He tightened the padded belt that transferred much of the pack's weight to his hips.

The morning passed with little interruption beyond switching back and forth between hiking boots and skis. He made good time and by the middle of the afternoon, was within a half mile of his cabin. It was a good thing too as the weather had shifted and he could feel snow in the air. Stopping at an open stream to refill his water bottle, Servy froze as the wind brought the sound of ATVs on the mountain.

Shit.

Jumping from the trail, he scrabbled down toward a thicket of scrub oak. Servy had been in such a hurry to disappear, he'd forgotten about the skis strapped to his backpack. The branches caught the slats, pulling him and eventually flipping him over and dumping him on his back.

Calm yourself.

With great restraint, he stilled himself and listened. Up on the trail, the motors had sounded nearby, but lying lower in the ravine, he realized the sounds were coming from the other side of the ridge, maybe as far as a quarter mile. An ache formed in his heart as he thought of his cabin. Servy knew he would have to clear out when spring hiking season started in earnest, but it was barely March. Blood rushed in his ears as he considered the implications. He barely held in the screams that threatened to escape his lips.

He shucked his pack and dropped it next to the stream and his mind raced as he considered his next move. His work. The cabin. He had to know. Without his pack, he ran swiftly back to the trail. It felt almost like he was floating without the extra weight. He slid to a stop as he approached the two-track trail that came up from west. It was a wider trail than the one he used to reach the cabin because even in the winter, the lower section was more heavily used and therefore to be avoided.

Fresh tracks.

Kneeling in the crusty snow, he discovered fresh tracks of four ATVs: three larger and one smaller. The trail was chewed up with activity, but he was no stranger to tracking. Servy quickly determined that the smaller vehicle had gone west toward the cabin and returned before the three larger ATVs had returned.

While concentrating had momentarily stilled his mind, the new information confirmed his fears. The trees started to close in and he was barely able to form a plan. He backed away and left the trail to head uphill. He would bushwhack his way to the cabin. It would be hard going, but he couldn't afford to be caught. He still had work to do.

Coming over the ridge, he looked down at the first of four cabins. The sun was low in the sky, but there was enough light to see the scene below. He settled next to a tree and allowed his heart to slow. The physical exertion of the climb had slowed his mind. His spirit buoyed as he realized the snow in front of the cabin was undisturbed. Perhaps the ATVs were just making a late run. Surely, they'd have to head home soon.

It's cold. Danger.

He stood and pushed further along the hill where he'd have a good look at the next two cabins. Closer to the trail, there were ATV tracks leading to both. His heart raced once again and this time, not from exertion.

Lost.

Blind with panic, he raced over the last ridge, only to discover his worst fears were realized. Three Game and Fish ATVs sat in front of his cabin. He cried out in pain and sank to his knees. A woman appeared in the doorway of his cabin and stared up at him, light blazing behind her. He froze. His camouflage jacket wasn't perfect, but just maybe her vision was ruined by the inside lights. She turned away as if to talk to someone and he ducked back, sinking to the ground.

I should die.

Horse hooves clattered on the rocky ground below.

"April, hold up," a woman's voice echoed through the draw. She was annoyed but not overly so.

Something about the name sounded familiar, but Servy couldn't quite recall why. The arrival of the riders was strange enough to pull him from his stupor. Carefully, slowly, he crawled back to the ridge and looked down at the cabin. Two women approached on horseback.

It's a child.

The girl, likely April, was ten yards ahead of the woman. She'd dismounted and was leading her horse toward the cabin. Even from the distance, he saw shock register on her face and he smiled. In the midst of such complete disaster, that moment was beautiful. Her face filled with horror and he wanted to believe he could see tears on her cheeks. A familiar sense of mania filled him with joy.

"April, no!" A man had exited the cabin and quickly pulled the door closed behind him.

"What's going on, Jasper?" the woman asked, dismounting.

"You shouldn't be here, Faith," the man answered.

"I'm sorry," April said.

"It's not your fault," Jasper said. "You shouldn't have seen that. I'm so sorry."

Servy felt growing excitement and he rolled onto his back, grabbing between his legs. He closed his eyes as euphoria washed over him. He struggled between enjoying the moment and missing the encounter.

"April, mount up," Faith demanded.

"I said I'm sorry, Mom," April snapped back.

"Where's Biggs?" Jasper asked.

"Up at camp," Faith answered.

"I'll be up in a few," he said. "I'm really sorry about this. I didn't know she was coming."

"I'm not a baby."

"You need to learn to listen better, then," Faith said. "Now get going."

Servy risked exposure and knelt next to a tree so he could watch the girl. He smiled as April's eyes crossed over the hillside where he hid. Her head snapped back, but he'd already melded into the shadows. His breath came fast as he imagined her staring at his position.

It's the girl from the hardware store.

He waited for what seemed like forever but was probably no more than five minutes. He could hear the officers working below and dimly became aware that snow had started to fall. The girl – she was so alive. She'd seen his work and understood. He fought the urge to touch himself again. He had a purpose. For the second time in two days, fate had handed him what he needed. It was a sign.

Find her.

Night had fallen and his survival depended on making good choices. He had to be disciplined like he'd learned in the army. Tracking required clear thinking. Survival required warmth and food. He recalled the survival pack he'd stashed. It was down the hill and across the two-track. Where were his skis?

Find the girl.

They were probably staying at the camp up the hill. He'd visited Gold Camp more than once – not much to look at, but there was reliable water. Retrieving his survival gear would take him out of his way and he desperately wanted to go straight to her. She would be his best work ever. It was time. She would be worth it.

He slunk back over the ridge with renewed purpose. The sky was dark and he carried no light, but that wasn't a problem. The falling snow reflected enough moonlight that he easily followed the path he'd just cut. Stepping in his original boot prints, he sought to minimize his presence.

When he reached the junction where the two trails met, Servy heard an ATV start up. He froze, worried that he'd been discovered. Only after the sound faded, did he risk a sprint across the trail. It took him almost ten minutes to locate his emergency supplies. When he'd originally stashed them, there had been no snow. The forest looked different with snow but eventually the details came to him.

Pulling off his jacket, shirt and pants, he added a layer of silk long johns. The process was a short-term loss in heat for a long-term gain. Shivering, he pulled his clothing back on and wished he could start a fire, although he knew better. He broke open an energy bar and forced himself to eat. Over the winter, he'd grown thin. Food was the last thing on his mind, but he knew it was required for survival.

The sound of an approaching ATV caught his attention. Sneaking over to the edge of the tree line, he saw two figures riding toward the cabin. There was a dog between them. He kept still. The dog was clearly a hunter and he wanted nothing to do with it.

April.

He decided not to cross back but instead, followed the two-track up the hill, staying several yards inside the trees. It was hard going, but the girl was worth any effort required. Focusing, he once again grew excited. This time he allowed his mind to wallow in fantasy. He replayed his encounter in the hardware store and the moment when her eyes found him on the hillside.

He reached Gold Camp, having lost track of how exactly he'd gotten there. Two silhouettes moved within a glowing white tent: a tall willowy figure and a smaller one. The sound of music was muted by snowfall. Vuk grinned as he watched April dance with her mother in an unguarded moment. His excitement grew and he found himself drawn to the tent.

A horse nickered and stamped at the ground behind him.

"Mom, did you hear that?"

4 / THE CABIN

I took one last look at the glowing horizon. A gentle snow filtered through the tall pines and I attempted to hold on to the serenity of the forest, but Ranger Bess Dawdry turned and pushed the cabin door open. Only through sheer force of will was I able to pull my focus to the evil wafting from the cabin. Once experienced, the smell of decaying flesh can never be mistaken for something else. I swallowed hard, adjusted my hat and followed her inside.

I blinked as my eyes adjusted to the bright lights. The momentary blindness was a final kindness from the forest, giving me a moment of peace. It was time to work. I scanned the cabin's single room. On opposite walls, wooden bunk beds had been built into the structure. The bunks had no mattresses, although one of them had a sleeping bag rolled out and a small pillow. On the other bunks, a total of eight small wire cages were lined up in neat rows.

Game and Fish Ranger Tom Elway was taking a picture of the interior of one of the cages. He must have felt my eyes on him and he turned, tipping his head back in recognition before returning to his work.

Diva pulled at her lead, uttering a low-throated growl.

"Easy girl," I said reassuringly as I continued to scan the room.

A single wooden chair sat directly opposite the stove and the small countertop along the wall with open shelving above was quite clean. If there had been a table or other furniture, they'd been removed and in their place were a couple of large cages. Movement from within drew my attention and I forced myself to move forward. Inside the cage was a cat, its body matted with blood. I crouched next to it and realized it was missing large patches of skin. It yowled sickly at me as it shrank to the far corner. Something was wrong with its leg and I understood where at least some of the blood had come from. One of the cat's legs ended in a bloody stump where its foot had been removed.

I pushed off my knees and looked into the other large cage next to the cat's. Within were the remains of what I imagined was a medium-size dog. Its head was missing as were a number of other appendages. The cage was thick with feces and other viscous matter.

"Damn," I said, trying to breathe through my mouth as the sights and smells threatened to overwhelm me.

I turned and scanned the other cages, realizing they all contained dismembered and tortured animal corpses. Some of the kills were fresh, maybe as recent as a couple of weeks. Others were long dead and desiccated.

My eyes moved to the cast iron wood stove that sat against the back wall. I took a quick step over to it and reached out.

"Careful of prints," Bess Dawdry warned.

I nodded. I hadn't intended to touch anything. Instead, I held my hand above the aluminum pot sitting on the flat top. There was nothing left in the pot except some scaly white residue and no heat was coming off the metal, indicating no recent fire. I accepted a nitrile glove from Dawdry and pulled at the heavy door handle. Holding my hand above the ash pile, I could feel a small amount of heat from coals that hadn't yet died entirely.

I closed the stove, stood and continued my inventory of the room. Someone had lived here for a good portion of the winter. The stack of firewood against the back wall had the marks of being gathered with primitive tools like an axe and hand saw. With the lack of debris, I was certain we'd find a woodpile outside where larger logs were split.

"First impressions?" Dawdry asked.

"Someone needs to put that cat down," I said.

"I'll take care of it," she said. "What else?"

"He's comfortable in the back country. He boils snow for water and cooks in the same pot," I said, pointing at the aluminum pot. I opened the lid of a plastic tote. All that remained was half a sleeve of crackers and two already-opened freeze-dried meals. "Looks like he ran out of food."

"I was thinking more along the lines of observations about the other stuff," Dawdry said.

"Those cages are live traps, but he keeps them inside, so he's not using them for food. Also, some of the animals have been dead for months. If he's comfortable in the back country and has the right equipment, what's the problem? He's either not a trapper or he's not willing to give up what he catches for food."

Dawdry's eyebrows raised. "That's interesting, so you think he's attached somehow to the trapped animals?"

"Not really my expertise, but if I wanted to stay in the mountains and I had all these traps, I'd be using them."

"How do you know he doesn't have traps outside?" she asked.

"He might. He certainly doesn't clean animals inside here, though. Despite the filth in those cages this place is immaculate. Also, he's not very well set up for cooking meat," I said.

"What do you mean?"

"He'd need a fry pan at least. Those freeze-dried meals were vegetarian," I said. "Of course, maybe he didn't like them."

"Anything else?"

"I think he hikes in," I said. "Everything is lightweight, but unwieldy. Getting this stuff up here would have required several trips. Did you see any ATV tracks on your way up?"

"The only ATV tracks we saw were from the group that discovered the cabin," she said.

"Why'd they open the cabin? Did they have a reservation?" I asked.

"No, it was a couple of teenagers from Crawford," she said. "They came over to the ranger station to make the report, but they were pretty shaken up, so I sent them home. We'll get statements from them next week."

"What else?" I asked. "Dead animals are creepy and all, but nothing you guys aren't equipped to handle. Why'd you ask for us?"

"Tom, you want to show him the hand?" she asked.

"It's in the cooler on the porch," Tom Elway said, not turning from the work he was doing.

She sighed and pointed out the front door. The storm was intensifying, but the biting wind was preferable to the putrid air of the cabin.

"At least it doesn't stink out here." She had to raise her voice to be heard over the wind.

Diva whined and pulled at her leash, trying to get off the porch. "I think Diva agrees."

Dawdry opened the top of a red cooler and retrieved a plastic evidence bag from among several. I pulled a tactical flashlight from my pocket and illuminated the bag as she held it up. Within was a small, withered hand. I accepted the bag from her and turned it over. It was hard to determine the age of it given its condition.

"It's small," I said.

"That's what I was thinking too," Dawdry said. "See the fingernails? I'd guess adolescent."

I turned the hand back over and brought it close so I could see through the bag, using my body to block the wind and snow. The conditions were horrible and I tilted the bag until the flashlight's powerful beam didn't reflect off the plastic. Having drawn my attention to it, I discovered what Dawdry had already seen. The ends of the fingernails still retained a small amount of bright pink fingernail polish.

"Dammit," I said, clenching my jaw. "Are you turning this evidence over to me?"

"If you want," she said. "We could bring it down with the rest of the evidence if that'd be easier."

"State Patrol might want it," I said. "Do they know about the hand?"

"No. They'll get a copy of my report," she said. "Why? Are you looking to hold onto the case?"

Dawdry had an honest face, like the majority of law enforcement personnel I worked with. Interagency squabbles for control of high-profile cases were common, but in the end, we all had to work together.

"No matter what, I'll need State Patrol's ISD to run this hand through their lab. Hopefully, they'll find who it belongs to," I said.

Dawdry looked out into the darkness that had fallen around us. "When I studied to be a ranger, I never imagined I'd have to deal with shit like this," she said.

I nodded, accepting her words. The truth was, bad people did bad things – exactly why I'd chosen to serve. I couldn't stop every crime, but at least I could make sure the dead found justice.

"Did anyone look for tracks when you got here?" I asked. "He had to come from somewhere."

"How do you know it's a man?" she asked.

"I don't."

"There are human tracks around the back side of the cabin," she said. "Heads up the hill to the northwest. I was going to ask the staties if they could bring in a tracker."

"If we get more snow, the trail will be lost. Diva and I could help," I said.

"You're not serious about going out in this, are you?"

"I'd like to see where it goes," I said. "Beats hanging out in that cabin."

She laughed mirthlessly. "Everything does."

I ADJUSTED my headlamp and scanned the packed snow behind the cabin. Dawdry was right; the ground was hard packed from constant use. I walked over to the neat wood pile and picked up one of the larger logs. The cut had been made by a hand saw. A makeshift wood-cutting cradle had been formed by lashing rough timber logs together. We weren't dealing with an amateur woodsman. Whoever this guy was, he was comfortable in the woods.

Diva whined as I paused to take in the entirety of the yard. There was no trash, nor gut piles, no fur. If the man was eating fresh meat, he was cleaning it away from the cabin. In fact, there was little evidence any human was in the area aside from the woodpile. We were dealing with a disciplined mind.

"Which way did he go?" I asked.

Diva barked and pulled at her lead.

The cabin faced southwest and sat within a bowl against a ridge-line. The map showed the two-track main trail leading due west for a quarter of a mile where it continued past two more cabins. Whoever had been hiding out here had gone to great efforts not to disturb the snow in front of the cabin, which eliminated the two-track trail as his destination.

Diva pulled to the northwest, her ears standing straight. Adjusting my headlamp to a longer-distance beam, I allowed her to pull me along. As we reached the edge of the trampled area, a clear trail emerged, leading up a steep incline. I withdrew an orange-topped wire flag I'd snagged from Jasper's ATV and flicked it into the snow. It stuck. I'd seen electrical company technicians do the same thing and I smiled at the accomplishment.

The trail was barely wide enough to allow passage, making for a clumsy climb. Facing south, much of the snow on the trail had turned to ice. I carefully scrabbled up, grateful for Diva's steady pull. We eventually crested the hill and joined a trail running along the ridge-line that ran behind the cabin.

Diva barked excitedly.

"Hold on there, girl," I said, dropping another marker flag. This one didn't stick and I had to bend over to replace it.

I stood at the edge of the trail, looking both ways along the ridge. To the left, the trail headed back in the general direction of the main trail and appeared heavily used, while the trail to the right looked like a game trail continued along the ridge. I was convinced I'd found the suspect's route to the cabin.

I followed the trail down the slope. Individual tracks were obscured from frequent traffic that had packed the snow. I was hopeful we'd find a usable print if we followed the trail far enough.

Exposed on the ridge, I became aware that the snow was getting heavier. I was careful to drop a marker whenever the tracks became difficult to follow. Whoever had made the trail had been careful to reuse their old footsteps anytime the old snow had been deep enough to leave prints, which made it difficult to estimate how many people or even how often the trail had been traveled.

After several hundred yards, we broke free of the tree line. A path had been cut through this section and there was enough moon-light to see shoulder rock stacked on the uphill side. I was looking at one of the spur trails that joined up with the main trail further to my left. The heavily-used part of the trail went to the right, away from the two-track, which made sense if the guy was trying not to be seen. Why then was there a newer, single line of footprints branching off to the left?

Pulling Diva in to heel, we walked slowly next to the prints. New snow hadn't quite covered all the tracks and I found a pristine boot print protected by overhanging scrub a few feet down the trail. I carefully crouched, placed a flag, and pulled out my phone. The conditions were poor for picture taking and falling snow had already done much to obscure the boot print. However, there was enough to identify a boot size, if not a make. I took several pictures then grabbed the black evidence ruler, carefully setting it next to the print and snapping a few more shots. I leaned down and blew gently to see if I could move any of the fresh powder. The icy imprint of a bear appeared on the boot's sole.

Hardly damming evidence, as the brand was common enough. I took a picture of the bear logo. Sometimes police work was about the small details and sometimes those same details were just noise.

As my excitement ebbed, it dawned on me that the print was too sharp. Based on the temperature changes and when the snow had started, this track was probably only an hour old, maybe two. I suddenly had the feeling that Diva and I might not be alone.

"Let's go." I tugged at Diva's leash.

My thighs burned as I jogged up the slope, playing out Diva's lead. I slowed, puffing from exertion, when my light caught an orange flag in the snow. I'd made it back to the trail that led down to the cabin. I continued up the ridge, inspecting it for fresh tracks.

My mind played out a scenario where the twisted individual who'd tortured animals and held a girl's desiccated hand as a trophy had followed the ridgeline up to April and Faith at Gold Camp. I breathed a sigh of relief when I discovered that only game had continued in that direction. Anxiety, however, had sucked away my will to continue tracking. It was time to get back to the girls.

Diva barked sharply and then jumped at me, pushing into me with her legs.

"Stop," I reprimanded, thinking she was trying to play.

She sat down, her ears perked and barked again.

Falling snow does a lot to dampen sound and had I been anywhere but on that ridge, I'd have never heard the faint sound of a gunshot. Diva looked up the hill and then back to me. She barked again, standing up and sort of lunging at me. I'd never seen her act quite like that before, but her intent was clear. She wanted me to act.

I reached for my radio and realized I wasn't carrying it. It didn't matter. I lunged down the steep slope, crashing through the trail as I used trees and shrubs to interrupt my chaotic path to the cabin. Diva continued barking excitedly.

"Quiet," I snapped and burst through the door at the back of the cabin.

"Keys," I said, a blast of snow and wind billowing in behind me.

"Evidence," Tom Elway shouted. "Shut that door!"

Jasper White looked up.

"I need your ATV keys, Jasper. I think I heard gunshots. April and Faith are in camp by themselves."

Jasper fumbled in his pocket, withdrawing a key and handing it to me. I raced to the front door and it swung open. Dawdry must have heard my entry and was coming to investigate. I pushed past her, but Diva's lead got caught around her legs. I released Diva and jumped off the porch, churning through the snow until I was on White's ATV.

The engine fired and I turned the handlebars hard to the right, gunning the engine and spraying snow in a rooster tail behind me. The ATVs were all four-wheel drive and they didn't skimp on off-road tires. The machine rocketed forward.

Diva had disappeared, but it hardly mattered to me as I raced up the trail. The girls were only a mile away, but it felt like a continent. I turned hard as I saw the glow of the panel tent we'd set up. In the dark, I missed the details of the terrain and plowed White's snow machine into a shallow gulley. It tipped forward at thirty miles an hour and threw me off.

I landed hard, the breath knocked from my lungs by the broad rock I'd discovered hidden by snowpack. I rolled over and pushed against the snow, gasping for air. I was so close. A gunshot and a woman's angry voice. I clawed at the snow, willing my body forward. There was pain, but it was fading.

Another gunshot.

"Get the fuck away from us," Faith yelled, turning in my direction.

I leaned down and plucked my hat from the snow. An angry bee buzzed over my head as she fired again.

"Don't shoot," I yelled back. "It's me, Biggs!"

A dark shape streaked from the woods and closed on her position. Faith swung her weapon over, but she would be too late. I raced forward. Diva must have taken a shortcut through the woods and had risked getting shot. She barked and swung around in front of the tent. She wasn't attacking Faith but rather, had come to protect her and April.

I ran forward and Faith turned to me, only this time she lowered the gun. "Biggs, was it you? Were you trying to scare us?"

I caught up to her and wrapped her in my arms. "Where's April?" I asked, ignoring her question.

"In the tent," she said.

"April?" I called.

"I'm okay, Biggs," April called back, her voice small and scared. Diva barked and ran to the tent, pushing on the soft door. A seam of light appeared as a zipper retracted and the door panel was pulled back. Diva wiggled her way through the opening to be immediately wrapped up by April's thin arms.

"What's going on, Faith?" I asked, holding her at arm's length. Even with the falling snow I could see the tears that stained her face.

"There was someone out here," she said. "He was over by the horses."

"He?" I asked.

"He called April's name," she said. "How does he know her

name?"

The sound of motors alerted us as two more ATVs chugged up the hill.

"You're safe," I said. "I'm not going anywhere."

Faith buried her head against my chest. "I was just so scared," she said. "I thought he was going to hurt April. Hurt us. I tried the radio, but no one answered. I looked for him and even fired into the air like you said. But he didn't leave."

"Diva heard the shots," I said. "You did the right thing."

"What's going on, Biggs?" Jasper White asked, running up to us with Bess Dawdry close on his heels.

"The girls heard someone outside the tent," I said, taking the gun away from Faith. "I think she scared him away."

I checked the .30-30's magazine. Only two rounds remained, which meant she'd fired seven rounds.

"Are you sure?" Dawdry asked.

"He called my daughter's name from outside the tent. Yeah, I'm fucking sure," Faith said, squaring up with Dawdry.

"Hey, no offense," Dawdry said. I knew Faith well enough to know she would remain fired up for a while. Fortunately, Dawdry had enough time as an officer to know how not to inflame a situation. "Did you get a look at him?"

Faith shook her head. "He was over by the horses."

"Hold on before we go poking around over there," I said. I unzipped the tent. We didn't have cots, but Diva and April had curled up into a sleeping bag.

"Heya kiddo, you doing okay?" I asked, staying on the mat next to the door. "I see you got a bunch of firewood for tonight."

"Is there really a bad guy out there?" she asked.

"I don't know," I said. "Did you hear him?"

She nodded but didn't say anything.

I pulled a box of cartridges from a bag and pushed it into my coat pocket.

"Don't worry, nobody's doing anything with Diva around," I said.

She tightened her grip around Diva's neck and Diva used the opportunity to lick her face. April giggled before pushing Diva's nose away.

"Don't go anywhere," April whispered. "Okay?"

I nodded but didn't say anything as I slipped back out of the tent and zipped it closed.

The problem with looking for evidence near the horses was that we'd spent a lot of time moving material to and from the corral and individual prints weren't distinguishable in the snow.

"See anything?" Jasper asked.

"Not yet." I started moving in larger arcs. Blood froze in my veins when I spotted tracks that couldn't be more than a few minutes old. Close by, the pink stain of blood marred the fresh snow.

"Here!" I called, pushing a flag into the snow next to the track and taking another bad picture.

"These aren't your tracks?" Jasper asked.

"Blood," I pointed out. "Faith might have gotten a piece of him."

"How old?" Jasper asked, crouching next to me.

"Fresh snow in the print," I shined my small flashlight at the track. "See how it's clean, not dirty? I saw a similar boot print down by where a spur trail joins up with the two-track."

"That's the northern loop," Jasper said. "Long trail."

"Do you think you can follow the tracks?" Dawdry asked, coming up behind us. "They'll be gone by morning."

I shook my head. "I'm not leaving Faith and April alone."

"One of us will stay with them," Dawdry pushed. "I'll get Elway to come up and help."

I shook my head. I wasn't leaving the girls with a man I barely knew.

"I'll stay, Biggs," Jasper said.

Faith had joined us and I looked at her. The hunter in me wanted to track this man, but I couldn't leave her again.

"Do you think you might have hit him?" I asked.

She nodded. "Yeah, I thought maybe I tagged him once."

"Why were you shooting again?" Dawdry asked.

"He told my daughter he was going to take her," Faith said, the muscles in her jaw clenching. "I wanted to make sure he understood the rules."

"I'd like to see if we could track him," Dawdry said. "This storm isn't supposed to last. Be a shame if he got away, especially if you winged him."

I shook my head. "I'm not going anywhere, Faith," I said.

"Why?" she asked. "I heard Jasper say he'd stay behind. You take Diva, we'll be just fine."

"You're not taking Diva," April's small voice called from within the tent, reminding us all that just because we couldn't see her, didn't mean she couldn't hear us.

"Are you sure?" I asked, looking at Faith.

"I'll get Diva for you," she said.

I shook my head. "No. Diva ran all day, she needs to rest. I'll do this."

"I'm coming too," Dawdry said.

"It's going to be tough," I said. "I move pretty fast."

"I'm coming."

I nodded. "We'll take water. Do you need any gear?"

"I'll grab my rifle," she said.

The March snow was soft underfoot which made for decent footing as Dawdry and I descended, following a clear foot-trail almost due west. Wearing a full kit, Dawdry was weighed down with an extra thirty-five pounds and I felt for her as she puffed behind me. She bore a common trait that I'd seen with most female peace officers and military personnel; she was tough and didn't complain.

I slowed after about a mile as we reached the ridge which led around the backside of the cabin and handed her my water. "Are you doing okay?"

"You're like a fucking gazelle," she growled between breaths, accepting my water.

I chuckled. To my knowledge, I'd never been compared to a gazelle.

"These tracks weren't here when I came through earlier." I pushed a flag marker into the ground next to a clean boot print. "There's more blood." I added a second pin.

"Brave woman," she said. "Like that she hit him. You two married?"

I shook my head. "No. Dating."

"Oh," Dawdry said. "Geez. Sorry. Kid seems to like your dog. Maybe you still have a shot?"

I chuckled. "I think we'll be okay."

"You dragged her into the forest where she got jumped by a psycho," she said. "Sure. It'll be great."

I rolled my eyes, which she couldn't see given the lighting conditions. "Good to go?"

"Me? Sure," she said. "I was just letting you catch your breath."

"It's three hundred yards until we hit the northern loop trail," I said and started down the ridge. A few minutes later, I realized I hadn't seen blood drops for a while and I hoped I hadn't missed his tracks moving off into the woods.

When we reached the intersection with the northern loop, I stopped. "Go that way, see if you can find blood. I'll do the same this way." I pointed Dawdry off toward the two-track trail that ran past the cabin and focused on the snow in front of me

"I've got something," she called out.

I jogged over to her position. "It's fresh, but that's my track from earlier. See my flag?"

"Sorry," she said.

"Good tracking," I said. "My trail isn't even an hour old."

I froze in place and slowly lowered to my haunches, waving Dawdry to do the same. She started to say something but must have seen the look on my face, because she became very quiet. Something was off. I couldn't immediately say why, but I knew we were being watched. I reached up, turned off my headlamp and doused my flashlight, gratified when Dawdry immediately followed suit.

We waited like this for several minutes.

"I know you're out there," I said, almost conversationally. "You need to turn yourself in. You're hurt and we've got your gear. We can help you. Don't let this go too far."

A fox scampered out of the forest and onto the trail about ten yards from our position. It looked at me and then, realizing its peril, dashed back into the forest. I slowly stood. Enough moonlight filtered through the trees and the falling snow to illuminate the trail we were following. I crept forward, certain I was within twenty yards of my quarry. The fact that I couldn't confirm that fact was of little consequence. I was good at this. Unfortunately, my quarry was a master.

"What do you have, Biggs," Dawdry whispered harshly.

I pointed off into the woods in the direction from which the fox had come.

She crept forward, the sound of her clothing scraping against itself filled the night. She gave me a pained look, but it wasn't her fault. The material had been chosen for temperature performance instead of tactical advantage.

"Hold," I said, but knew it was already too late. He was on the move.

I stood, took a few steps forward and heard the sound of running feet at least forty yards ahead of us.

"He's moving," I said, unable to keep the excitement from my voice.

"Careful, Biggs," Dawdry said. "He could be drawing us in."

I shook my head. If this guy were inclined to use weapons, I was certain the night would have already gone in a different direction.

"Let's go," I urged and started after him.

`Ahead, I saw a dark figure vault onto the trail and pause only long enough to look back at us. He turned and raced away. Man, he was fast. I pushed myself but found that the trail was too uneven. I was in danger of stumbling or even falling. That would be a mistake with this man.

I almost overran the point where he left the trail. We were just about to cross a stream. Plum thickets had grown up along the banks, partially covering the trail.

Dawdry chugged up behind me. The woman had a lot of heart, as I'd been pushing her hard for over a mile trying to catch this guy. I held up my hand as I expelled long clouds of vapor. I pointed into the thicket and flipped my head lamp on, giving my .30-30 a single pump of its lever to bring a round into the chamber.

"He's in there," I whispered. "Stay close."

"I've got your back," she huffed.

I found footprints and followed them, expecting to be jumped at any moment. I heard rustling and swung around. There was nothing but a backpack lying on the ground. I jumped over it and found long thin tracks exiting the small clearing. Cross-country skis. I ran after him, but knew I was already too late. The snow was almost done and the moon shone brightly on the side of the hill. In the distance, a dark figure disappeared around the curve of the hill.

I walked back to where I'd left Dawdry. She held something fat and wiggly in her arms.

"What's that?"

"There was a puppy in that backpack. I think it belonged to our perp," she said. "He's frozen."

I doffed my backpack and unfolded a space blanket for Dawdry. The puppy was shivering but looked like it would live.

"Did we lose him?" she asked.

"He skied out," I said. "Never catch him on foot."

Dawdry cooed at the puppy in her arms. "You're a lucky little fella. Matter of fact that's your name now. Lucky. You're lucky because we found you and that bad, bad man can't do awful things to you," She'd switched from professional-ranger voice to puppy voice. I grinned. No doubt the dog was well named.

WE TOOK turns carrying Lucky as we retraced our tracks back to Gold Camp. My respect for Dawdry grew as we continued. She had shorter legs and carried considerable gear. Tracking the suspect, we'd dropped about a thousand feet of elevation and the return climb was exhausting, especially after a long day.

"You must be a runner," I said. We'd just crested the final rise and I could see the yellow glow of the tent ahead of us. The snow had stopped up here, as well. The scene would have been idyllic except for the pall the events of the day had placed over everything.

"I'm dying inside. Just too proud to let on," she puffed. "In the summer, I organize trail runs and volunteer as the women's strength training coach at Crawford High School."

"Organized trail runs are a thing?" I asked.

"You should come out. Our kick-off event is in two weeks," she said. "We'll be running Lower Sandy Trail over on west slope. It's a 5k with two thousand feet of elevation change. We'll have eighty or more runners."

"Sure. If I'm not working," I said.

"You should talk to your chief," she said. "It's good community outreach."

"Biggs, that you?" Jasper White called out. If he hadn't spoken, I wouldn't have been able to locate his position.

"Dawdry and Biggston," Dawdry called back.

Jasper stepped out from behind a tree and allowed the barrel of his rifle to slump toward the ground.

"What'd you find?" he asked.

"Chased the suspect down to Northern Loop trail," Dawdry said. "He'd stashed a pair of cross-country skis and got away."

"Storm was interfering with the radios," Jasper said. "Seems to be better now."

I pulled the radio from my belt. "Butte-Base, this is Butte-2. Over," I called.

I raised my eyebrows as the response was both clear and immediate. "Butte-2, this is Base. Go ahead."

"I'm coordinating with Ranger Bess Dawdry. We have a suspect at large we believe will be exiting on Sage Creek Forest Trailhead-4," I said. "Could we send a patrol unit over there and see if they find anything? Approach suspect with extreme caution. Butte-2. Over."

"Copy that, Butte-2. Suspect at large on Sage Creek Forest Trailhead-4. Will approach with caution. Base over."

I looked at Dawdry.

"I'll follow up with your chief in the morning," she said.

"Base, tell Butte-1 that Ranger Bess Dawdry will make contact tomorrow. Butte-2 out," I said.

"Copy, Butte-2. Stay safe. Base out."

"I hope your boys grab him," Dawdry said. "I wouldn't get too hopeful, though."

Lucky took that moment to twist in her arms and she had to set the puppy on the snow.

"Who's this?" Jasper asked.

"I'm going to check on the girls," I nodded and walked around the pair. "I'll see about getting that ATV out of the ditch in the morning."

"No worries," Jasper called after me. "We've got cables. It didn't look like it was in there too bad.

I waved over my shoulder.

Diva growled as I approached the tent. She was funny like that. I couldn't imagine she didn't recognize my voice but until she got a whiff of me, I'd be treated as suspect.

"It's me. Can I come in?" Snuffling next to the door was replaced by a recognition whine.

A moment later, the door's zipper slid up and Faith stuck her head out. "Did you get him?"

I shook my head. "Dawdry and I tracked him for about a mile and a half. He had skis stashed and we lost him."

"Is he coming back?" April asked, wiggling in next to Faith.

"No," I said. "We have the equipment he left in the cabin. He'd have a hard time surviving on the mountain without it."

"I'm sorry. You must be freezing," Faith pulled on my arm and I stepped into the tent. In truth, Dawdry and I had generated more than our share of heat running up the mountain and the tent felt almost unbearably hot.

I levered the bolt on my rifle and withdrew the round from the chamber. I rested the rifle against the corner of the tent and unzipped my coat. My chest was damp with sweat and the cool draft was welcome.

"What do we do now?" Faith asked, eyeing the holstered pistol on my belt.

"Finish the night up here. The snow's stopped. We'll head down in the morning," I said.

"What if he comes back?" Faith pushed. I appreciated her protective instinct. The man had threatened April and it was understandable that she would want to get her daughter away as quickly as possible.

"He'll have a bad night," I said.

"But what if he comes when you're sleeping?" April had withdrawn herself from the bedding and stood next to us. Diva joined her and pushed against my hand.

"I won't be sleeping," I said. As a Ranger, I'd been trained to operate in sleep deprived situations. Staying up through the night was well within my skillset. "I just need to see if Jasper or Bess need anything."

"Bess?" Faith asked, her eyebrow lifting.

"Ranger Dawdry. National Forest Service."

I got the impression that wasn't the last of that conversation, but it was neither the time nor place. I exited back into the night and stood for a moment, allowing my eyes to adjust.

"They doin' all right?" Jasper asked.

"On edge, like all of us," I said. "Look, thank you for looking after them while we tried to run that guy down."

"Know you'd have done the same for me," he said, nodding. "Bess, what do you say we take a run at pulling Biggs out of that ditch. It'd save us from heading back to the cabin. You know we're sleeping down there, right?"

"I've got a chain on my rig," Dawdry said. "Biggs, any chance you could look after the pup tonight? I just hate putting him in one of those cages in that hell hole."

I nodded, accepting transfer of Lucky. "You going to turn him over to the Humane Society?"

"No," she shook her head. "I've been having a tough run on boyfriends lately. Maybe Lucky's more my speed."

I chuckled.

"Don't say that in front of him," Jasper said, feigning horror. "If that gets back to Bigg's day-time dispatcher, Hollie Wilder, she'll have you married off in a week."

"Won't say a word," I said and turned back to the tent.

Before I was even through the door, Diva's long nose was busily snuffling against the package in my arms.

"What is that smell?" Faith asked.

"A puppy!" April shrieked and pulled it from my arms.

"Oh, my gosh," Faith said. "Is that what smells so bad?"

"Found him on the side of the mountain," I said. "He'd been left in a backpack."

"You just found a puppy on the side of the mountain?" she looked incredulous, until understanding hit her. "He had a puppy?" Her voice raised an octave.

"I have a rag in my pack." I gave her a quick nod and sat on the chair we had set up next to the front door. "Did you set in all this firewood?"

"Jasper got some too while we were waiting," she said.

I unclipped my overalls and pulled them off, leaving them inside out, then rummaged through my pack for a clean rag and a package of baby-wipes. I handed both to April and sat back down, letting out a sigh of relief.

"You must be exhausted," Faith said.

"More hungry than anything," I said.

I was caught off guard when Faith knelt next to me and pulled me into a hug. I wrapped my arms around her as her chest shuddered and she cried silently into my shoulder. I had no idea what to do, so I simply stroked her hair and held on.

"I knew you'd come back for us," she whispered.

"If it was the last thing I did," I said. "You and April are my everything."

Apparently, that wasn't the right thing to say because she began to weep in earnest. At some point, April recognized her mother's distress and wrapped her thin arms around the two of us.

"It's okay, Mom," April said. "Biggs is a real badass. We're safe."

I grinned. It was great that April thought of me that way, but I needed to set the record straight. "Your mom was the badass tonight," I said. "She tagged that creep. I found blood beside his trail."

"Is he dead?" April asked as Faith pulled back.

"Flesh wound most likely," I said. "But he learned something tonight. He learned that Hudson girls bite."

April grinned and flopped back onto the floor, gathering Lucky into her arms.

"Did I really?" Faith's breath shuddered in her chest. Even with tear streaks on her cheeks, her face a picture of fierce determination.

"Oh, yeah," I said.

"I want to get a conceal carry permit," she said.

"That's a great idea."

———

It was after two when Faith finally drifted off to sleep. I extracted myself from the pile of bedding where dogs and girls were comfortably stretched out. Staying inside the warm tent next to Faith would be the kiss of death for the early-morning watch. I stoked the stove's dwindling fire and pulled my clothing back on. The overalls were still a little damp, but I'd be fine.

Diva popped her head up when I unzipped the tent. When I motioned for her to lie down she gave me no argument and settled her muzzle along April's hip so she could watch me.

I crouched next to the tent opening and allowed my eyes to adjust to the dark, sensing only peace from the quiet forest around me. The man I'd tracked was comfortable in the woods and the quiet could have been deceptive. He could have circled around, thinking our guard would be down, but I didn't think it likely.

There's a certain exhilaration shared by any who have stood the last watch and witnessed the breaking of a new day. The unsteady glow that eventually bursts from the horizon is a hopeful moment as it marks departure from a long night.

"Any trouble?" Faith quietly exited the tent, handing me a cup of coffee. The coffee was welcomingly warm.

"All quiet." I sought her eyes, knowing I had to get something off my chest. "Faith, I'm sorry this happened."

She gave me a quizzical look. "You didn't make this happen," she said.

"I know. I shouldn't have pushed the season," I said. "I wanted to share my love of the outdoors with you and April."

She smiled and leaned into me, pulling at my cup and taking a drink. "It's pretty out here in the morning," she said.

I exhaled tension I didn't realize I'd been holding. "Something hopeful about sunrise."

She nodded and I wrapped my arm around her shoulders.

"Think Jasper and Dawdry would like some breakfast? We brought a lot of food. I assume we're headed down this morning and won't need it all."

"That'd be really nice," I said. "Why don't you get started and I'll see if I can raise them on the radio."

"I completely forgot. Did you eat anything last night?"

I smiled. "I grabbed a couple granola bars from my pack. I'm all about breakfast, though."

———

We turned onto the gravel lane leading back to Hudson Ranch in the middle of the afternoon. "Do you want to go in to work tonight?" I asked.

In the Hudson family, there was no such thing as a vacation day and even though we'd returned a day early, Faith was feeling pressure to join her sisters, Reagan and Lexi, at the family-owned Hootskill Bar.

"It's Monday. They'll be okay. I'm not leaving April alone," she said.

"After we get unloaded and cleaned up, we could head over to my grandparents'," I said. "They could probably use help moving boxes."

My mom had taken off when I was young and left me in the care of her parents. Oddly, I still carried my father's last name of Biggston, even though he'd left even earlier than Mom. Lester and Pearl had provided a stable environment and I'd never known anything different. I'd always called my grandfather Pappi, but Pearl had talked me out of calling her Nanna. I still did, on occasion, but she wasn't the sort to hold a grudge.

"How is it you're still awake?" Faith asked.

"I am tired," I admitted.

"I thought they were still at the Sage and Rosemary Inn."

"I just got a message from Pearl," I said. "Movers showed up early and she thinks they'll be out before five. We could take pizza."

"April?" Faith asked.

"Do I really have to move boxes?" she complained. I'd learned complaining was just the nature of the ten-year-old girl beast.

"We got the wi-fi up," I said. "Have you ever watched *Ranchers* on a one-hundred-two inch, 4K screen with theater sound?" I caught a raised eyebrow from Faith and knew I'd struck a chord.

"Lester and Pearl have a hundred-inch TV?" April sounded skeptical.

I shrugged as Faith swung the long trailer around to line up in front of the horse barn.

"That's Mr. and Mrs. Ploughman to you," Faith prompted.

I flashed April a smile. "Pearl likes to watch knitting videos."

"Oooh, that's ... tell me that's not true," April said, frowning.

"It's not," I said with a laugh. "Theatre room came with the house." Then I noticed Faith looking at me expectantly. It was a well-known rule that whoever rode shotgun had the responsibility of opening all gates and barn doors. I jumped out and started for the barn.

"Hey, next time, could we camp out in that theatre room?" April shouted out the truck door before I closed it.

———

"This place is amazing," April gushed from the back seat as we turned onto the asphalt drive from the highway.

A white fence lined both sides of the drive, just as it had paralleled the highway for three hundred yards before that. Fruit trees had been evenly spaced along the drive and I looked forward to their blossoms in a month or so. The sun was just setting and the brightly lit log cabin sat proudly backdropped by the forest to the north.

"I didn't know you were rich, Biggs." April had released her seat belt and was leaning over my partially restored 1979 Ford Bronco's bench seat.

"April," Faith warned.

"I'm just saying! That barn could hold twenty horses."

I grinned. She'd looked right past the half-million-dollar home to the barn. The previous owner, Sheriff Cal Leonard, had been forced to sell the property when it had been discovered he was running a drug ring – amongst other sins. I'd been surprised when my grandparents swooped in and purchased it at auction, although I suspected they'd paid a pretty penny for it. Twenty acres backing to National Forest didn't come cheap.

Pearl must have heard us pull into the drive because she appeared on the wide porch and stood behind the rustic wooden balustrades, waving.

I jumped out of the truck and jogged up to give her a warm hug. "Heya, beautiful."

"You don't look well, Henry," she tsked as she pulled back and released me, turning as April cautiously stepped from the truck. "I'm so delighted you came too, April." April giggled and ran over to collect a hug. The two had only met a few times, but Pearl was a pied piper with kids.

"Mrs. Ploughman," Faith nodded to Pearl as the two made eye contact.

"Oh, dear, please call me Pearl. And I'm a hugger. No excuses." Faith grinned as Pearl pushed right through her personal space. When they separated, Pearl kept one of Faith's hands. "You're tense, dear. Is Henry being irritating? Is that why you came back early? He's not always the best communicator, but he means well."

Faith's expression turned serious. "We had some problems at the campground. It wasn't Biggs. It was something else."

Pearl patted Faith's hand and then wrapped her free arm around April. "Henry, be a dear and bring the pizza in. We'll toss a salad."

Diva stretched as she jumped from the Bronco. My grandparents had taken ownership of the property only a week previous and I hadn't been here since it had been owned by the ex-sheriff. Diva whined and turned into the light breeze.

"There you are," Pappi said, approaching from the garage, wind at his back. "They here for you?" He was looking toward the highway, across the unused horse pasture, where a sheriff's vehicle was approaching with lights but no siren.

"I imagine," I said.

I'd told Shelby Cantrell, afternoon dispatcher, that I'd be out at my grandparent's new place, but I hadn't expected they'd need me. I pulled out my phone, wondering why I didn't know what was going on and wasn't particularly surprised to discover it was dead.

"Let me grab those," Pappi said, relieving me of the pizza boxes. "Come on, girl." He clucked his tongue and Diva fell into step, happy to be following the food.

The approaching vehicle was a brand-new white Tahoe and when it turned onto the asphalt drive, acting Sheriff Gene Ellis turned off the lights and pulled to a stop. There was a lot of information implied in the way Ellis had driven in. Lights but no siren told me he was in a bit of a hurry, but when he slowed significantly after entering the drive, I knew things weren't critical.

"Sorry for the intrusion," Gene said, exiting his Tahoe. He was a middle-aged man with thin, graying hair. I was on the fence about his cop skills but overall he was a decent enough person.

"Hey, Gene," I said, holding my hand out in greeting.

"Heard you had some excitement up in the forest," he said. "You doing okay? You look beat. Girls okay?"

"We're good. Did you get that evidence bag from Bess Dawdry?"

He nodded. "What happened up there?"

I turned so I could watch the house and quietly gave Gene a Reader's Digest version of the events. I hadn't yet had a chance to write an official report, although I had notes in my pad. His face turned ashen as I described the state of the cabin and what'd been found inside.

"I'm turning the investigation over to ISD," he said.

I nodded. For a cop, Gene was mild mannered and I wasn't surprised he would ask for help from the State Patrol Investigative Services Division. He'd been thrust into his current position as acting sheriff, a position he readily admitted he was ill-suited to. I respected the fact that even with reservations, he'd stepped up.

He sighed. "You did good work up there tracking him. How long you suppose you'll stick around?"

"Probably spend the night," I said. "I've been up for a couple of days."

He shook his head. "I mean Butte County," he said.

"I don't plan on going anywhere," I said.

"Figured if you were sticking around, you'd have thrown your hat in the ring for sheriff," he said.

"I've got a lot to learn, Gene," I said.

It wasn't humility that prompted the statement as much as it was fact. Sure, if you needed someone to kick down a door, take up a sniper's position or track someone through the forest, I was your guy. If anything, watching Gene assume the mantle had taught me that being a sheriff was a lot more than being a tough guy.

"You're a man of action. I can respect that. Hope you stick around," Gene said. "Did you see Reba Wiley has signs up around town?"

A special election had been scheduled at the end of April. I'd been surprised to see Gene's name on a few signs. I'd also recently seen *Wiley for Sheriff* posters but hadn't given the race much thought.

"Comes from money," he said, as if that explained everything.

I nodded and looked at him. I wasn't sure what he wanted, so figured I'd let him get it out at his own pace. He held my gaze for a moment and then looked away.

"So, like I was saying, I'll need you to run that hand over to ISD in Platte City tomorrow. State Patrol wants your report," he said.

"I'll be by the station, first thing," I said.

"Get some sleep, Biggs. You look like crap." He smiled and slipped back into his rig.

I COULDN'T TELL what time it was when I startled awake in the windowless theater room. I'd been dreaming of being beaten and I scanned the room, alert for danger. My movement caused the tiny figure next to me to rustle. April's neck was twisted around and her breathing was ragged.

The events of the evening flooded into my mind. After pizza, April had convinced Pearl to let us watch an episode of *Ranchers* instead of unpacking. We must have fallen asleep, as a large blanket had been draped over the two of us. I worked my way free from the unconscious girl and gently turned her so she lay straight. I couldn't imagine how the kid had wormed herself so completely around my heart in such a short time, but I was all in.

Strip LEDs glowed along the edges of the tray ceiling. The light was dim and I wasn't immediately aware of Faith's lean figure as she unfolded from one of the loungers on the opposite side of the room. She quietly stood and walked toward the door, meeting me at the back, placing a finger to her lips, smiling wanly.

"You're sexy as hell when you take care of my kid like that," she said and then furrowed her brow. "I didn't mean that in a weird way."

I smiled at her awkwardness and stepped into her, lifting a lock of her sandy brown hair to push it over her ear.

"Didn't even cross my mind."

She held her hand over her mouth. "My breath."

"Just one kiss."

With her lips firmly pressed together, she leaned in and her hand somehow found its way to my backside. I pulled her to me and returned her kiss but kept my hands safely in the PG zone. Faith had been abused in a previous marriage and was skittish about physical affection beyond kissing.

I'd fallen for this woman almost the first moment I'd seen her. She'd been bartending at Hootskill, one of the Hudson family's bars. I'll admit, there was some serious physical attraction. She was a willowy five-ten, with sassy brown eyes in a beautiful face framed by wavy locks of sandy brown hair. Her tanned complexion hinted at a person who enjoyed the outdoors and when I'd first seen her, the twisted knot of her t-shirt had displayed a toned stomach. A bar fight had broken out that night and she'd been all business when she slid across the bar with a pink bat in hand. I'd stepped in and nearly had my head caved in by the brute of a man who'd been at the center of the fight. The mixture of beauty and fearlessness had sealed my interest and I'd been glad when she didn't fight me off.

Later, I'd learned of the abuse she'd suffered at the hands of Raff Butler who still worked as a deputy. To make matters worse, Raff was also April's father and Faith's high school sweetheart, turned husband, turned nightmare. I'd give Faith whatever space she needed and enjoy whatever relationship she was able to give me.

"You've got that far-off look again," she said, pulling back. "I know I'm sending mixed signals. I'm not sure why you stay with me. I do want to be with you. I'm ..."

I pushed a finger to her lips. "I need to go to Platte City today."

She narrowed her eyes and scrunched her brows. "Don't you want to talk about it? Most men would have taken off by now."

The fact that she didn't even need to say what *it* was, was proof of how much she still lived with the burden of her abuse. "If you want to talk, I'm all ears."

"Don't you find me attractive?"

I smiled. "You know I do."

"But you never push."

I shook my head. "Not how I work," I said. "You'll know when it's right. Trust me, I'll be right there when you do."

"You're too good for me," she said, tucking back in to lean her head against my shoulder.

"I'm no picnic," I said, stroking her hair.

We stood there long enough that my body relaxed. It was Faith who broke the silence. "What's in Platte City?"

Together we walked up the basement stairs and padded our way into the kitchen. It was still dark outside and dim lights illuminated the long granite island. I chuckled as I noticed a pair of new jeans and unopened packs of fresh underwear and t-shirts. Next to the clothing were three toothbrushes, towels and soap with a note. *Coffee is set for* 5:30. *Turn on the oven. There's a casserole in the fridge. Forty minutes at* 350. *Love – Pearl.*

"Thought I heard someone up," Pappi said.

The sound of paws on the carpet of the basement stairs warned of Diva's approach. Pappi crossed over to a sliding glass door that led to a deck. The log cabin styled home was a walkout and the deck looked over the forest to the north. Diva touched the back of my leg with her nose as she passed and ran out, not missing a beat.

"Morning." I nodded to Pappi.

Faith had worked her way over to the oven.

"You conked out pretty quickly last night," he said. "Did you run into trouble on your trip?"

I nodded. "Had a problem at one of the cabins. Had both state and fed rangers. I got a call on the way up." As a retired police officer, Pappi was more than familiar with interagency operations. "Things got a little close to the girls. Faith was forced to defend herself and April."

"Oh?" Pappi said. There could be no doubt from whom I'd learned my communication skills. "Sorry to hear that. You get him?"

"We tracked him off the mountain," I said, "but not before he threatened April."

Pappi's eyebrows rose as he poured a cup from the still-in-process-of-brewing coffee maker.

"That sounds serious," Pappi said.

"He's good," I said. "I'm guessing military. Maybe special ops."

"You and April are welcome here as long as you want." Pappi turned to Faith. "I haven't paid much attention to that security system, but I'll give Biggs' buddy, Alan, a call. I'll have it up by this evening."

Faith shook her head. "I don't want to make too big of a deal about this," she said. "April has school and her activities."

"Offer stands," he said.

I expected her pushback. The Hudson women had been through plenty of hard times and it would be a sorry individual who underestimated them.

Sliding my backpack off the counter, I pulled out my Walther CCP 9mm. I kept it unloaded in my pack but had a magazine next to it in the leather pouch. "Nobody in Butte will give you trouble for carrying this," I said. "Don't carry out of the county until we get you through a conceal course."

"Are you going somewhere?" Pappi asked.

"Platte City," I said. "Ellis wants me to turn over some evidence to ISD."

"That man needs to grow a pair," Pappi said.

"He's a good man."

Pappi didn't argue but raised his eyebrows. That signature move could communicate any number of different ideas. In this case, he was probably letting me know he had a stronger opinion but would let it go.

"How will we get home?" Faith asked.

I slid my keys to her. "I'll see who's on patrol," I said. "I'm sure I can arrange a ride into town."

"I could drop you off," she said and then dipped her head bashfully. "I mean if it'd be okay if I left April for a few minutes."

Pearl padded into the kitchen and smiled. She got up every morning at the same time as Pappi but spent a few minutes getting ready. She wore what she called a house dress. Per her description, the dress wasn't formal enough for company but was suitable for working around the house. The only time I'd seen Pearl in jeans was when she'd owned horses and worked in the barn. That hadn't been for a number of years.

"Thank you for getting the oven started, dear," she said, running a hand down Faith's arm. "I just can't get over how pretty you are."

Faith melted under the spotlight and blushed, something that was fairly unusual for her given her line of work.

"How did you know it was her who started the oven?" I asked, feigning offense.

She didn't miss a beat. "Because I don't smell anything burning, Henry."

Faith caught a laugh in her throat and coughed.

"You okay if I take a shower?" I asked.

My question had been directed at Faith, but Pearl answered. "We'll take good care of her. Now go shower. I can smell you from here."

———

"When do you think you'll be back?" Faith leaned out the Bronco's driver's side window after we switched in the alley behind the sheriff's office.

"Could be late," I said. "I haven't written my report yet and they'll want to interview me firsthand. There's a possibility someone will contact you to get your take on things."

"What do I say?"

"Just walk 'em through it," I said. "You're not in any trouble."

"But I shot a man."

"In self-defense," I said. "I want you to keep that Walther with you at all times. Hank, over at the hardware store, has a conceal course this coming weekend. I'll get you signed up. You should see if any of your sisters want to join you."

"Do you think that's necessary?" she asked. "I always have a rifle in the truck."

"It's necessary."

A siren broke the morning quiet and Faith jumped. An older Crown Victoria cruiser pulled in behind my Bronco and had illuminated the flashing strobes. Faith looked at me, panicked.

"I've got this," I said. Behind the wheel of the vehicle was Raff Butler. He grinned broadly and whooped as he slapped the steering wheel with his open palm, laughing.

I walked back to the car and stood there as he gave me a goofy look, still laughing. Finally, he rolled down the window.

"You should have seen your face," he said, "and Faith jumped about a mile."

"She's trying to back out," I said. Raff had pinned the Bronco in.

"Aww, come on, don't be such a buzz kill," he said. "I'm just messing around."

"Back up, Raff," I said. He rolled his eyes and I walked alongside his car so he didn't get any ideas. As soon as the Bronco's front end cleared the building, Faith tore off, wheels spinning on wet pavement.

"I should ticket her for reckless," he chortled.

"I wouldn't," I said, allowing a warning into my voice.

He sighed. "Geez, you too?"

Raff Butler had been something of a sports star a decade ago when he and Faith were in high school. While she and her older sister, Reagan, took their volleyball teams to state, Raff enjoyed winning seasons and popularity by excelling in several other sports. However, the decade since then hadn't been kind to him.

I was concerned he'd follow Faith, so I placed a hand on his door. "You comin' up?" Since it was six fifteen, his shift wasn't technically over for forty-five minutes but under Gene Ellis, there would be no one to question him.

"Hang on," he said and turned into an open parking spot next to my rig. I keyed open the station's back door and waited.

"Anyone in the tank?" I asked as I turned into the small locked room used for temporary evidence storage. Butte County wasn't overly large, but there were plenty of locals who treated drinking like a sporting event and spent a lot of time in a cell sobering up.

"Quiet weekend down here," he said. He looked surprisingly refreshed for a man who was getting off a graveyard shift. "Heard you had some excitement."

I nodded. "State Patrol case now."

"Big surprise. Thought Gene would nut up when he got the call. Guess I was wrong," he said. "You gonna vote for him?"

"Hadn't given it much thought," I said.

"That Reba Wiley is a looker for an old girl," he said. "Bet she's a bitch, though. All those rich old ladies are."

I pulled out a small cooler from the refrigerator and opened it. Inside sat the desiccated hand Dawdry had found in the cabin. I closed the cooler and signed the evidence log.

"Can't say I know her," I wasn't interested in engaging Raff in locker room talk about someone I didn't even know.

"People been askin' why you aren't running," he said.

"Only been a cop for a year," I said.

"Wiley's never been a cop," he spat. "Her claim to fame is flying choppers in the dirt box."

"Sandbox."

Raff looked at me like I'd grown a second head. "You leaving now?"

"Might be a long day," I said. "I'd like to get a run at it."

"So long," he said.

"Stay safe."

I sighed as the station door closed behind me. My relationship with Raff was complex. In addition to his broken relationship and continued edgy behavior toward Faith, he was my co-worker. Further, the two of us had been through some crap of our own when we'd had to rely on each other for our survival. I found it a lot easier when people were consistent in their behavior. Either be an asshole or a hero, because the gray areas in between sure made things a lot harder.

I beeped open the year-old F-150 Interceptor pickup assigned to me and stuffed the sealed cooler into the back seat next to my backpack.

"Butte-Base, this is Butte-2," I called as I started the truck.

"Go ahead, two," Hollie Wilder answered. Her desk was maybe fifty feet from where I was parked. I probably should have just stopped in and talked to her, but I wasn't in the mood to run into Raff again.

"I'm headed out for Platte City. Over," I said.

"Copy that, Two," she answered.

"Butte-2, out." I hung up the mic.

I'd like to say that my old Bronco was a superior vehicle to the F-150 Gene had assigned to me. The fact was, the new truck was about as nice a vehicle as I'd ever driven, aside from the lingering smell of chemicals used to clean up the barf which was common in all sheriff's vehicles.

My destination was Platte City which was mostly south and a little east of Wood Creek. I'd take 385 past my grandparents' new home and meet up with the interstate after about ninety minutes. Thirty minutes at eighty miles an hour going east and I'd arrive at one of ISD's two installations in the state. The other facility was in the state capital of Sutherland another four hours further east.

I'd no more than cleared the national forest when a large, pearl-white SUV pulled into the passing lane and blasted past me. The speed limit was sixty, but both Gene and his predecessor routinely pitched any tickets for less than fifteen miles over for any plates bearing the county designation of 69 – which was Butte County.

My radar showed seventy-three. I shook my head and flipped on lights and sirens, pulling the radio transmitter off to let Base know what I was up to. The plate was local, but the move had shown blatant disregard and I couldn't let the offense pass.

I pulled in behind the new Escalade and jotted down the license plate before I got out. Glancing into the back windows as I walked toward the driver, I saw a spotless interior occupied by only one person. Country music wafted out from the open driver's side window.

"Thank you for stopping," I said, keeping back from the window just enough that it would be difficult for the woman in the driver's seat to turn quickly on me. "License and registration, please."

"What's the problem, Officer?" I put the woman in her late forties. Her auburn hair leaned toward red and she had a serious twang to her voice.

"Got you at seventy-three," I said. "Speed limit is sixty through here."

She handed her license through the window along with her registration. She flashed me a bright smile and I felt like I recognized her but wasn't sure why. Given her driving, it was probably another traffic stop.

"I was hoping you'd pull me over, Officer Biggston," she said.

I'd already started back to my rig and her familiarity surprised me, stopping me in my tracks. "Do I know you?"

"Call it in. We can talk after you give me my ticket," she said.

I looked at her and then mentally shrugged. If there was a universal constant in pulling people over, it was that you never knew what you were getting into. I looked at the license so I could punch in her information. I had just pulled over none other than Reba Wiley, candidate for sheriff.

The search on her license came back clean and I wrote her a ticket, wondering if Gene would dismiss it. I chuckled as I considered his quandary: follow the pattern or stick it to his competition. It was exactly the sort of thing he'd struggle with.

"I just need you to sign this," I said, returning to Reba's vehicle.

She raised an eyebrow suggestively. "You're really giving me a ticket?"

"I knocked it down to nine over," I said. "You should keep it down. There are lots of animals moving around this time of morning. I'd hate to see you get hurt."

She signed and handed the ticket book back to me. I tore off her receipt.

"We good?" she asked.

"Absolutely, ma'am. I'll let you get back to your morning," I said, tipping my hat.

She opened the door, which was a no-no with most patrolmen. The fact that I knew who she was, was the only reason I didn't move for more provocative engagement.

"Please stay in your car, ma'am."

She shook her head and leaned against her car. "No threat," she said. "I just wanted to talk to you a moment."

I considered the source and made a quick decision. "We can talk in the truck," I said, nodding at my F-150.

"Thank you," she said and followed me back.

I opened the passenger door for her.

"Why aren't you running for sheriff?" she asked as soon as I was back in my seat.

Her question caught me flat-footed. "You got a speeding ticket so you could ask me that?"

Wiley's smile bordered between wolfish and friendly. "I've got something of a lead foot," she said. "But I saw the opportunity, so I grabbed it. You and I both know Gene Ellis isn't the right man for the job. Best I can tell, you're my only real competition." Her grin was decidedly wolfish.

"To be honest, running never crossed my mind," I said.

"I looked up your service record," she said. "At least what wasn't classified. I even made a few calls. I've got some friends over at Army. Far as I can tell, you're the genuine article." As she said genuine it sounded more like *gen-you-eye-n.*

"I heard you flew helicopters in Iraq," I said. "Army?"

"Air Force actually," she said. "Your endorsement would go a long way in getting me elected."

I sighed. I hated politics. "That'd be pretty hard on Gene. He's a good man."

The wolfish smile returned. "What I just heard was you don't believe he's the right man for the job either."

"Didn't say that."

"Didn't deny it either. Do you plan to endorse Gene?" she asked.

"Nobody cares what I think."

Her eyes locked onto mine. "I do."

I shook my head. "Anyone asks, I'll tell 'em what I told you. Gene Ellis is a good man."

"Mortimer Cook isn't willing to print that as an endorsement," she said.

I grinned, recognizing the woman was at least a few steps ahead of me. Mortimer Cook and Denholm Campbell ran the local newspaper and were also my current landlords at the Sage and Rosemary Inn. Newspaper men from Chicago, they'd come to Wood Creek for retirement. Both in their mid-sixties, they were as sharp as they come and had already pressed me on the matter.

"Guess that's your answer, then," I said.

She placed a hand on the truck door handle and opened it. When her feet hit the ground, she turned and waved her speeding ticket. "Best seventy-five bucks I ever spent."

AT JUST AFTER EIGHT, I pulled up to the State Patrol Western Division headquarters building, only a few hundred yards from busy Interstate 80. The building itself was an austere, one-story brick building that sat next to a large fenced-in parking area. I felt a certain pride for the organization. State Patrol recognized its mission and hadn't built a monument to themselves. They were all about officers in vehicles, protecting and serving.

I parked in a smaller lot that sat adjacent to the building, backing into a spot that gave me easy access to the exit. I jumped out of my truck, stretched and then twisted around to limber my body. I'd racked up a fair amount of scar tissue and sitting for long periods of time was uncomfortable.

"Deputy Biggston?" A uniformed man had stepped from his vehicle and was walking toward me. I'd missed his approach when I'd leaned in to grab my cowboy hat that completed Butte County's uniform requirement of a uniform shirt with an open collar, jeans and hat.

The Army in me wanted to stiffen to attention at seeing the bars on the man's shoulder and I had to force myself to relax. "Captain ..." I said, pushing a smile onto my face and my hand out in greeting.

"Jack Arnold," he said, grabbing my hand and locking eyes. "You're still a bit fresh from the field, aren't you?"

I narrowed my eyes. I wasn't sure if he was insulting me because I worked in a rural area like Wood Creek or what he meant.

"Sir?"

"Old habits die hard, Sergeant," he said. "I'm afraid your reputation precedes you. I understand you're here to see Detective Cropsie."

"Yes, sir," I said. "Rangers found the partial remains of a young female, her hand to be exact. We were hoping ISD would help identify our victim."

"Why don't you grab your evidence and I'll walk you in," he said. I opened the truck's back door and extracted the cooler. "That was quite a deal up there in Butte County with Sheriff Leonard. Detective Cropsie's report was rather eye opening."

I closed the truck and looked back at the man. He was in his early fifties and in decent shape.

"I don't believe I've read it, sir."

He smiled. "She also said you're not a big talker."

I nodded and stepped forward, walking up to the building so I could open the door for him. I wasn't in his chain of command, but it was in me to respect the uniform.

We entered a small lobby that had exactly one desk and a single door with an electronic lock. Behind the desk sat a uniformed officer with two stripes on his sleeve, marking him as a corporal. The officer watched us enter with interest but did not stand at attention as I would have expected given the appearance of his superior officer.

Arnold ignored the corporal and turned back to me. "Maybe we could catch lunch before you head home. Say eleven thirty?"

"Of course, Captain Arnold," I said, my head suddenly spinning with questions I knew better than to ask. "I look forward to it."

Arnold grinned as he pulled a white plastic card from his pocket and swiped it across the electronic lock. "Corporal James will get you checked in."

For a moment, I watched as Arnold disappeared behind the door.

I wondered if meeting the Captain in the parking lot had been purely accidental. Why in the world would he want to go to lunch with me?

"Can I help you, Deputy?" the corporal asked, breaking my contemplation.

I gripped the cooler in my hand and turned back to the man. "Sure. I'm here to speak with Detective Cropsie and I have some evidence to drop off."

"Keep the evidence," he said, handing me a clipboard. "Please use the unloading station to clear your service weapon and use one of the lockers that has a key."

I followed his eyes over to a large cylinder mounted to the wall. About the size of a plastic five-gallon work bucket, the sides were made of steel and there was an inch-and-a-half thick plastic liner that I knew to have ballistic material behind it.

Setting down the clipboard, I withdrew my Springfield 1911 .45ACP and placed it within the bucket. Pulling back the slide, I ejected the chambered cartridge, locked the slide open and ejected the magazine.

Next to the unloading station was a bank of maybe a dozen mailboxes built into the wall. We'd had the same thing back at Sutherland PD, so the idea wasn't new to me. I placed my unloaded weapon into an open box and withdrew the key.

"Deputy Biggs."

I recognized Roseland Cropsie's voice behind me. She'd been the ISD investigator in the murder of a Butte County deputy the previous year. Mid-thirties and standing at a slender five foot four inches, she was far from imposing. At first glance, a person might mistake her for an office worker, given her plain gray wool skirt suit and sensible shoes.

"Detective Cropsie." I acknowledged her approach by touching the brim of my hat. "Good to see you."

I happened to notice the expression of surprise on the corporal's face. It was understandable. Not everyone likely enjoyed meeting Roseland Cropsie.

She shook her head slowly, a rare grin spreading across her face as she looked at the cooler in my hand. "Are you really turning over this investigation to ISD before you've even started?"

"Not my call. Either way, we need to see if we can get this identified," I said.

"You bring a statement with you?"

"I've got notes, but haven't had time to write anything up." I picked up the clipboard. The form required basic contact information and purpose of visit.

"Corporal Thompson, Deputy Biggston will return your clipboard in a few minutes," Cropsie said. "I'll have him at Corporal Otto's desk."

"Yes, ma'am," the corporal answered.

Cropsie played out line attached to a security card clipped to the waistband of her skirt and swiped the electronic lock. "With me, Biggs," she said, pushing through the door.

She led me down a hallway to a grouping of desks. Mentally, I had a picture of Cropsie's desk as being tidy – to the point of questioning if someone actually used it. I couldn't have been more wrong. The desk she sat at was piled with manila folders and large white envelopes. If there was an organization to the piles, it escaped me.

"Mind if I take a look?" she asked, eyeing the cooler.

I handed the container over. Without hesitation, she pulled out the plastic-wrapped, desiccated gray arm. A model of professional detachment, she carefully inspected the entire piece, focusing for a while on the chipped paint on the fingernails.

"Not good," she summarized as she replaced the arm in the cooler. "You found this in a cabin?"

"Bess Dawdry of Game and Fish found it," I said.

"So, three departments," Cropsie said. "What a cluster."

"I think Sheriff Ellis would love to have Butte County sidelined," I said.

"I'm sure he would." Cropsie snorted derisively. "How about you write up a statement for me and then we can talk it through. Don't leave anything out. Take Otto's desk. He's on patrol today. I'll get your evidence to the lab."

In contrast to Cropsie's desk, Otto's was completely clean except for a picture frame of a woman and two kids posed beneath a tree in full fall color. Already on the desk was a blank lined notepad and a pen. I placed my hat on a corner of the desk, sat in the chair, and started writing.

———

Three hours, four cups of famously horrible coffee, two donuts and an interview that rivaled a rectal exam later, Cropsie sat back in her chair. "I received a call this morning from Dawdry at Game and Fish. They discovered a shallow grave behind the cabin. They've recovered remains from at least two DBs. We don't think the arm you recovered belongs to either of those remains. They're bringing in equipment to further excavate the ground. Sheriff Ellis will be pleased, State Patrol is taking over the case."

"Is ISD overseeing the excavation?" I asked.

"No. Jasper White, the senior ranger in the region, agreed to oversee the site. ISD is stretched too thin and Game and Fish already had people deployed," she said.

"Why don't you think the arm Dawdry recovered is related to the recovered remains?" I asked. "Did you identify who it belongs to?"

"A ten-year-old girl, Una Servy," she said. "She died in a car accident three years ago."

"Parents?"

"Natasa Savic and Vuk Servy," she answered.

"Did the dad have military service?" I asked, flashing back to the impressions of the man I'd tracked through the forest with Dawdry.

Cropsie shook her head. "The parents emigrated to the US in 2002," she said. "Una was born shortly after that. They divorced a few years after Una's death. Mom's been in jail a couple of times for minor drug offenses. Nothing recent."

"Anyone feel like lunch?" I'd seen Captain Arnold's approach and was expecting the question.

"Almost finished," Cropsie said, stiffening.

"Anything you can't finish over a Chinese buffet?"

Cropsie pursed her lips but to her credit, didn't respond with the irritation that radiated off her. "No sir."

"Good, we'll take my car," he said.

The walk out to the vehicle felt awkward. I couldn't tell if Cropsie and Arnold didn't get along or if Cropsie's often surly disposition was just making for an odd dynamic.

"So, Biggston, I understand your grandfather was SPD," Arnold said as we climbed into his dark gray Buick Enclave. Cropsie took the back seat before I could offer, which left me in front next to the captain.

"Most people call me Biggs," I said. "And that's right. He retired about eighteen months ago."

"Good for him," he said. "Ploughman, right? I know the name but don't think we ever met. You know, some might argue that taking a position as a deputy sheriff is a bit beneath a man with your experience and training. Tell me how that all worked out."

"My grandfather was Sheriff Leonard's TO back when they were in SPD together. Leonard reached out for help," I said. "But I'm sure you know that whole story."

"Didn't know your grandfather was Leonard's TO," he said. "Talk about misjudging the situation."

"How's that?"

"Cropsie's report pretty much framed you as the central figure in bringing Leonard down," he said. "Can't imagine why he'd hire you unless he thought his relationship with your grandfather would come into play."

"I see what you're saying. I'm not sure I understand what Leonard's motivation was," I said. "I'm not even sure Cal knew he was doing the wrong thing."

"There had to be a point where he offered you money to keep his secret," he said. "We recovered over twelve million in cash from his residence. Odd, considering he was neck deep in debt. No doubt he had trouble laundering it all."

"In Afghanistan, my team ran into money all the time," I said. "I know of a few who thought they could hold some back. Never worked out in the long run."

"So, he did?"

"Offered to split a couple million in cash," I said.

Arnold whistled. "Good for you, son. Tell me, do you know what my position is with State Patrol?"

"You head up western division's ISD," I said.

"Any idea how much staff we have?" he asked, pulling into a parking spot.

"Website says eleven full-time investigators," I said. "Best I can tell, Detective Cropsie is either second or third in your chain of command."

"Well, damn. Explain again to me why you're a deputy in Podunk Nowhere?" he said.

The restaurant wasn't overly busy. Arnold waved to the hostess instead of waiting and led us to a table.

"Butte County suits me," I said. "Good people and beautiful country. I've got nothing to prove."

"Plates are on the buffet." Arnold pushed away from the table, unceremoniously leaving Cropsie and me sitting alone, watching him walk away.

"Any idea what this is all about?" I asked, looking for help from the equally perplexed woman.

"Yes. You're doing fine," she said, getting up to follow her captain.

I found it difficult to load my plate at the buffet and ended up with a random selection.

"By design, the western division is understaffed," Arnold picked up the conversation again after taking a few bites.

"Why ..." I started. No one would plan to be understaffed.

"Let me finish," he said, even though he'd paused for another bite.

"*By design*, in this case, means we don't want to build an ivory tower. Our territory is just too darn big to manage it all from Platte City. So what we do is hire civilians to fill out our ranks. One of the problems is, the more rural we get, the more difficult it is to find qualified individuals. And I don't have to tell you that the further north and west of Platte City you go, the more rural it gets."

"But I'm not a civilian," I said.

"Which makes you all the more qualified," he said. "I'd like your permission to formally request that you join our task force as an investigator for your region."

"How would that work?" I said.

"According to Cropsie, not much would change since you have trouble keeping your nose out of our business as it is," he said. "We'd reimburse Butte County for your hours and you'd get a small bump in pay. Most of the time you'd be like every other deputy in Butte County but when the situation arises, we'd tap you to get involved."

"What happens when Butte County needs me and I'm on an investigation?" I asked.

"Your chain of command doesn't change. Butte County runs the show," he said. "When you're working on an investigation, you report to Detective Cropsie. If you run into problems with your command, you let her know and she'll take care of it."

"Have you already talked to Sheriff Ellis?" I asked.

"He knows we're having a conversation."

"I'm surprised he's good with this," I said.

"I might have told him that it was either this conversation or I was going to actively recruit you for State Patrol," he said. "The fact is, I need someone in the northwest right now who fills that bill."

"Why now? We've got nothing on the case I just brought over," I said.

"We have four ongoing investigations in your region right now," he said. "A local guy would give us a chance to make progress. And from what I've seen of this whole Sage Creek mess, we're going to need all the help we can get."

"We need to get ahead of this thing," Cropsie added. "I've looked at the pictures from the cabin and read the rangers' statements. You have a psychopath running around Butte County. We're particularly disturbed by the attention your perp gave to your girlfriend's daughter."

"Does that mean I should be recused from the investigation?" I asked.

"If this was Sutherland PD and we had three hundred officers, I'd say yes," Captain Arnold said. "Fact is, we have one officer for every four thousand square miles. What I see in front of me is a man who can't be intimidated, has a love for the law, and has proven himself under fire. I'll accept the risk that you might go a little overboard in protecting that little girl. In fact, I'll sleep better tonight because of it."

"Where can I find Vuk Servy and Natasa Savic?" I asked, turning to Cropsie.

"You'll take the position?" Arnold asked.

"I accept," I said.

"What was the deciding factor?" he asked.

"One thing war taught me was to recognize the enemy," I said. "We're on the same team. We all want the same thing: put the bad guys down and keep the good people safe."

"State Patrol motto is *pro bono publico*," he said and then translated. "For the good of the public."

"The father, Vuk Servy, is off the grid, but the mother, Natasa Savic, lives in Sutherland. I have a last known address," Cropsie said. "You want to interview her?"

"Seems like until those corpses are identified, our only lead is that arm, which leads to Servy and Savic," I said. "Do I need permission?"

Arnold chuckled. "Would you ask if I wasn't sitting here?"

"Probably not."

My answer caused Arnold to guffaw and Cropsie to look down at the table with a slight grin.

"Maybe you don't need to be quite so honest," he said holding out his hand. "Work it out with Cropsie and welcome to the team."

⊏⊐

"What do you mean you're in Sutherland? Did you even pack any clothing?" Faith asked. "I thought you were just going to Platte City."

"I'm running down a lead on the remains that were recovered in the cabin," I said.

"I thought Ellis turned that over to State Patrol."

The heavy bass thump of country music in the background came through the call. It was Tuesday night and early enough in the week that Hootskill wasn't in full swing. They'd still be busy for the dinner rush, even though they had a limited menu.

"State Patrol asked me to work with them," I said. "I'm lead on this case."

Someone yelled out an order in the background and I knew I'd caught Faith at a bad time. She didn't sound like she was in a rush, though. "I left April with Pearl after school. I figured you'd be back tonight so it wouldn't be a big deal."

"I'll call and make sure everything's okay," I said. "I can tell you the answer, though."

"Am I making a mistake?" Faith asked. "Maybe I shouldn't have introduced April to your grandparents. I can tell they're already bonding. What if we don't work out? April would be crushed."

These were unexpected questions. "Is there something I need to know, Faith?" I asked. "Am I pushing you too fast?"

"What? You? No!" she said and muted the phone as she talked to someone. Faith was more than capable of multitasking her time while on the phone. "Geez, if anything, I'd say maybe you're being too much of a gentleman."

"I don't think that's right." I hoped she heard the smile in my voice.

Faith was silent for several moments. I was content to just be on the phone with her while she worked out what she wanted to say next. "I scheduled an appointment with a psychologist," she finally said, her voice small. "I really want this to work with us and I know I need to fix my shit."

"That's a big step."

So far, Faith had been all over the board with physical intimacy. Sometimes she was on me like it was prom night and other times she was so closed off I felt like I was alone in the room. Early on, I'd decided I wouldn't let things go too far, even though I desperately wanted that. Although, part of my hesitance might have been a result of my last relationship, which had started with a flash and ended with a gun pointed at my head.

"You'll give me time?" she asked.

"I'm not going anywhere," I said. "Do you need me to join you in counseling?"

"Maybe? Not yet?" she said, unsure. "I guess I have no idea."

"Do you have to drive far?" I asked.

"There's a woman down in Hemingford," she said, her voice trailing off. "That's weird."

"What's that?" I asked.

"One of April's scrunchies is holding something to this beer bottle," she said. "I'm not sure how it got here."

My heart slammed into the front of my chest. "Faith don't touch that," I yelled into the phone.

"What in the hell? Oh shit ... fuck ..." Faith's alarmed voice faded and a moment later the phone clattered to the ground.

"FAITH?" I shouted into the phone.

I'd parked behind Alan Snerdly's, electronic repair shop, planning to visit my best friend before attempting contact with Natasa Savic.

"Biggs, I gotta hang up," she said. "I've gotta find April."

The line went dead.

I dialed Pappi's number and waited impatiently.

"This is Lester. I'm not available at the moment. Please leave a message."

As much as I'd like to suggest I was capable of remaining calm, I found my chest gripped with panic. It was one thing to come at me directly. I could take that kind of stress but to go after a ten-year-old was too much.

I stabbed angrily at the phone, punching in Pearl's number and waiting impatiently for the ridiculously slow lines to make their connections.

"Hello, Henry," Pearl's cheerful voice answered after an impossibly long wait.

"Nanna, where's April?"

"Why she's outside with Lester, Henry. Is there a problem?"

"I don't know," I said. "I need to talk to Pappi and make sure April is inside with you. Did he get the security system running?"

"I guess I don't know. Henry you're scaring me," she said. I heard a door open and rustling on the other end of the phone as she placed the microphone against her chest. "Lester, April, come in, please. I have Henry on the phone and he's all worked up."

In the background I could hear the theme song to the TV show *Ranchers*. It was April's ring tone.

"Henry?" Pappi asked, picking up Nanna's phone. "What's the trouble?"

"Is April with you?"

"She's right here," he said. "We were just headed out to the paddock."

"Are you carrying?" I asked.

"Yes. What changed, Henry?"

"I don't know. I was talking to Faith on the phone. Something happened at the bar and she hung up to call April," I said.

"We've got Diva and she hasn't alerted on anything," he said. "All that said, we'll keep it inside. Unless you need me to run over to the bar?"

"No. It's a busy public place. Faith just needs to know April's okay."

"They're talking on the phone right now," Pappi said. "Where are you? I thought you'd be getting back fairly soon."

"Sutherland, following a lead."

"I thought Butte was turning the case over to State Patrol." he said. "Henry, you need to be careful about stepping over the line on this one. Staties aren't going to like you sniffing around in their investigation after Ellis gave it up."

"I'm working for ISD," I said.

"You quit Butte County?" Disappointment filled his voice.

"No. ISD is contracting with Butte County so I can be part of their remote investigation team," I said.

Pappi was quiet for a while and finally responded. "Unorthodox, but I guess it makes sense. Not like you'd have left it alone either way."

My phone beeped, announcing I had another call coming in. "Hey, I gotta go. I think that's Faith on the other line."

"Be careful, Henry, and don't worry about April. We'll take good care of her," he said. "Diva never leaves her side."

"Thanks, Pappi," I said and hung up.

"Henry Biggston," I said, answering the other line.

"Biggs, Bess Dawdry." I pulled the phone away from my face and looked at the phone number. Yeah, not Faith's number.

"Bess. Hey, I'm kind of in the middle of something. Can I call you back?" I asked.

"I'm at Hootskill, Biggs," she said.

"What are you doing at Hootskill?"

"Following a hunch," she said. "Although if my supervisor asks, I'll tell him I was just taking a break for dinner."

"Make contact with Faith," I said.

"I'm looking at her. She's talking to April."

"What happened?"

"Honestly, I missed most of it," she said. "There's a pink hair tie around the neck of a beer bottle. I think that's what set Faith off. There's a wad of what I think is horse hair under the tie. I saw a man put the bottle on the bar but didn't know it was trouble until Faith started getting worked up. I tried to follow him, but I was too far behind."

"You did good, Bess," I said, trying to keep irritation from my voice. "Have Faith give you a plastic bag so we don't contaminate fingerprints or trace on that bottle. I'm in Sutherland right now. I've got no right to ask, but any chance you could stick around the bar tonight?"

"Believe it or not, I'm a pretty good line-dancer," she said, although I couldn't tell if she was being serious. "What are you doing in Sutherland?"

"I got recruited by ISD," I said, launching into another explanation of my new job situation.

"That's smart on their part," Dawdry said. "Still don't know why you're in Sutherland."

"We were right about that hand belonging to a girl," I said. "Ten-year-old, Una Servy, died in a car accident. Accident report didn't have a lot of details. The mother Natasa had alcohol in her system but wasn't impaired. She lives here in Sutherland. I'm going to reach out to her."

"When are you coming back?"

"Not sure," I said. "Depends on if I can find the mom."

"Hey, Faith just hung up," she said. "Give her a call. Tell her I'm her new bestie for tonight."

"Thank you, Bess."

"Don't thank me, you're paying for drinks," she said and hung up.

———

It took me the better part of an hour to get Faith calmed down. She wanted to go out to Pappi and Pearl's ranch, but I convinced her that if she was being watched, it might be best if she didn't lead someone back there. During this time, Snert had discovered me sitting in his parking lot and was waiting patiently for me in his shop.

"Hey, buddy," I said, when I finally entered.

"Henry, what a nice surprise," he said, eyeing my uniform shirt. "I didn't know you were coming to town. Business trip?"

I nodded. "Can't really stay, but I wanted to stop by and say hi."

"You still ready for us to come out next weekend?" Snert asked. "Melinda is real excited for the trip."

I almost told him not to come, but we'd already cancelled several times due to our crazy schedules.

"Yeah, sure," I said, trying to keep doubt out of my voice.

"What's going on, Henry?" Apparently, I hadn't been convincing enough.

Without hitting the details too hard, I explained what we'd been through.

"Hootskill have a decent security system? You could probably get an ID from the video," he said.

I shook my head. "No video."

"Mel has the week off," he said. "We'll come out early and I'll bring a demo unit. Once this thing is over, I can pull the unit. No charge. That way, I can write the whole trip off as a business expense. Everyone wins."

I didn't know much about business expenses and trips, but I doubted it was quite a simple as he explained.

"I don't know, Snert," I said.

He smiled. "You remember that phone security program I wrote a couple of years back?"

"Sort of? Something about blocking outgoing internet traffic from spyware?"

"Sure, let's call it that," he said patiently. "I just sold the rights to it. I'm thinking about closing the shop."

"What? You built this shop from nothing. It's part of who you are. You love this place," I said.

He shrugged. "Life changes, Henry," he said. "I was going to talk to you about this when we came out. I'm not sure what I want to do right now. What I know for sure is that I don't want to run a retail shop."

"Can you afford to do that?"

A small grin broke out on his face. "For a few years at least," he said. "Maybe longer. Depends on how spendy we get."

I raised my eyebrows. "Who are you?"

"Don't you mean congratulations?" Melinda Garcia's voice echoed in the stairwell in advance of her arrival. Five-foot nothing with long black hair that made it to the middle of her back, the curvy Latina woman looked every bit as good as when she'd chosen my best friend over me. I smiled and accepted her welcoming hug.

"Absolutely. Congratulations," I said, releasing Mel. "Hey, look, I wish I could stick around, but I've got to get going. Snert, tell Mel what I told you. If you guys decide to come out another time, I get it."

"I will," he said as I pushed my cowboy hat back onto my head.

"So mysterious," Mel said, a glint of humor in her eyes as she looked from Snert back to me. "Do love a man in uniform, though."

———

Natasa Savic's apartment was on the third floor of an old house that was in bad need of paint and repair. The number C in the 1C hung precariously from a single remaining nail. It was the sort of place I visited a lot back when I'd trained with SPD. The types of calls we received ranged from burglary to domestic squabbles. Almost always, there were either drugs or alcohol involved. I didn't miss being a cop in Sutherland. Sure, Butte County had plenty of problems with alcohol and domestic abuse. Without prevalent hard drugs, however, my new home didn't feel quite so hopeless.

I glanced up the exterior staircase to Natasa's apartment. The wood wasn't in good shape and as I started to climb, I became concerned I might actually break through. I'd just passed the second-floor landing on my way up the next set of stairs when the apartment door opened.

"You looking for Natasa?" asked an older woman in a cotton nightgown. Smoke billowed out from her apartment and she held a cigarette in her hand.

"That's right," I said.

"She done something wrong?"

I climbed back down the stairs so I could look at the woman. "And you are?"

"Dawn Smith," she said, coughing as she gave me a good once-over. "You're not a local."

"Do you know when Ms. Savic will be back?"

"I might. Got twenty bucks?"

If I'd been SPD, I probably would have handled it differently, but I pulled a twenty out of my wallet and held it out.

"You know you got no jurisdiction here," she said, snatching at the bill. I was quicker and pulled it back.

"Just need the information," I said, holding the bill where she could still see it.

She scowled. "Waitress at the 24-Hour on Highway-2."

"When does she get off?"

"Two in the morning," she said. "Gimme my money."

I let her take the money and turned to go back up the stairs.

"Hey, I told you she was gone," the old woman said.

"Yup."

My phone rang as I knocked on the door. There was a small window in the door and I peered through. I couldn't see the entire apartment, but it didn't look like anyone was home.

"Biggs," I answered.

"Have you talked to Savic yet?" Cropsie asked.

"Not yet," I said, knocking on the door again. "Got word she might be working at 24-Hour Diner. I'm headed over there now. We had an incident at Hootskill earlier. Might be our guy. Not sure."

"What happened?"

I described the events.

"Might be nothing. Putting a lot on a hair tie," she said.

"Faith recognized the hair of April's horse. It was either mane or tail," I said. "Bess Dawdry happened to be there. She bagged the whole thing for me, including the bottle the tie had been looped around. I'll send a deputy over to collect it."

"Yeah. That's weird. Keep me updated. When you get back to Wood Creek, check your email. We've got preliminaries on those DBs," she said and hung up. I think one of the reasons Cropsie and I got along so well was because neither of us enjoyed talking.

I knocked a third time and called Natasha's name. With no answer, I slid my phone into my pocket and jogged down the stairs.

"Told you she wasn't up there," Dawn Smith called after me as I passed.

"Ma'am," I acknowledged her, touching the brim of my hat.

It was a short drive over to 24-Hour Diner. The diner was a one-story dark-brown building with faux stone beneath the windows that faced the highway. Old metal highway signs and a variety of non-working vintage neon signs adorned the walls. The whole place had a certain unpretentious charm.

I found a booth that looked out onto the highway and set my hat on the bench next to me. It was six thirty and if I were to guess, we were just at the end of the dinner rush.

"Coffee?" an older woman asked.

I turned my cup over and slid it to her. "Thanks."

"Know what you want?" she asked, filling the cup. The woman was in her mid-fifties and I knew Natasa was closer to early forties.

"Natasa Savic work here?" I asked.

The old woman shook her head. "What's she done now?"

"Just have a few questions," I said, sliding another twenty onto the table. I kept my hand on the bill and looked up at her.

The woman smiled, showing a few missing teeth. "Take a booth at the other end," she said. "That's Natasa's section."

I lifted my hand and she grabbed the money. I sure hoped I was about to find Natasa soon, as I was running out of cash. I moved to the other end of the restaurant and sat in a booth as I watched the older waitress disappear between swinging doors. Leaning back, I sipped at the hot coffee. As a cop, I had low expectations for coffee and the diner's brew met those expectations.

I was starting to become suspicious after I'd been left to sit for several minutes. Finally, the older waitress ambled her way over to my booth.

"Is there a problem?" I asked.

"No. No problem," she said, waving her hand at me. "Natasa got off her shift just before you got here. Sorry, I didn't realize that."

I looked at her skeptically and noticed that she was looking over my shoulder and out the window. I followed where she looked and saw a woman, wearing the same gray uniform dress, climbing onto a city bus.

"Damn," I scooted out of the booth, pushing past the waitress.

"You can't have your money back. I told you the truth," she called after me as I jogged through the dining room.

I jumped back into my truck and tore out of the parking lot. If I'd been in Butte County, I'd have tried to chase the bus down and pull it over. Natasa's neighbor had been right, however. I had no jurisdiction as a Butte County deputy. I wasn't sure if my State Patrol contract gave me any extra juice, but I wasn't ready to push the issue.

Instead, I drove back to Natasa's neighborhood and parked the truck. Getting out, I retraced my steps to her apartment and started back up the long wooden staircase.

"Back already?" Dawn asked, before I even made it to the second floor.

"Got a hunch," I said and continued past her until I was at the top, where I turned around and sat with my back leaning against Natasa's front door.

With nothing else to do, I pulled out my phone and opened my email program. Most people I cared about had long ago learned that sending me emails was primarily a one-sided affair. It wasn't that I didn't want to talk to them, I just didn't know what to say. I grimaced as I found an email from Snert, from over a week ago. The title of the email was: *Big News – Sold Mongoose Program*. I needed to be a better friend.

The email at the top of the list was from someone at the State Patrol. I opened it and read through. They'd created a new email address for me for official business. I shook my head. Like I needed another email to ignore. I tapped the email's embedded link and was soon presented with a logon and registration process.

Movement near the busy street caught my eye. Given there was a lot going on, I'm not sure what caught my attention, but my eyes fell on a haggard-looking woman wearing a gray uniform dress, looking up at me from the sidewalk in front of the apartment building.

Recognizing that I'd seen her, she abruptly turned and started fast-walking down the sidewalk. I stood, shoved the phone back into my pocket, and took the stairs two at a time.

"Ms. Savic," I called as I easily overtook her. "Stop."

She flinched and stopped her flight as I placed a hand on her shoulder.

"I'm clean," she said, turning to me, holding her hands out to her sides.

"Ms. Savic, why are you running?" My eyes fell on the name tag on her dress which read *Natasa*. According to the information I'd read, she was forty-two years old, but the woman who stood in front of me could have been ten years older.

"I can't go back to jail," she said.

I shook my head. "I'm here about Una," I said.

Shock registered on her worn face and she took a step back. "Una is dead. Why would you say that to me?"

"Ms. Savic. I'm Deputy Biggston," I said. "Can we talk somewhere?"

She eyed me warily. "What about Una?"

The sounds of cars passing by made it difficult to hear her and I wasn't about to continue interviewing her on the sidewalk.

"Not here," I said.

"Take me back to the diner. I can't afford to lose my shift," she said. "Things will settle down after seven. I'll talk to you then."

I nodded. "My truck's around the corner."

"So, you found her?" Dawn yelled from her front porch on the second floor as we passed by.

I glanced in her direction and tapped the brim of my hat. I had no intention of getting into it with her, but suspected she wouldn't stop calling after us if I didn't at least acknowledge her.

"Hateful woman," Natasa hissed as we turned the corner.

I ushered her to the truck and helped her in, concerned she might try to escape given an opportunity.

"Tell me about Una," I said when I jumped in the truck.

"She was my everything," Natasa said, her voice thick with an accent. "I'm abet without her."

"Abet?"

"Specter. Ghost."

"Tell me about the accident," I said.

"Why do you care? Why now?" she spat quietly, looking out the window.

The words came out so quickly and with such venom that I didn't quite know what to think.

"You were close?"

"What is your name?"

"Deputy Biggston," I said, repeating myself.

"Your real name, Deputy Biggston."

"Henry Biggston," I said.

"Henry, do you have children?"

"I don't."

"Then you cannot understand. A child is precious beyond life. There is nothing a mother would not do for her daughter," she said. "I failed my Una. I am dead."

I pulled into a parking space at the diner and Natasa rattled the door handle, attempting to get out. Given the nature of my typical passenger, the doors remained locked unless I released them. She turned to me and wiped tears that hadn't yet fallen to her cheeks. For a moment, I thought about how a twenty-year-younger Natasa might have been pretty. Hard living had changed that.

"Please. I must go back. This job is all that I have," she said.

I pressed the automatic door lock so she could escape. I gave her a minute and then followed her in.

"What are you doing back?" the older waitress asked as I passed her in the dining room.

I ignored her and made my way to the booth I'd given up an hour previous.

After several minutes a rumpled middle-aged man approached the table. "Officer? Very sorry to bother you. Do you have a moment? I'm the night manager here."

"Any chance I could get a coffee?" I asked.

"Certainly. Of course," he said nervously. The man reeked of marijuana and his eyes were bloodshot.

"How can I help, Mr. Goodall?" I asked, reading the nametag on his shirt.

"Um, Natasa Savic," he said. "I fired her."

I raised an eyebrow. "Why are you telling me this?"

"I figured you'd want to pick her up before she got away," he said.

"You guys really have something against me getting a cup of coffee," I complained. "Tell me, Mr. Goodall, what car do you drive?"

"Car? Why?"

I slid out of the booth and put my hat back on my head. "I'll shoot you straight," I said. "You smell like marijuana. Thought I'd check out your vehicle. See if there's anything visible. Maybe get a K-9 unit over here."

"You don't need to do that," he said, holding his hands out. "What do you want?"

"I'd like to talk to Natasa," I said and gave him my best cop stare.

"You ... you want me to call her?" he asked.

"And?" I prompted.

"Give her the job back?" he asked.

I tossed my hat back onto the seat and slid into the booth.

"What's the wi-fi password?" I asked.

"*Magic toast*. All one word," he said, looking nervously at me. "Thanks."

I FINISHED SETTING up my State Patrol email account and logged in. There were already several emails waiting for me, but I ignored them in favor of two from *r.cropsie*.

Biggs –

I need to discuss a few matters of protocol with you. The region you've been assigned is greater than Butte County. While you are outside of Butte, you will need to contact the sheriff's department for the county in which you're visiting. While not required, you might consider dropping in and introducing yourself to the local sheriffs. It'd go a long way toward reducing inevitable stress of multi-agency operations.

Further, please keep track of both miles and hours used on State Patrol business. Our HR will coordinate with your paymaster to make sure people are paid correctly. You're expected to submit this information each week. Failure to do so will result in non-payment.

Finally, you should discuss arrangement with Sheriff Ellis. He's been contacted but will likely want to give further instructions.

Cropsie

I chuckled at the terseness of her message and archived it for future consideration. I wasn't great at logging things, but I'd make an effort. Her second message held a lot more interest for me.

Biggs –

On-site identification of the DBs recovered from Sage Creek forest shows females in their late teens or early twenties. There was evidence of torture. The bodies are in transport to our lab in Platte City and we won't know more for several days. I've instructed the coroner to copy you on initial and formal findings.

Cropsie

I scowled at my phone. A man was running around in my county torturing and murdering people and animals alike and I had virtually no leads on who he might be. How is it that we hadn't heard of these missing girls? Worst of all, I'd somehow dragged April and Faith into the middle of this mess.

"Deputy Biggston?" Natasa's small voice interrupted my thoughts. "Are you ordering tonight? My boss said he was picking up the tab."

"When can we talk?" I asked, not interested in her boss.

"Things are already slowing down. I only have one table left because Norma took all my others," she said. "Give me twenty minutes?"

"Meatloaf any good?" I asked, trying to push away angry thoughts.

"Lots of people like it."

"I'll do that with the mashed potatoes and brown gravy."

"Anything to drink?"

I flipped over my coffee cup, although I was losing hope that I'd ever get any.

Faster than I thought possible, Natasa delivered a steaming plate with a generous slab of meatloaf and a heaping mound of gravy-drenched potatoes. I caught the night manager's eye mostly because he stood directly behind Natasa with a dumb smile on his face, giving me a thumbs-up.

Instead of leaving, Natasa slid onto the bench opposite mine. "I have a few minutes," she said. "Thank you for making Mr. Goodall give me my job back."

"Tell me about the accident that killed Una."

Natasa stiffened and sat back in the booth with a far-off look on her face. Her eyes flitted around, and I imagined she was recalling the events she was about to recount.

"We weren't a happy family," she said, her voice thickly accented. "Vuk and I emigrated from Bosnia at the end of the war. He was a police officer. You must understand. It was a different place. Bosnia was in the middle of a civil war. Neighbors killed neighbors. It was horrible. Men in power were horrible."

"Like policemen?" I asked.

She stilled. I suspected she hadn't intended to be quite so direct.

"War changes people," she said. "Did it not change you?"

"How do you know I was a soldier?"

"A woman knows," she said. "You did not answer my question."

I nodded. "War changes everything," I said quietly.

"When I met Vuk, he was so young and full of energy," she said. "What was the question?"

"The accident."

"I've never told anyone this," she said. "I don't care anymore, though."

I sipped my coffee, which tasted like it had been filtered through a cardboard box. I kept my eyes on Natasa as she waited for me to say something. I didn't.

"My husband hurt me," she said. "It started shortly after Una was born."

"How?"

"He hit me when I said stupid things," she said, "or when he was frustrated because the men at work belittled him."

"Where did he work?"

"Here and there," she said. "He never could hold a job more than a few months. He had a violent temper."

"Did he hurt Una?" I asked.

She shook he head. "Not at first and he could be sweet with her. He loved giving her presents."

"But that changed."

"She started to look more like a woman. It changed everything," she said.

"Wasn't she ten when she died?" I asked.

"She was murdered, Deputy Biggston."

I shook my head. I'd only seen part of the investigation. Una had been killed in a car accident, but the circumstances were suspicious. The child's body was in poor shape. The investigation, as well as the coroner's report, had been shoddily done.

"Ten doesn't sound like a woman," I said.

"She wasn't a woman," Natasa spat. "Vuk was the only one who thought so. She was tall for her age, that's all. She hadn't even started the change."

"You said murder. Who murdered Una?" I asked.

"Vuk."

"The report didn't put him in the car."

"He wasn't," she said. "He disabled the brakes. I was taking her to school. There was a big hill. I could not stop."

"Did you tell the police?" I hadn't seen anything about faulty brakes in the report, but then I didn't have a lot of time to read before I'd been rushed off to lunch.

"Of course," she said. "But Vuk talked to them. He showed them pills I used for sleep. He said I had taken them, that it was all my fault."

"They didn't check your brakes?"

"Why would they?" she shrugged. "They had what they wanted. Vuk can be very charming when he wants. They believed him."

"Are you certain Una died?" I asked.

The question shocked her enough that she sat back. When she'd recovered, she leaned forward and narrowed her eyes. "What's going on, Deputy Biggston? Something has happened. Something bad."

"Answer the question."

"Yes. They only let me see her face. It was enough. A mother knows her daughter's face." The words came out angrily and were accompanied by a flood of tears. I sat quietly as she cried, her head turned toward the window overlooking the highway so the staff and dwindling dinner patrons couldn't share in her grief. Her pain was hard to watch.

When she finally composed herself, I continued. "Did Vuk have any unusual hobbies?" I asked.

"Vuk did not have hobbies."

"Pets?"

She narrowed her eyes. "He hated animals as much as he hated people. If Vuk came across a stray cat or a dog, he would kill it. Animals did not understand that he was evil. They were drawn to him."

"Was Vuk in the military? Beyond his job as a police officer?"

"Yes. He excelled in the beginning," she said. "But something happened and he was released. He would not talk about it, except it made him very angry. But then, the war came and men like Vuk were important again."

"Why do you think he sabotaged your car?" I asked. "Did he want Una to die?"

"Oh, no," she said. "Even though he was starting to hurt her, he loved her. It's difficult to explain."

I thought about how Raff Butler had said he loved Faith, but he would also hurt her. In some twisted way, I believed Raff did love Faith, but his choices were unhealthy.

"How about you?"

"Me he had grown to hate," she said. "I planned to run away with Una. I was saving money. I didn't have enough, but I was getting close."

"You think he found your money?"

"I know he did," she said. "When I got back from the hospital, my money was gone – just like Vuk."

It was four in the morning when I punched in the code to Pappi and Pearl's house. Diva brushed the back of my leg with her nose as I moved through the house. The move startled me, and I was grateful she'd recognized my scent. While on patrol, Diva had been trained to be quiet. If she hadn't recognized me, no doubt I'd have had an arm or ass full of her long canines.

"Hey, girl," I said, sinking to one knee so I could rough her up. She wiggled around on me like a six-month-old puppy and plastered my face with her tongue. I pushed her face away as I wasn't really into the whole dog-washes-man thing.

"Heard your truck in the lane," Pappi said from the darkness of the hallway that led to the kitchen.

"Girls still here?" I asked.

"They're sharing the guest room," he said. "Faith only got in an hour ago. I was planning to give April a ride to school in the morning."

"Sorry I dropped this on you," I said.

"Don't be silly," he said. "I haven't been retired for that long. They're safer here under my roof and you know Pearl, she loves to take care of people."

"Faith is pretty stubborn," I said. "She'll probably want to go home tomorrow."

"Then you make sure you're laying your head down on a pillow wherever that precious little girl sleeps," he said.

I nodded. "Love you, Pappi," I said, sliding my backpack to the floor. "Which room?"

"Door before the bathroom," he said, giving me a hug. "Glad you're back in town."

I pulled off my boots and hung my hat on a coat tree that hadn't been in the foyer the last time I'd been here. After a quick restroom stop, I carefully pushed open the door where the girls slept.

I hadn't intended to stay in the room. I just wanted to see them before I found a bed somewhere. The room smelled faintly of Faith's perfume and I listened to the breathing of the sleeping girls. For a moment, the tension in my stomach eased as everything seemed right with the world.

"Lie with me for a while," Faith whispered.

"There's not enough room," I said. I'd seen April sleep before. The girl was a sprawler. A queen bed was barely big enough for the two of them, much less three.

"Just for a minute."

April's even breathing was interrupted as she turned over. It was almost comical the way her frame contorted while she slept, making her look a bit zombie-esque. Faith's plea was too much for me to resist, so I made my way around the bed. Diva pushed past me and jumped onto the bed, landing directly between the two girls.

"Diva!" I whispered harshly. I didn't allow her to sleep in the bed with me.

Faith rolled out of the bed and walked over to me in her long-sleeved satin pajamas, a finger over her lips. "Don't. It's the only way April will sleep," she whispered.

I grinned. Diva should have been born a coyote for as wily as she was at breaking rules and avoiding the consequences.

"I just wanted to see you guys," I whispered back as she stepped close and picked my hand up with her own. Tipping her head to the side she leaned in for a kiss. I ran my free hand up her back and beneath her hair, cradling her head gently, holding her to me.

After a few moments, she released and pulled me toward the bedroom door. "We'll have to lie on the couch," she said. "The other bedrooms haven't been set up yet. I think your old bed is still in the garage."

"Are you okay?" I asked.

"Other than the weird *gift*, nothing happened," she said. "Bess Dawdry stayed at Hootskill the whole night, nursing a couple of beers. She closed the place down. That your doing?"

"I think she came to the bar to check in on you," I said. "I might have asked her to stick around a little longer."

"I figured," she said. "You know she has a law degree? Apparently, her family is loaded and her dad all but forced a fancy education down her throat. He's a big-time criminal defense lawyer who represents the rich and famous."

I smiled. It was nice to hear Faith talk about something other than the bad weekend we'd had. I pulled my belt from my pants, coiled the length and placed it on the end table. When I shrugged off my t-shirt and hung it over a chair, I realized Faith had stopped moving. Tension rolled off her.

"Sorry, that's the end of the show," I said, making no move to remove my jeans.

She relaxed and sat on the couch. "You have to be exhausted."

I scanned the room and found the familiar blanket chest I was looking for. I pulled out a pillow and one of Pearl's oversized quilts.

We'd both been going for almost twenty-four hours. "You must be, too."

"I can sleep on the chair," she offered. I dropped the pillow at the end of the couch and gently nudged her so she would lay down. "Where are you sleeping?"

I draped the quilt over her and slid into the open space she'd left. For a moment, she seemed okay. Then she stiffened, panic rippling through her body. I dropped a foot onto the floor and extracted myself from the couch.

"I'm sorry."

"No, stop." She rolled off the couch and stood next to me. "I just can't be trapped. You first."

I knit my eyebrows, thinking this was likely a ploy to get me onto the couch while she took the chair as she'd first suggested. She nodded encouragingly, so I stretched out on the couch. Surprisingly, she sat next to me and stroked my cheek. "Gentle warrior. You're such a contradiction." Tentatively, she lay down with her back to me.

I pushed her hair from my face, adjusted the quilt so it covered both of us and rested my arm along her hip and leg. "Better?" I asked softly, my mouth only inches from her ear.

"I'm sorry I'm such a freak."

"Wait till I smack you in the head because I'm having a dream," I said. "You won't be apologizing."

"You shouldn't joke about that."

"I'm not joking."

She reached down and interlaced her fingers with mine and then pulled my hand around her chest. It was one of the most intimate moments we'd shared. Using little force, I pulled her to me and kissed the back of her neck. This time her tension drained away and her normally sharp edges softened into me.

I allowed my neck to relax as my head sank into the pillow. I'd had more comfortable sleeping positions, but wouldn't have traded my spot for any place I could imagine. As the room quieted, my mind turned to Natasa Savic. Her story lined up with everything we knew, but something was off. No doubt her estranged husband, Vuk, was a bad man, maybe even the man from the forest. I couldn't shake the feeling that there was more to this story.

Faith's breathing slowed as she drifted off to sleep. Even as she did, she gripped my hand with both of hers, clasping it to her chest.

I awoke to the smell of bacon and the sound of excited whispers from another room. The lighthearted banter brought a smile to my face as Pearl and April chatted about horses. I reached over to the table for my phone. At seven-thirty, April had an hour before she needed to be at school and I had an hour and a half before I was due at work. I was operating on four hours of sleep, but with coffee, I'd be okay.

As artfully as I could, I extracted myself from the couch. Faith rolled over and pulled the quilt up around her neck, tightly squeezing her eyes shut. With her work hours, I suspected she was pretty good at getting back to sleep once the sun had come up. The thought gave me an idea and I scooped her, quilt and all, into my arms.

"Biggs," she complained.

"I'll make it better." I carried her through the hallway and into the guest bedroom.

"I should get up," she said. "April needs to go to school."

Faith's hair stuck out at all angles as she blinked her eyes and sat up. I moved to the window and pulled the shades.

"We'll get April to school," I said, moving back to the head of the bed. I leaned down and kissed her head. "Go to sleep. We've got this."

"Love you," she said and drifted back to sleep.

I stood there dumbstruck. The *L word* was something Faith had yet to bring up and it wasn't something I said casually beyond Pappi and Pearl. I wasn't about to wake her to clear the air, so I returned to the living room and recovered my clothing. Well, I found my belt, boots, phone and armored vest. Conspicuously missing were my uniform shirt and tee.

"Oh, dear, you're awake," Pearl said as I entered the kitchen. She crossed the room and gave me a quick hug. "Your clothing is on the counter."

"What are all those scars?" April asked, frozen in place and staring at me. "Are those from bullets?"

"Nothing much. Just stuff from my days in the Army." I plucked a freshly washed t-shirt from the pile and pulled it over my head. "Body armor in the hall?"

"Yes, dear, beneath the gun cabinet." Pearl had a rule about guns in the house. She'd made Pappi install a special gun safe in the front hall of the home they'd raised me in. Apparently, she'd been keeping Pappi busy in her new home as well.

"I could give April a ride to school," I said.

"Nonsense," Pappi said, coming up from the basement. "I told Mrs. Hudson I'd deliver her to school by eight-twenty and I'll be darned if I'll be usurped."

"What's usurped?" April asked, pushing eggs away from the pancake she'd drenched with syrup.

"Put out to pasture, replaced, made to feel like a useless old man," Pappi explained.

She giggled up at him. "You're funny."

"Do my best," he said, scooping scrambled eggs and toast onto a plate. "Say, Henry, Pearl was thinking it might be nice to take a run out to the old Quinn farm. Maybe make an afternoon out of it."

"Is that Biggs' new house now?" April asked. "I heard its real rundown."

"If he wants it," Pearl said. "The house is very old. I lived there when I was your age."

"Ooh, that's old," April's face was innocent for a second, until she realized what she'd said. "I didn't mean it that way. I just know the Quinns didn't take care of things very good. They used to raise beef but had to stop because the cows kept dying." She was talking faster and faster as she tried to dig herself out of the hole she'd dug.

"I've got the next three shifts," I said, "but I'm free on Saturday unless something comes up. Otherwise, we could run over after work, but it'll be dark."

"Saturday would be just fine, dear," Pearl said. "And make sure you don't schedule anything the whole day. We're working on a surprise."

"Surprise? What kind of surprise?" I asked.

"Loose lips, dear."

I PULLED into the parking lot behind Sage and Rosemary. While Pearl had washed my shirts, I still needed a fresh pair of pants and a quick shower. Diva barked happily at the sight of Mortimer. I chuckled as he made some effort to hide a cigarette, pretending to look at Denholm's newly potted flowers. Diva had taken an instant liking to the two old newspaper men and she scrambled over me to greet her friend.

"Still no endorsement on the sheriff's election?" he asked. "It's only a week away, I could get it into this Friday's paper."

I grinned, doubting he really expected me to give him anything new. "I met Reba Wiley. Seems like she's squared away."

"Can I quote you?"

"Prefer if you didn't," I said. "What do you know about her?"

"Air Force helicopter pilot in the first gulf war," he said. "Got into a few scrapes and has a chest full of medals to prove it. I could pull a couple articles if you'd like to read 'em. When she got back, someone did a fluff piece on her Air Force career."

"I'd read it," I said. "Any idea why she didn't re-up? Lots of upward mobility for a hotshot like her."

"Reading between the lines, I'd say she doesn't play well with others, especially if *others* include an entrenched boy's club," he said. "Nothing specific, but she was turned down for a promotion right before she got out."

Morty was trolling me. We'd had several conversations about the military while tossing back drinks in his den. He often expressed his distaste for military brass. Personally, I had no real beef with the Army cake eaters and typically left the conversation about a woman's place in combat or chain of command to smarter people than myself.

When he figured I wasn't going to take the bait, he continued. "She bought a nice place down by Hemingford after a messy divorce to her husband of twenty years. Apparently, her being back in the states cramped his style."

"Why Hemingford?"

"It's where she grew up. She's got a sister who still lives in town. I've got a piece on her in the Friday edition. It'd go well with a comment from one of Wood Creek's finest."

"Leave the man alone, already," Denholm said, joining us. "He's smart enough not to be making statements about anyone who might end up his boss."

"Hey, Den," I said, shaking his offered hand. "You think Ellis has a chance against Wiley?"

He shook his head. "Depends on how big this Sage Creek thing is. Ellis is a follower and people know it. Word is they recovered bodies yesterday. Might be enough to keep people from wanting a change just now. Anything you want to say about your trip up the mountain, Biggs?"

"Sorry, talking to the paper is beyond my paygrade," I said. For the most part, Morty and Denholm respected my desire not to get caught in the middle between what was newsworthy and what needed to be kept sheriff's business.

"He's not going to say anything, Mortimer," Denholm said. "We're not on the crime beat anymore. Leave him alone."

"So you say," Morty said. "I'd say Ellis will be lucky to have a job if Wiley does get elected, though."

"You think she'd fire him?" I asked.

Morty shot me a look, one eyebrow raised. "Would you keep him? Are you telling me Ellis never saw what Leonard was up to? He had to have turned a blind eye at some point."

"Are you planning on moving in with your grandparents now that they're in town?" Denholm asked, apparently bored with the conversation.

I shook my head. "Nah. Just helping them get settled in."

"Anything you want to say about Faith Hudson having a meltdown at Hootskill last night?" Morty asked. "Something about a bottle and one of April's hair ties."

"How do you hear about all this?" I asked.

Using his best mobster voice, he said, "I know people."

"I can't say anything."

"I heard there were body parts," he pushed.

I raised my eyebrows. Morty knew just about everything there was to know. I wanted to press him on how he came about the information, but he would just use that as confirmation of the facts.

"Can't get into it with you," I said. "Mind looking after Diva while I shower? I've got to get to work."

"You're getting better at dodging questions." Denholm smiled at me.

"Give me a break," Mortimer said. "I'm going easy on the kid."

⸻

"Oh good, you're here," Sheriff Ellis said.

The Butte County sheriff station sat across the street from the courthouse, which occupied the center square of the town of Wood Creek. The public entrance also faced the courthouse, but visitors had to take stairs up to the second floor. I'd come through the secured back entrance and up past the holding cell.

The space we all shared wasn't large, but it didn't need to be. None of the deputies spent time here except to turn in paperwork.

The back of the station was separated from the stairs and atrium by a wall of glass. Two desks flanked the double entry doors. On one side was Holly Wilder, our daytime dispatcher, receptionist and shift scheduler. If you wanted something done, Holly was the woman you talked to. Opposite Holly was the sheriff's desk.

Along the front wall were the desks the deputies used. Currently, our staffing was at a low point. I'd only recently learned that Leonard's hire from South Dakota had fallen through. With Ellis stepping up to acting sheriff, Raff and I were the only remaining deputies. The department had a budget for five and two wasn't enough to field any sort of regular patrols.

Standing next to Ellis was a thickset, shorter man with dark hair. They both looked at me as I crossed over to them. His bearing told me the man had military background.

"Henry Biggston," I said, shaking his offered hand. Callouses on the ridge of his palm and a firm grip suggested he was a weightlifter. I found further confirmation of my guess as his arm pumped up and down. He had powerful muscles under the denim jacket he wore.

"Julio Ocampo." He introduced himself with a strong Hispanic accent.

"Julio is joining Butte County," Ellis said. "As First Deputy, your job is to evaluate him during his probationary period."

I nodded. "Welcome to Butte County, Deputy Ocampo," I said and looked to Ellis to continue.

"I've got Holly setting up his schedule to match yours for the next two weeks," he said. "It'll be your responsibility to get him checked out on gear and qualify him on the firearms course."

"Can do," I said, giving Ocampo a reassuring smile. I had no idea of Ocampo's skills or background, but we'd figure that out.

"Before you go, can I talk to you in the conference room?"

I nodded. It was easy to forget that we even had the room as it was used more for storage than anything else. Besides the holding cell, our "conference room" was the only other place where a private conversation could take place.

"What's up, Gene?" I asked as he shut the door behind him.

"You okay with Ocampo?" he asked. "I mean, we're really short-handed and he's got experience."

"Seems like a good guy." I shrugged, not catching where the conversation was going.

"Twenty percent of Butte County is Hispanic," he said. "I know Raff has trouble with wetbacks. He seems like a good one, though."

I fought to keep my eyebrows from shooting off my head. Between the Army and SPD, I'd heard more than my share of derogatory terms to describe race, but I'd never heard it from someone in command. Moreover, I'd served with all manner of people and as far as I could tell, skin color didn't factor into job performance. If anything, some folks worked harder for their success as they struggled against attitudes like the one I'd just heard.

"I'm sure Deputy Ocampo will be a great addition to the force," I said. "How long of a probation is he on? I thought you said he had experience." According to Ellis, probation was reserved for fresh deputies.

"A month will get me past the election," he said. "I'd like you to run him down to Hemingford and Alliance this week. Stop by the market and Marie's."

"What happens after a month?"

"Don't be naïve, Biggs," Ellis said. "Mayor will never let us keep him. We'll get some relief on shifts and I'll get a bump in the election."

My stomach soured at his bald admission. "Don't you feel bad using a man like this? If he's a good officer, we shouldn't care what the mayor thinks."

"Politics, Biggs," he said, shaking his head. "You don't need to understand them. I just need you to do what I ask. That work for you?"

I nodded. "Yes, sir," I said.

"So, what's all this with the State Patrol? You want to be their boy?" he asked.

His hostility surprised me. "State Patrol keeps taking our cases. I don't want to be in the back seat on these things. Wouldn't you rather have Morty and Denholm reporting about how we solved some big crime for once?"

He grinned. "Maybe you're not such a political dunce after all. Just keep track of time and make sure I get the benefit, not the state. It's about time they ponied up for what they use. And be sure to get your work around here done first."

I nodded. Ellis' perspective was what I thought it would be... he wasn't exactly onboard. He wanted as much financial reimbursement as possible and didn't mind me working extra hours. I could work with that as long as I wasn't squeezed out of the Sage Creek Forest investigation.

"Anything else?"

"Nope. Go make me look good."

I'd had some pathetic pep talks in my career, but that one was top of the list. I pushed my way back into the main office. Holly Wilder had laid out a pair of uniform shirts on the desk and Julio was filling out paperwork.

"Any calls we need to look into?" I asked.

Holly was a middle-aged woman with a sharp wit. The realization that Sheriff Leonard had played her for a fool had changed her attitude for the worse.

"Mildred Fosum says someone broke into her chicken coop and took a couple of chickens. I told her it was probably a fox. Let's just say she gave me an earful." She handed me a pink slip with the information.

I picked up the clipboard from her desk that served as an informal police blotter. Each morning, Holly added calls to the list. My eyes caught on a few items as I scanned past the drunk and disorderlies and regular traffic stops. Extremely interesting was the report of a stolen puppy from a display in front of the pharmacy. The second significant item was a hunting rifle stolen from a farm truck. I jotted down the make and model of the rifle.

"Can you get me the address of the stolen puppy's owner?" I asked.

After a few deft strokes at her computer, Holly scrawled a name and address on a note pad. "Norma Hendricks. They live about halfway down to Hemingford on 385. Do you think that's the puppy from Sage Creek?"

"Hope so," I said. "Would you mind sending the evidence Raff recovered from Hootskill over to Cropsie at State Patrol?"

"Already on its way," she said.

"Julio, you're with me. Leave your paperwork on the desk over there. I'll drop you off before end of shift so you can finish up," I said, which earned me an indignant grunt from Holly.

"Okay, boss," he said.

"Grab your shirts and we'll get on the road."

Julio avoided looking directly at Holly as he picked the uniform shirts from her desk and followed me through the double glass doors at the back of the office.

"The only thing you missed on the top floor is the drunk tank," I said. "On the first floor we have the armory, prisoner intake and evidence. Courthouse security and the county jail have their own staff and we only get involved if there's a problem. You shouldn't have to mess with that."

Julio nodded as I filled him in. "That is how we did it in Texas."

"Whereabouts in Texas?"

"Concho County. Middle of the state. Smaller than here," he said.

I raised an eyebrow. "You like working there?"

"Yes. Very much."

"Why are you looking all the way up here in Butte County?" I asked, opening the armory and beckoning him to join me in the crowded space.

"I met this girl," he said. I grinned. All good stories started that way.

"Hold on. I've got you at a large for body armor, right?" I asked.

"That's correct," he said.

"Choose a service weapon, but I'll have to control it until I get you checked out," I said, pointing to a display of pistols on the wall.

"Prefer a Glock .45," he said, pointing at a column of black semi-automatics.

I pulled a utility belt from the wall, handed it to him and removed the Glock from the wall. I checked the chamber and locked it open.

"You'll need to get a hat," I said, tapping my own cowboy hat.

"I already have one," he said. "It's in the truck."

I slid open a drawer beneath the pistols, extracted three magazines and handed them to him.

"You wearing a t-shirt?" I asked.

"Si," he answered and then caught himself. "Yes."

"Put on your vest and uniform shirt. Let's make sure those fit," I said. "How long were you a deputy in Concho?"

"Two years," he said. "Army before that."

"Hooah, brother," I said.

"Figured you for Special Forces," he said. "You regular Army?"

"Ranger," I said.

"You guys always have a look," he said.

I grinned. I missed hanging out with my team. "I think that's all we need here. Tell me about the girl." I locked up the armory behind us and ushered him through the back and out to where I'd parked.

"Mia," he said. "It was kind of a chance thing. I got invited to a party. She was visiting family. We just hit it off."

"Hang on a sec," I said as we approached the truck.

Diva barked at our approach and Julio slowed, looking apprehensive. His caution was smart. Under the wrong circumstance, Diva could be a real problem.

"Setzen." I rarely used the German commands Diva had been trained with, but the foreign commands tended to be more forceful. Diva calmed and I opened the door so she could jump out. She whined and looked to me for reassurance.

"Perro demonio," Julio said under his breath.

"Not a demon," I chuckled. "Diva, this is Deputy Ocampo. He's one of the good guys."

Julio didn't move a muscle as Diva sniffed him. Diva gave the dog equivalent of a shrug, which was to simply walk back and sit next to me.

"We didn't have K-9 in Concho," he said.

"Diva is easy," I said. "Don't ignore her when she growls."

"Si," he said warily.

"Diva, kennel," I said. Diva jumped into the back seat. "Julio, let's get you checked out on the range and then we'll run down these calls."

"Not a bad set of groupings," I said when he came back from retrieving his paper targets. We were alone at the shooting range, which was nothing more than four posts set in front of a sculpted embankment, a couple of wooden rests and a shed where we kept targets and a few other supplies.

"Not bad?" Julio asked, affronted. "They're all torso shots and within six inches of center."

"Don't sweat it. I'm passing you. I'll grab the broom and we can get cleaned up and go." Since we were done shooting, I started over to the truck to release Diva so she could stretch her legs.

"Are you some sort of hot-shot shooter?" he asked. He was taking my words harder than I'd expected.

I turned and faced him. "You anticipate the gun's recoil, Julio. That's why your shots tend down and left. You're also jerking the trigger pull."

We locked eyes for a moment and I saw gears churning in his head as he tried to figure me out.

"Shit," he said, finally.

I grinned. "Look, Julio, I'm not trying to bust your balls. I've had a lot of firearms training. I'd be happy to share what I know. As your supervisor, it's my responsibility to point out areas that need improvement. Your shooting is good, but it could be a lot better."

"I cannot tell if you are truly a cowboy or if you have simply managed to stuff yourself into that shirt," he said, a grin breaking on his face. "A wager, then?"

"Stakes?"

"Loser buys breakfast mañana."

"I'm in," I said. "We'll each shoot two mags. Goal is to fire as quickly as you can under control. Winner is assessed by closest overall grouping."

"How will we ever judge that?" he asked.

"Easy. I'll let you make the call," I said. "At worst, I'm out breakfast."

"And you get to judge my integrity along the way," he said. "Very tricky."

"Go set up the targets," I said. "I'll grab more ammo."

I grabbed one of his empty magazines from the table and walked back to the truck. Diva whined, wanting desperately to join us, but I wasn't about to subject her to the concussive damage of repeated gunfire.

Julio and I were about to learn a lot about each other. First thing Julio needed to know about me was that I could care less about pissing contests. If this man was going to have my back, I wanted him to excel at the fundamentals, which meant he needed to spend more time honing his shooting skill. I loaded six rounds into the thirteen-round magazine, slipped a snap cap in and added the remaining six rounds. Snap caps are devious little fake cartridges that operate just like live rounds, except they have no bang. The snap caps are great tools to demonstrate just how a shooter moves in advance of the bullet firing.

"Do you want to fire a couple of warm-up rounds?" Julio asked.

I handed him his magazine and pulled out my phone, selecting the camera. "Nope, but I'm going to record you. You can do the same for me if you want to compare our firing rate."

"You're pretty cocky," he said, pulling on his ear protection.

"Give me a countdown," I said, holding my camera up so I could catch both him and the target.

"Three ... two ... one ..."

I hit *record* on two and watched as he fired off six shots in rapid succession. The seventh, of course, was the snap cap I'd put in. Sure enough, Julio's gun jerked forward.

"Misfire," I called. "Clear your weapon, Deputy."

He racked the slide and neatly caught the snap cap. "That's dirty pool, Biggston," he growled. "Cheating on a bet disqualifies you."

"Sounds fair," I said. He stuffed the snap cap into the front pocket of his uniform shirt, giving me a rebellious look. "Want to tell me what happened when you hit the snap cap?"

"I anticipated," he said.

"Every shooter does it," I said. "It's a habit you constantly have to work on."

"Does this mean you aren't shooting?"

"I already owe you breakfast," I said.

"I feel like you need to back up your words," he said. "Or are you all hat, no cattle?"

I tapped my electronic ear protection to indicate he needed to put his back on. We turned back to face the targets.

"Ready?" I asked, looking at him.

"Go," he said.

In a smooth stroke, I pulled my Springfield 1911 from its holster and kicked my right foot out to the side and a little back, settling into my stance. The target appeared in the V of my rear sight and a nanosecond later the I-beam of the front sight raised into view. I squeezed the trigger and willed my breathing to slow as I pushed the gun's barrel down until the sight-picture showed itself again. I'd done enough shooting that my actions weren't entirely conscious. It was as if I could hear a tone when the target was perfectly in the picture and my body reacted on its own. I had no idea how long it took to empty the magazine, but it wasn't long.

"For the record, I've never raised cattle." I ejected the magazine, replaced it with a fresh one and pushed the pistol into my holster. "Let's get cleaned up."

"YOU'VE DONE A LOT OF SHOOTING," Julio said, climbing into the truck. "Heard you caught a bullet last year. That true?"

I nodded. I didn't love the conversation. "We practice so when we're in the field, we can rely on muscle memory. Shooting accurately is harder under stress."

I wanted to drive home two critical factors to a deputy's survival in a confrontation involving weapons: time on the range and attention to the fundamentals. Accuracy in the field is harder than on the range. At a minimum, your sight picture drastically changes. That can be anywhere from poor lighting, innocent bystanders, moving targets or other unexpected moves suspects come up with in their desire not to get shot. Add return fire to the situation and a deputy needs every advantage available.

"I didn't see much real combat in the army," he said. "We had a few times that were tense, but mostly we just wondered when all hell was gonna break loose. It never did, but the possibility sure played on my nerves."

I'd heard similar stories from other regular army. It didn't match my own experience. As Rangers, we'd been on the go constantly, bringing the fight to the enemy. While I missed the comradery of my elite team members, I was grateful to have stepped back from the constant danger. Like Julio described, it wore on a person.

"Good news is, we're chasing down a chicken burglar today," I said. "Likely to be masked and thirty pounds."

He chuckled at my description. "Raccoon?"

"That's my guess."

The shooting range was on the north side of town and it was a twenty-minute drive to Folsum's farm. I'd been by the place several times on patrol but had never been on a call. Like many farms in Butte County, the buildings were old and in need of paint. Looking past the disrepair, there were decades of back-breaking work given to hewing life from the unforgiving Sandhills.

"Once you break out of the trees, there's not much around, is there?" Julio said. "Kind of reminds me of Texas, except everything's not all brown."

I looked at him sideways, trying to figure out if he was making a racial observation. "Brown?"

"Brown. Red. The dirt has a different color. So much green out here," he said. "Even when we're out of the trees. I thought this was the Sandhills."

"It is," I said. "Vegetation is barely covering the sand. Look where the rain has washed out the hillside. It's all sand beneath. Farms really struggle to produce much. That's something you want to pay attention to. If they say *farm* around here, they're talking about crops. *Ranch* is likely a place with cattle in the fields. Some people do both."

"I don't see any crops," he said as we pulled to a stop at the end of a gravel drive, behind a worn home.

"Mrs. Folsum's husband died a couple of years back. I don't think anyone actually works this farm right now," I said.

The slap of a screen door drew our attention to an older woman who was making her way over to us. I opened the door, slid out and made my way around the front of the truck.

"Deputy Biggston! Boy, am I glad they sent *you*. That lazy Butler boy just ignores me whenever he comes out," she said. "I've just been so worried since it happened."

I put Mildred Folsum in her early seventies. She had worn, weathered skin that spoke of a hard life of physical labor. Over her shoulder, a large garden had already been tilled and low plastic hoop-houses sat atop rows of bright green plants. Past the garden was an enclosed chicken yard and coop where a couple dozen chickens wandered around behind the wire fence, searching for food.

I extended my hand and she grinned as she shook it vigorously. The old girl still had a strong grip and I imagined she'd be running the farm for several years to come. "Mrs. Folsum, meet Julio Ocampo," I said. "First day on the job for him."

"Welcome to Butte County, Deputy Ocampo," she said. "You listen to Deputy Biggston and you'll do right, you hear me? He's one of the good ones."

"Yes, ma'am." Julio grinned and he tipped his hat. "Good to learn from the best."

"You betcha." She turned abruptly and waved over her shoulder for us to follow. "Now, come with me and I'll show you what happened."

I pulled out my notepad and quickened my step to keep up with her. Obviously old and with an uneven hitch in her gait, the casual observer might not have expected her to move so quickly. In fact, we had to step it up to keep pace.

"What time did the trouble start?" I asked.

"Claude, my border collie, was up making all sort of racket about two in the morning. I'm a light sleeper and I generally sleep down-stairs on the couch, so I got up right away," she said.

"Was Claude outside?" I asked.

"Oh, heavens no. Collie like that is likely to chase a coyote off to who knows where. I'd never see her again." She was facing away from us and I thought I heard her voice crack. "Old girl was tough as nails, just like me."

She reached for the gate clasp that held the chicken coop closed.

Her hands trembled so badly that she had difficulty unlatching it. "Mrs. Folsum, did Claude get hurt?" I asked.

She turned and I saw tears rolling down her proud face. Her piercing grey eyes held mine for a moment. "Dammit. I said I wasn't going to cry about this."

I think Pearl had permanently given me a soft spot for older women. I looped an arm around her back and gave her a light hug. "I'm sorry, Mrs. Folsum. Sounds like Claude was a good dog. I know I'd be upset if my girl got hurt."

"You should've let her out for a run," she said, patting my chest. "I'll be okay. I'm just a sentimental old woman. At least that's what my Calvin always said." This time when she reached for the gate, it opened easily for her.

"What happened to Claude?" I asked.

"That's just it," she said. "I don't know. I let her out the back door and she took off like a bullet. I heard her yelp and then nothing. I've been out looking for her all morning."

We followed her over to the coop. "If coyotes got her, they might have dragged her off. I'll take a sweep with Diva after we look around here," I said. "Hollie said you were missing chickens."

"Four Rhodies," she said. "And all the eggs were gone too."

"A lot of eggs?"

"Oh, yes," she said. "I hadn't cleaned them out yesterday. There'd have been at least two dozen."

"Do you close up the coop at night?" I asked.

"Fence goes into the ground eighteen inches," she said, as if that answered my question.

"Julio, walk the fence line. Look for any breaks. See if you can figure out how *whatever it was* got in," I said.

"The fence is cut just over there." She pointed to a section of fence that had obviously been recently repaired, the edges pulled back together by rope. "It wasn't no animal that broke into my coop. It was a man."

"How do you figure?" I asked.

"Look at the cuts in the wire," she said. "They're clean."

"She's right, boss," Julio called as he crouched next to the fence to inspect it.

"And no animal takes eggs without breaking the shells right where they find them," she said. "I took a shot at him."

"You saw who did this?" I asked.

"Didn't say that," she said. "But I knew he was out there and gave him a piece of my mind. I'm no helpless pantywaist, you know. I'll defend what's mine and be dammed what the law says."

I suppressed a grin. "You're within your rights to defend yourself, Mrs. Folsum," I said, "but you should be careful shooting off into the dark. What if it'd been teenagers? You'd feel really bad if you hurt one of 'em."

"Says you. Way I figure it, if it's kids, they'll tell their friends to leave me alone," she said. "Nothing wrong about picking a little double-aught outta their hides."

I pulled a tactical flashlight from my utility belt and shined it into the coop, inspecting the roost bars and laying boxes. She was right. There were no eggshells, nor did it look like anything had been disturbed.

"Looks pretty clean," I said. "A fox or coyote would have made a mess if they'd gotten in there in the middle of the night. There'd be blood all over the place."

"That's right," Mrs. Folsum said. "You didn't think I'd call you out here because my coop got broken into by animals, did you?"

"We have to eliminate everything," I said. "Let me grab Diva and we'll see what we can find on the outside. Julio, see what else you can find."

"Roger that, boss," he said.

Diva was beside herself with excitement by the time I released her. Something about being clipped to the long leash got her fired up and she pulled hard as we jogged back to the chicken yard. We circled around the outside of the fence, stopping near the broken section.

"Hunt 'em up, girl," I urged.

She snuffled next to the fence and along the ground, turning around and around as she gained scent. Then all of a sudden, she pulled away from the fence, her clawed feet digging into the loose soil as she dragged me along.

"Good girl," I encouraged.

Along the north side of the Folsum farm was a long row of tall, scraggly cedar trees. It was a common scene, as farmers and ranchers planted the hardy trees to block against the battering arctic winter wind. It was this shelterbelt that Diva raced toward and I did my best to keep up with her. Just as we approached the tree line, she stopped suddenly and sat. I slowed and carefully crouched next to her.

"What'cha got girl?" I asked.

She responded with a whine. I looked at the ground and caught a dark red splash of blood on the brown, matted grass. I withdrew my phone and snapped a couple of pictures. I estimated at least a pint of blood in that spot, if not more. I sat on my haunches and parted the grass so I could run my fingers along the ground. They came up smeared with blood. I'd most likely just discovered Claude's kill site.

I scanned the area. If Claude had run into wild animals, the grass would be disturbed and torn up. I found it eerie just how much that wasn't the case. I found evidence of something passing through the area, but they'd been careful to avoid open patches of dirt and hadn't left any discernible tracks. I did, however, discover a handful of red feathers on the ground, probably where the suspect had set down a bag of chickens to meet the charging border collie.

I withdrew a plastic evidence baggy and used my knife to collect some of the blood. I'd send it to the State Patrol lab to determine if it was indeed dog.

"Hunt," I ordered once again. Diva glanced at me as if to say I hadn't properly rewarded her for her fine work. I raised an eyebrow and shook my head as I tossed her a treat from my pocket. "You're getting spoiled."

She gave a happy woof and was off again. We wound through the trees and I could tell she was losing the scent. She started doubling back, following a different track and then stopping to look around in confusion. In the back of my mind, I started to build a picture of the person who could kill an angry dog in a single stroke and had the woodcraft to cover his tracks enough to evade Diva's nose.

My thoughts were interrupted as Diva's ears perked up and her head snapped to the side. She'd caught a fresh scent. She pulled me through the trees, panting heavily as she beelined to the opposite side of the trees. With a single bark, she sat and I would swear she had a grin on her muzzle as she looked back at me.

"Well, that's something," I said.

In front of where Diva sat, was a shallow impression of a single boot print. I placed a ruler next to the impression and took a picture. Just past the boot impression were fresh tire tracks.

"Good girl, Diva." I pulled her away from the fresh evidence, scrubbed her head and unclipped her leash. Knowing the suspect had driven away, I wasn't quite as worried that Diva would run off in pursuit. She soaked up the praise and wriggled around with me, demanding as much attention as I was willing to give her.

After a few minutes, I stood and slowly walked around the boot print, spiraling outward. I found a blood trail roughly behind where I imagined the back of the vehicle had been. We wouldn't be finding Claude's body.

I traced our path back through the trees and stopped at what I assumed was Claude's kill site. I repeated the spiral search and found nothing new.

"Such a good girl." Mrs. Folsum grabbed a fence post and lowered herself to her knees so she could greet Diva. Diva, the world's foremost attention seeker, laid her ears down and dove in for a thorough loving.

"What'd you find, boss?" Julio asked.

"Let's go with Biggs," I said. "Found some blood and a track. Mrs. Folsum, where did you hear Claude's yelp this morning?"

"It was dark, but I know this farm like the back of my hand. It was right up by the trees where you were looking," she said. "She's dead, isn't she."

"I think so, Mrs. Folsum," I said. "There was a lot of blood."

She looked up at me, holding Diva's head away just enough to keep the dog's tongue off her face. "You do me a kindness by telling the truth."

I grabbed the brim of my hat. "In the end, that's all we have," I said. "I'd appreciate it if you'd lock your doors for a while. Especially at night and I was wondering if you had someone who can come over and make a more permanent fix for your fence."

"That rope'll hold just fine," she said.

I shook my head. I'd expected the response. Farmers and ranchers were a tough lot. It was their job to make do with what they had. Hiring someone to fix something wasn't in their nature. Julio looked at me and raised his eyebrows. "I used to run fence for a fella down in Texas," he said. "Maybe if a person had a few eggs to trade, I could probably get that fixed right up. You know, if that's not frowned upon by the county."

"Mrs. Folsum, you know anyone who'd want to trade some eggs for a little fence work?" I asked.

"Eggs are two-fifty a carton," she said. "How many you suppose you would want to fix that fence?"

"Two dozen would just about do it," he said. "I'd need pliers and some wire."

"Wire's in the shed and pliers should be on the bench," she said, struggling to stand. Julio was faster than me and reached out to help her up. "Just make sure you put things back where you found them."

"Yes, ma'am," he said.

Back in the truck, I typed in the incident report. As disturbing as it was, we were still in misdemeanor-land, especially if the dog was never found. I'd send the evidence off for identification but beyond confirming the sample was canine, I had no reason to expect anything enlightening. If our guy from the cabin had been here, I hoped Claude truly was dead.

"Gracias, Mrs. Folsum." Julio had finished repairing the fence. He tipped his cap respectfully as he backed toward the truck. I smiled as the old woman stuffed a bag of something under Julio's arm as he tried to separate from her. Grateful gifts from the people we served were something we ran into from time to time. The good people of Butte County were a giving type and often tried to slip us small tokens of their appreciation, all without expectation of compensation. Technically, we weren't supposed to accept gifts, but try to tell that to a seventy-year-old woman who'd just lost her dog. Thankfully, Julio graciously accepted whatever it was and climbed into the truck.

"Will you catch him?" Mrs. Folsum asked through Julio's open window.

"I don't know, Mrs. Folsum," I said. "We don't have a lot to go on. I can promise you, we'll do what we can, though. We don't want someone like this running around."

"Now, Julio," she said, patting his arm. "You make sure you give that bread to Mia. That's Julio's girlfriend, you know. Tell her you helped a helpless old lady today. A woman needs a good man to be her hero."

I chuckled and tipped my hat as I pulled slowly away from the house. "That's quite a haul."

"Hope you don't mind," he said. "Most people I know won't accept charity as easily as they will a trade."

"Just need to be careful taking gifts," I said.

"Simple trade of labor," he said.

"What'd you get?"

"Three dozen eggs, a bag of frozen cookies and a loaf of bread," he said. "She also offered that if I wanted to pick up some work once in a while, she'd be open to it."

"Sounds like you hit it off."

"I've got a way with women. You'll see," he said. "What's next? Going to the high school?"

I shook my head. "Let's take a drive first," I said. "We had some excitement last weekend and I'd like to look at something."

"What kind of excitement?"

"Mostly just disturbing," I said and set about giving him the high-lights of the events in the forest.

"That is some loco shit," he said.

"There's only one place the POI could have come out if he had a vehicle waiting," I said. "I'd like to get a look around."

"How far?"

"It's close, only ten minutes or so," I said, accelerating. "Why don't you pull up a map on the computer so you can get your bearings."

He worked the computer and after a while he gave a low whistle of surprise. "I knew this was big country but mierde, this county is gigantic."

"Perimeter can't be patrolled in a single shift," I said.

"You've got this much territory with three deputies?" he asked.

"Our numbers are down. Ordinarily, we should have five deputies," I said. "People up here are independent, though. They generally take care of things before we get there. Not always a good thing."

He smiled. "We got a lot of that in Texas, too. You know how you hear that saying not to mess with Texas?"

"Yeah?"

"Well, it's because every last one of 'em carries," he said.

"That's good you have that in mind," I said. "We have a lot of that here, too, although more likely to be a rifle than a pistol."

I pulled into the parking lot at the base of the trailhead that we were pretty sure our POI had taken. There were a couple parked cars which I assumed belonged to park visitors. I wondered just how safe they were given the circumstances.

"What are you looking for?" he asked as we both jumped out of the truck.

"I don't know," I said, walking over to where the trail formally started. "Deputies and rangers did a thorough search and didn't come up with anything interesting."

The crunch of gravel beneath tire treads drew our attention to a vehicle entering the parking lot. It was the dark green of State Game and Fish and Ranger Bess Dawdry was behind the wheel.

"Howdy," she said as she pulled up next to us.

"Bess," I nodded, touching the brim of my hat.

"Who's the new guy?" she asked.

"Julio Ocampo, meet Ranger Bess Dawdry," I said.

Julio offered his hand through Bess's open window. "Nice to meet you."

"Find anything?" she asked, not bothering to pretend we were here for any other reason than the investigation of what happened on Sage Creek. I imagined she was here for the same reason.

I told her about what we'd found out at Mrs. Folsum's farm. "My gut puts the two events together."

Dawdry waggled her eyebrows. "Seems plausible," she said. "So, I've been thinking. There's an abandoned barn across the road about half a mile up. I was on my way over to check it out. Want to come along?"

"Sure," I said. "We'll be right behind you."

"You guys work pretty close with the Game and Fish folks?" Julio asked as we piled back into the truck.

"We help each other out. It's a lot of country for all of us," I said.

I picked up the radio mic. "Butte Base, this is Butte-2. We're at Sage Creek Northern Trailhead. We're assisting Game and Fish on the north side of the highway. Over."

"Copy, Butte-2."

Dawdry left the road and pulled to a stop so she could unhook an old chain that sagged between two rotting fence posts. Jumping back in her truck she slowly bumped over an overgrown gravel path. From the road, you could barely see the barn as it sat behind a copse of evergreens. The barn, as so many others in the county, had seen better days and sagged just as much as the gate chain.

"There's a car in there," Julio said. "Way that grass is matted down, looks like it's been used recently."

"Be a good time to unclip that holster," I said, my stomach fluttering a warning.

"Yeah," he said. "Kind of got the creeps going."

"Get on the radio. Have Hollie patch us through to Dawdry," I said. "We need to pull back."

Diva sat up abruptly and barked a moment before Dawdry's driver's side window exploded followed by the muffled report of a high-powered rifle.

DAWDRY ACCELERATED and veered away from the gunfire, her truck bouncing wildly over the rough ground. In quick succession, two more shots rang out and her truck ran into a tree.

"There!" Julio pointed.

I followed his arm and caught the tail end of the muzzle flash from our previously unseen assailant. I looked back at Dawdry's truck and watched as her door flew open.

"Shit," I said. While her truck didn't provide significant protection against a high-powered rifle round, the visual block was critical. Out in the open, she was easy game. "Hold on."

I stepped on the accelerator and the truck lurched forward, throwing up a rooster tail of grass and gravel behind us. I had to block the shooter's lane. We bounced unmercifully as I pushed the truck into the underbrush.

"Metal stuff," Julio warned a moment before the truck pushed up and over the top of what I would later learn to be an old harrow, a farm implement with metal teeth that are dragged over a field to break up dirt clods. Probably the most significant detail is that an old harrow is not something a truck is designed to traverse.

Jerked to a stop, I pushed my door open, slid out into the V between my door and the truck frame and started firing. Without being ordered to, Julio followed suit. I ran through the eight rounds of my 1911 as our fire chased the figure from his shooting position and to the barn. We were thirty yards away and I was certain I hadn't tagged him. Julio continued to fire, although neither of us could see the gunman anymore.

I ejected my magazine and slid a fresh one in. "I'm going for Dawdry," I said. "Cover me."

"Copy," Julio said and continued firing at the building. I appreciated that I didn't need to tell him to keep the pressure up. While he wasn't likely to hit our assailant, it would keep the guy from sticking his head out for another shot at us. At least that was the theory.

I ran behind the truck and into the open area between us and Dawdry. Bullets tore up the ground in front of me and I dove to the side. I could hear the report of Julio's .45 as he returned fire. I came up to my knee and oriented on the building, counting on Julio's fire to throw off the shooter. I caught a glimpse of our guy up in the barn's loft and returned fire. At thirty yards, I could hit him fairly confidently. He seemed to sense that, because he ducked back inside. For good measure, I peppered the barn's siding both below the window and on either side.

Dawdry, only a couple yards from my position, groaned. I gritted my teeth and raced to her, grabbing her vest to pull her around the front of the truck. Acrid smoke wafted from the truck and I realized the engine was on fire.

"Hold on, Bess," I said, dragging her into a ditch on the other side of the tree she'd hit and out of the line of sight of the shooter. "Where are you hit?"

"Leg," she grunted.

"Partner, you okay?" I called as I noticed the shooting had stopped.

"Called it in," Julio yelled back. "But the GPS isn't transmitting. They need our twenty."

I nodded and pushed the information down. Dawdry needed my

immediate attention. Fortunately, I had some experience looking for battle wounds in the heat of things and ran my hand across Dawdry's uniform from top to bottom. She wore a vest and I found a crease along the side of her arm. The wound was bleeding, but not critically. I continued down her body and grimaced as I found a bullet entry on her thigh. Unmercifully, I turned her over and found an exit on the back of her leg.

"Through-and-through," I said, pulling my knife out and cutting away her pant leg. "Got weapons in the truck?"

"Shotgun behind the seat," she grunted. "Chamber empty."

"Keep pressure on that," I said, wrapping a strip around her leg and trapping a wad of fabric against the back of her thigh. I handed her a second wad of cloth and guided her hand to the bullet hole.

"Get him, Biggs," she grunted.

I set my 1911 and my final magazine on her chest and raced back to her truck, grabbed the Benelli M4 and cycled the chamber. If I could get to the barn, the shotgun would more than even things up. The loud report of rifle fire drew my attention. The telltale thump of bullets hitting my truck was followed by Julio returning fire.

I looked over the back of Dawdry's truck bed. The shooter had made his way down to a car inside the barn. I fired the shotgun, spraying a nice grouping of pellets into the darkened opening. A grunt of pain told me I'd tagged him. One of the car doors swung open. When I lost sight of the shooter, I fired a round into the back window of the vehicle.

"He's making a run for it," I shouted for Julio's benefit.

"I'm out," Julio answered.

I ran around the back of the truck and zigzagged my way to the barn as the car started up. I slowed just long enough to steady my aim through the back window of the vehicle and fired. Dirt sprayed up from the rear tires as the car leapt forward and crashed into the barn's back wall. I ran after the car and fired again, even though I'd lost much of my sight picture. Wood boards crashed down onto the vehicle as it punched through the opposite side of the barn. I fired again in frustration at the fleeing vehicle.

"Dammit." The car bumped through the ditch and up onto Highway 20. I considered shooting again, but it was beyond my range and already speeding away.

I pulled at my radio and unclipped it from my belt. "Butte Base this is Butte-2. Over."

"Biggs, where are you?" Sheriff Ellis's voice came over the radio. "We've got your last twenty at Mildred Folsum's. Deputy Ocampo called in but couldn't give us a location."

"Copy," I said. "We're on the north side of Highway 20, half a mile east of the Sage Creek North trailhead. I'm requesting emergency services. We have an officer injured. Over."

"Dammit, Biggs, what's going on?"

"Butte Base, probably best to have that conversation in person. We're on live radio," I said. "Over."

"Stay put, Butte-2," he answered.

"No choice," I said. "We're going to need a couple of wreckers out here too. Over."

"You wrecked your truck again?" Ellis asked angrily.

"Vehicle is inoperable. Over. Butte-2, out." I placed the radio in its pouch and walked to the partially collapsed barn wall. I didn't think for a moment that the shooter's exit through the barn's back wall had been a spur of the moment decision. He'd exited the barn and been on the highway seconds after taking off. This guy was highly organized.

"What's the plan, boss?" Julio had retrieved the shotgun I carried in my unit and taken a position behind a tree trunk, peering warily into the barn. "Got a bad smell in there."

"Fall back until more units arrive," I said. "Dawdry's hit."

"Copy."

Diva's frantic barking drew me to my truck where I noticed three large holes in the grill. The shooter had intentionally disabled the vehicle, apparently not trusting the harrow's embrace.

"Heel," I ordered as I opened the back door, releasing Diva and grabbing my first-aid kit. Off leash, Diva wasn't solid with the heel command. She darted toward the barn. With the shooter gone, her protective instincts would be valuable in the quickly changing situation. If I'd let her out during the incident, she would have rushed the shooter without hesitation, likely ending up dead.

"How you doing?" I asked as I made my way back to Dawdry. She'd crawled over to a tree and propped herself up against the trunk.

"Truck's on fire," she said, referring to her Game and Fish vehicle.

"I know. Emergency services are on their way," I said.

"Your truck done too?" she asked.

I released the field bandage to replace it with a better dressing. "Julio mentioned something about a farm implement shortly after we mounted it," I said, grinning wryly.

"You cut off his line of fire," she said. "Probably saved my life. I don't know why I jumped out of the truck."

I looked into her face and leaned forward to push the bangs away from her forehead. She had an egg half the size of my fist growing just below her hairline.

"You got shot, ran into a tree and banged your head," I said. "You reacted in the moment."

She misread the moment. "Biggs, I'm ... I'm not available."

I let her bangs drop back and smiled. "Need to take your shirt off," I said, pulling at the Velcro that held her vest in place. "You've got a nasty gouge near your shoulder."

She nodded and helped me remove the vest and uniform shirt, exposing corded muscles beneath a wife beater t-shirt. Her physique wasn't surprising. I'd met plenty of women in both law-enforcement and the military who made up for their smaller stature by bulking up. Toned muscle was a good look, although I was mostly interested in seeing what damage the 7.62 round had done to her arm.

"Stings," she said as I liberally sprayed antiseptic into the wound. I knew for a fact that it more than stung.

"Just about done." I squeezed antibiotic ointment into the wound and placed an oversized bandage on it.

"I'm glad you guys followed me in. He really got the jump on me."

"You get a look at him?"

"Not a very good one. Tall and thin. I'd say six foot, maybe a buck-eighty. Assuming that's the guy from Sage Creek, why didn't he shoot at us that night?"

"He didn't have the gun then," I said. "We got a report of a truck break-in not far from here. A 7.62 assault rifle was taken, along with a hundred rounds of ammo or so."

"He's escalating."

"I hope not. You good for the moment?" I asked.

"Thank you for having my back." She looked over my shoulder. I'd heard Ocampo approach while we'd been talking. "You too, Officer Ocampo."

"My pleasure," Julio answered. "Boss, I need you to look at something in the barn."

"Aww, hey, girl," Dawdry said as Diva loped into view and approached. Lifting her uninjured arm, she reached for Diva who instantly switched from soldier mode back to pet mode and nuzzled the ranger's hand.

I followed Julio back to the barn. "What do you have?"

"It's kind of gruesome." He led me into the barn and around a partition to an interior room. "Guy's been camped out here for a while." The smell of rotted flesh hit me in a wave and I followed Julio's flashlight beam over to an old wooden workbench. On top sat the ruined body of what I imagined had once been Mrs. Folsum's dog, Claude.

"Sick bastard," I said.

"I think there's a light over here," he said and reached for a pull string.

"No!" I yelled, but I was too late. A stream of fluid struck Julio in the chest just before a shower of sparks rained down from the ceiling, igniting the flammable substance. Julio screamed and raced for the exit as his chest turned into a ball of flame. Without hesitation, I launched myself at him, tackling him to the ground. The flame transferred to my hand, but I scooped at the dirt floor, depriving the fire of much-needed oxygen. Flames licked around Julio's vest and I splashed dirt onto his neck as he rolled against the floor, smothering the fire. Heat at our backs warned of another growing problem. The old barn was a tinder box. I grabbed Julio's belt and hauled him up as we both stumbled toward the door.

"What kind of crazy place is this?" he asked when we made it clear of the barn.

"They tell me it's a quiet neighborhood," I said and pulled out my cell. "Sorry, I need to make a call."

He looked back at the spreading flames. "That whole barn is going to go up."

The distant wail of sirens alerted us to the approach of emergency vehicles. I was a little annoyed that it was the sound of Fire Rescue and not that of a sheriff's vehicle.

"Cropsie," came the terse answer on the other end of the line.

"It's Biggs," I said. "We've had an escalation in that Sage Creek incident."

"What kind of escalation?"

I gave her a reader's digest version of the events and included details about the missing chickens and stolen rifle.

"Why can't anything be simple with you?" she asked. "Dawdry going to be okay?"

"She's tough," I said. "Might have a limp for a while."

"What's your next move?"

"I'll talk to Sheriff Ellis," I said. "We'll have to tell people there's a fugitive running around and to be on the lookout."

"Don't you have an election coming up in a week or so?"

"Yes."

"That'll play well for Ellis," she said. "Take pictures and send them my way. If there's anything left after the fire, send it to the lab."

"I've got evidence ready for overnight processing," I said. "Blood samples from Mildred Folsum's farm. Probably the dog's but maybe we'll get lucky."

"You have anything else to go on?" she asked. "From this end, it sounds like you're outta leads."

"That puppy we recovered from Sage Creek," I said. "I think I know where it came from. Might get a physical description of the guy who took it. Dawdry got a look at the guy. Gave a description. We'll get a BOLO out on his vehicle."

"That'd help," she said. "Keep me posted." She unceremoniously hung up.

First on the scene was the fire engine, closely followed by Ranger Jasper White and finally, Sheriff Ellis. With only the water they'd brought in their truck, the firemen focused first on Dawdry's burning rig.

"What a shit show," Ellis said, as he got out of the newly repaired Yukon. White gave me a nod but beelined for Dawdry. "What happened to your F150?"

"I ran over a farm implement when I was cutting off the shooter's firing lane," I said. "He also dropped three slugs into the engine block."

"What the hell were you doing over here?" Gene asked, irritation clear in his voice.

I explained how Dawdry had seen us in the trailhead parking lot and asked for our assistance. He didn't seem impressed. "You think this is the guy from Sage Creek?"

"Heck of a coincidence if it isn't," I said.

"People aren't going to like it. We can't let a psycho run around the county. I'm holding you responsible, Biggs," he said.

I nodded. "I'm on it."

"What's your plan?" he asked, then quickly added, "And it seems like this is a State Patrol case. I want you to bill them for your hours today."

I bit back an angry response. I hadn't gotten into law enforcement to play politics and worry about who was picking up the tab. The problem was, I didn't have the foggiest notion of where this shooter was or where to look for him.

"We need to warn people," I said. "We have a basic description and I have an idea about how to dial it in even further."

"I think you're right," he said excitedly, then pulled out his phone, holding his hand out to shush me.

"Denny, this is Sheriff Ellis." I shook my head. Nobody who knew Denholm called him Denny. Gene listened for a minute and then continued. "That's right. I'm on scene right now. A Game and Fish officer got hurt. Our boys are fine, though. Bit of a shootout."

Gene listened for a minute and the old newspaper man's voice came clearly through the line, pumping Ellis for information.

"That's right. We believe it's the same perp as the Sage Creek incident. We're really circling in on him. Thing is, I was thinking we get something into the Friday edition. I'd like to have a community meeting to let people know what's going on. We're going to need community involvement to get this thing into the endzone. I'll stop by your office late this afternoon once we've processed the scene," he wrapped up. "Sounds good. See you then."

"Are you sure a community meeting is a good idea?" I asked. "We don't have a lot of information."

"You've got a description of the perp and his car. We know this guy is dangerous. People are going to hear about it one way or another," he said.

Talking with the public wasn't something I knew much about. From my perspective, though, I'd have thought a simple warning in the newspaper with a rough suspect description was more in order. It seemed to me that if details of what this guy had done got out, it could cause the wrong kind of response.

"Sheriff?" Mark Thompson, Fire Chief of Wood Creek's primarily volunteer fire service approached.

"What can I do for you, Chief Thompson?" Ellis asked.

"Not much we can do for the barn aside from let it burn down. I'd say from how fast it went up, an accelerant was used," he said.

"We'll keep it contained, but there won't be much to look at once it's done."

"Deputy Ocampo got sprayed with an accelerant right before the whole thing went up," I said. "He got lucky the liquid hit his vest and not his face."

"You're saying this was intentional?" Thompson asked.

"The barn was booby-trapped," I said. "Julio pulled on a string he thought was the light. It triggered the release of diesel and a shower of sparks."

"Thanks. I'll make sure that gets into the formal report. Like I said, though, we can't put the fire out. We just don't have enough water aboard."

"Thanks, Chief," Ellis said. "You mind if I get a copy of that report when you're done?"

"Of course. We provide all suspected arson cases to both county and state law enforcement," he said, excusing himself with a nod.

Ellis rolled his eyes once Thompson turned away, apparently irritated by the man's correction. "I'll get Raff to run you back to the station. I'll need your report on this ASAP so I have my ducks in a row for my conversation with Campbell and Cook. We'll leave Ocampo out here. He can get a ride home with the Chief."

As if on cue, Raff's old Crown Victoria patrol unit turned off the highway and bumped along the uneven drive to where we were standing.

"What's with the EMT?" Raff asked as he got out of the car and struggled to pull his pants over his expanding girth.

Ellis ignored him. "Raff, need you to run Biggs back to the station."

"Killed another one, eh?" Raff chuckled, looking at my high-centered truck. "Bet you wish you'd made me number one now, don't you, Gene."

"Both Julio and I fired our weapons," I said, refusing to look at Raff. "Don't you want to get our statements before we go?"

"Negative," Ellis said. "Put it in your report. I assume you didn't hit anything, since the perp isn't here."

"Got you there, Biggs," Raff said, grinning. "Knew I'd be around when you fucked up. Just a matter of time."

"Leave it alone, Raff," Ellis growled. "I'll talk to Biggs once we're back at the station."

"Sure," Raff shrugged innocently. "Forget I said anything."

"We got a problem, Gene?" I asked.

"You guys go busting in on an armed suspect and don't even call for backup?" he said. "Yeah, I've got a problem with that. Damn careless if you ask me."

"That's BS, Gene. We *were* the backup."

"I'm getting damn tired of cleaning up your messes, Biggs."

"I NEED you to drop me at my folks," I said as Raff pulled into town, moving considerably faster than was needed. He'd kept his lights on the entire way back and blooped his sirens to move slower vehicles out of the way.

"Ellis said to drop you at the station," he said with a nasty grin. "What'd you do to get him all pissed off?"

"You need to know some things," I said. "Ellis didn't want to tell you, but that evidence you picked up at Hootskill was April's hair tie attached to some of her horse's hair. I think that guy from Sage Creek is fixated on April."

Raff jammed on the brakes, not even bothering to move to the side of the street, abruptly sliding to a violent stop.

"Say that again?" he growled. "That fucker's after April?"

"The suspect came in contact with Faith and April while we were up at Gold Camp," I said.

"And you're just telling me this now? You're a bastard, Biggston, you know that? First you take my wife and now you don't tell me my girl's in trouble? I'm gonna end this shit right now. Get the fuck outta my car."

"Raff, you don't even know where he's staying or what he's driving. He's dangerous," I said. "You can't go after him by yourself."

"Seriously, get the fuck outta my car," he said, unclipping his holster. I wasn't sure if he was threatening me or trying to make a case that he was every bit as dangerous as the suspect.

"Diva, heel," I ordered as I opened the door. She jumped over the back seat and barely escaped before Raff slammed the car into drive.

"I'm not done with you, Biggston. I thought we were friends," Raff called as his patrol car's tires spun against pavement and careened out of control down the street.

I pulled Diva onto the sidewalk and turned toward the station. We were a good ten blocks away but after the morning I'd had, the walk was welcome. I pulled out my phone and dialed Faith.

"I found missing hair on Hermione's tail where someone cut it. He was here, Biggs," she said.

"Where are you?"

"Home, finishing up chores. I was going to get cleaned up and head over to Hootskill," she said.

"April at school?"

"Yes. Reagan is watching her tonight," she said. "And before you say anything, Pearl invited us to stay. The thing is, I talked to my family and we decided April needs to be at home. We don't want to make this a bigger thing than it is. To be safe, we've got Jimmy hanging out at the house with them."

I nodded. Jimmy provided security at Hootskill on the weekends. A large, barrel-chested man, he often relied on his size to intimidate, although he had no trouble mixing it up if pushed. More importantly, he'd worked for the Hudsons for years and would take the job seriously.

"I think I ran into the guy today," I said. "Bess Dawdry got shot."

"Shit, Biggs, is she okay?"

"I think so. She was wearing a vest."

"Did you get him?"

"Not even close," I said. "He was expecting trouble and escaped. That's not why I called, though."

Faith grunted and, in the background, I heard metal scraping against cement. I suspected she was in the middle of cleaning one of the stalls, a job typically left for April.

"Why'd you call?"

"I'm without transportation," I said. "My work truck got disabled."

"Well, you're in luck," she said. "I had Lester drop me off at home. We left the Bronco at the station. Hollie has the keys."

"Thank you."

"See you at the bar tonight?"

"If I have time," I said.

"Just call. I can get you something to go."

"I'd like to see you."

"Me too."

Instead of entering through the front of the station, I took an alley entrance and circled around to the back. At the end of the small lot where we parked, there was a steel container where we stored bulky equipment. I thumbed through my large keyring, operated the lock and swung open the door. With my phone as a light, I located the light-bar I'd removed from the Bronco only a couple months ago and hoisted it over my shoulder.

My instructions to the guys at the garage had been to leave the mounting brackets for the lights in place. The light bar was easy to install, only requiring a few stainless-steel nuts from the plastic bag I'd taped to the bar. Twenty minutes later, my Bronco was ready for service. I'd have to rely on a portable radio and work without a computer until my cruiser could be repaired, but I was in business.

"Tough morning?" Hollie handed me my keys when I finally walked into the station.

"More excitement than I'd like." I grabbed a notepad and a stack of report forms and sat at the small desk. "Gene has Ocampo stranded at the scene. I don't think Julio has a radio if he needs to contact us. Do we have his cell?"

Hollie tipped her head forward with a motherly glare. "Did he fill out his paperwork?" she admonished. I looked guiltily at the papers that still sat on top of my desk. She continued the ruse for a moment and then grinned. "You're lucky I still have his resume." She pulled a folder from her desk, extracted a piece of paper and rattled off the phone number.

"You know, Gene is mad at you for not endorsing him," she said, also putting the number on a sticky note and pressing it to the surface of my desk.

"I don't see why anyone cares what I think," I said. It wasn't an entirely truthful statement. Gene's actions at the scene had me even more convinced he wasn't the right man for the job.

"They say politics makes strange bedfellows," she said. "Reba Wiley wouldn't hold it against you if you supported Gene."

"You know Wiley?" I asked.

"Of her," she said. "But my point is, you're not looking at all the angles. Not supporting Gene will make your life hard if he's elected. Wiley will just see a man being loyal to his friend. People read between the lines, Biggs. Your silence looks an awful lot like a lack of confidence in Gene to some people."

"That how you see it?" I asked.

"I've known Gene for most of my life. Did you know he was a deputy even before Cal took the reins?"

"That's not an answer."

She rolled her eyes. "That's what I get for working with cops! Butte County used to be a sleepy little place and Gene was well suited to that. What I'm trying to figure out is if my recollection was all a fantasy. Have there always been these bad people out there and I just didn't see it? If the last two years is how Butte County will be like going forward, then I don't see Gene as being the right man for the job. You're walking a fine line with Gene, trying not to hurt him. My question to you is, can Butte County afford for you to be quiet?"

I shook my head. "I don't think you give people enough credit."

"What do you know about a town meeting on Friday? I got a call from the mayor a few minutes before you came in. Sounds like we're going to hold it at the high school. Mayor is worried we won't have enough room for everyone."

"Gene wants to get word out about the suspect," I said. "We do need to let people know what's going on."

"We've always done that by putting an article in the paper," she said. "I hope this wingding doesn't backfire on him."

"How so?"

"Paper goes out on Friday morning. People will be pretty fired up by Friday night. If Gene doesn't have answers, it might not go that well," she said.

"In that case, I better get this report done."

I didn't love writing reports, but I had enough experience to know how important recording every little detail could be. I started with the investigation at Mrs. Folsum's farm. The crime itself wasn't all that exciting, but if this was our shooter, the fact that he'd stolen food was interesting. He was living off the land and I wondered how many other things were missing across the county. Four chickens and a couple dozen eggs wouldn't last him very long.

I had just finished the reports on both Mrs. Folsum's farm and the shootout and was feeding the pages into the scanner when Ellis entered the office.

"Done with your reports?" he asked, catching my eye as he sat back into the plush office chair behind his desk.

"On your desk, Sheriff," I said. As much as I didn't love Gene's job performance, I had no trouble respecting chain of command.

He held my gaze for a moment. "Hey, Biggs, I'm sorry about what I said out at the scene. I was irritated that this thing got the better of us and then I saw the damage to your truck. That guy was hitting pretty hard back there. From the way Ranger White and I see it, you saved Dawdry's life today."

"Appreciate you sayin' so, Gene," I said.

"Oh, look! My boys have kissed and made up," Hollie cooed, just before her phone rang.

"What's your next move?" Ellis asked, ignoring her.

"I'd like to talk to Dawdry again. She's the only one who got any sort of look at this guy. I'd like to see if she can fill in our description." I picked the blotter off Hollie's desk and slid it in front of Ellis. "Look at line seven."

"Paul and Norma Hendrick ... stolen dog ... last Saturday."

"What are the odds that's the same dog Dawdry found on the mountain?" I asked.

"I took that call," Ellis said. "Guy grabbed a pup in front of the drug store and disappeared. Crap, they've got a security system. We might have a picture of this guy."

"I was going to run out to Hendrick's farm and talk to the wife," I said. "I might learn something about him."

"That's good work, Biggs," he said, starting to get more excited. "If we have a picture, we'll have something to show people. We're gonna get this guy."

"You need me for anything else?"

"Go get 'em," he said. "But not before Friday."

"Gene!" Hollie said, scandalized.

"I'm just kidding."

"Deputy Biggston." Jasper White greeted me in the hallway just outside of Dawdry's room at the hospital.

"Jasper," I said, acknowledging him. "She doing okay?"

"They're changing the bandage on her thigh," he said. "Got a little personal for me so I thought it best to step out for a minute. Sure appreciate you having her back out there today. Feel like things might have gone differently if you hadn't been there."

"She took some hits," I said. "Tough lady."

White grinned. "That's an understatement. Tougher than twice any man has to be."

A nurse opened the door but didn't leave. "You can come back in, Ranger White."

"You here on official business?" White asked.

"Yeah, 'fraid so. I need to see if Bess can give me a better description," I said. "We're setting up a manhunt, but no one has really gotten a good look at this guy."

"Go ahead," White said. "I've got a few calls to make."

I nodded, brushing past him to enter the room.

"Biggs!" Dawdry said, with more cheer in her voice than I thought likely without painkillers. "My hero!" She reached out for me and I placed my hand into hers.

"You doing okay?"

"Kind of like drinking. You know it's going to hurt in the morning, but you don't care," she said.

"How bad is your leg?" I asked.

"Doc says I'll need PT, but I should be back to light duty in a couple of weeks. I hope it doesn't screw up my trail run this spring," she said. "You still up to helping with that, right?"

"Of course," I said as the nurse moved around busying herself with buttons on various monitors. "So, Bess, are you in any condition to give me a description of the guy?"

"Nothing I didn't tell you before," she said. "I just barely got a look at him as he got in the car. Like I said, six foot, maybe a hundred and eighty pounds."

"Did you get a look at his face? Hair? Maybe close your eyes and try to remember."

She closed her eyes and her face screwed up with concentration. "Nope. It was in shadow," she said. "Do you think you could do me a favor? That puppy we found on the trail. It's at my apartment. I have paper out, but it's going to need to be let out and to have fresh food for a few days."

"I might have found its owner," I said.

"Really? Who?"

"We had a stolen dog report this weekend. Guy took a puppy on

Main Street in Wood Creek," I said and pulled out my notepad. "Belonged to a Norma Hendricks."

"You should give it back to her then," she said.

"I think she was trying to sell it. Are you in the market?" I asked.

Dawdry shook her head. "Maybe before, but definitely not now," she said. "I'll have my hands full getting back into shape as it is, and that puppy already chewed one of my best hiking boots."

"Think about that description some more," I said. "Write down anything that comes to mind. The smallest detail might help."

"I know the drill," she said. "I'll work on it. Probably be easier after the drugs wear off."

"Butte-2, this is Butte-Base," my radio chirped.

"Sorry," I said. "I gotta get this."

"Go," she said.

I stepped outside her room. "Base, this is Butte-2. Over," I said.

"We just got a call from Wood Creek Middle School. They've got a suspicious person on premises. They're in lockdown," Hollie said.

"Responding." I nearly bowled Ranger White over as I bolted for the stairwell at the end of the hall.

Taking the steps three at a time, I was out the back door in seconds. Reorienting, I noticed a long walkway hugging the building that led to the front of the hospital and the emergency entrance. A small creek separated the walkway from the lot on the north side where I'd parked. Opting to take the shortcut, I charged forward, running down the dormant grass in the shallow ditch, jumping the water, and then scrabbling up the other side.

Diva barked wildly, feeding off my frantic energy as I jumped in the truck and fired up the engine. I rocketed out of the visitor's parking lot with sirens blaring and lights flashing, nearly plowing into an unsuspecting civilian. I pushed the thought from my mind. If the suspect was at the elementary school, April and other children were in danger. It was a cop's worst nightmare.

I tried to tamp down the speed as I flew down the streets, but it was hard to maintain any discipline. I'd never felt so afraid in my life and even as I drove, I tried to negotiate with that fear as I had so many times before. Fear made for irrational decisions and the kids at the school deserved better. April deserved better.

The school was south and east of the hospital and I wracked my brain for the right cross street. I chose Fifth Street but after a block, I realized I'd turned too early. So much for not being paralyzed by fear. I blew out a hot breath and steeled myself. I had to push thoughts of April from my head. Finally, I became aware of Diva barking madly behind me and my peripheral vision started to widen. It was a good sign.

I slowed to turn onto Chapin Street, which would dump me almost directly into the Middle School parking lot. Aware of the danger I posed to any children or adults who might be fleeing the school, I slowed even further and doused my siren. I pulled through the teacher's lot and parked up on the sidewalk in front of the school.

"Diva, stay," I ordered as I jumped out, slamming the truck door behind me. In the distance, I heard another siren on approach. I unclipped my holster but didn't draw my weapon. The parking lot was only half full and I realized that school was over for the day. The only teachers and students still here were those in after-school activities. I pushed myself to recall April's schedule. I was pretty sure she had basketball practice.

A harried-looking middle-aged woman in a business suit met me at the front door. She held a large ring of keys which she used to unlock the door and let me in.

"Thank you for coming so fast, Deputy Biggston," she said.

"Tell me what's going on," I said. "You are?"

"I'm Assistant Principal Mandy Jones. About ten minutes ago, a man tried to force his way into the school through the girl's locker room door – the one that leads out to the field. It's supposed to be closed at all times, but sometimes the girls prop it open," she said.

"Is he still on premises?"

"We don't know," she said. "One of the girls saw him approach and tried to close the door. It's one of those doors with a panic bar in case of emergency. The girls can get out, but it can't be opened from the outside. Well, apparently, the man got his fingers around the edge of the door, but enough girls were able to scream and pull on the bar that the man gave up. The girls pulled the door closed and ran for help."

"Is everyone accounted for?"

"Again, we're not sure. We're after hours, so we don't have a good count. The girls in the locker room were getting ready to play basketball," she said, opening the next set of doors and locking them behind her.

"Take me to them," I said.

"Marge, I'm taking the deputy down to the gymnasium," she said. "Only law enforcement with a real badge gets through that door."

"I know, Mandy," Marge answered.

"Tell me about your lockdown procedures after school," I said as Ms. Jones started down a long hallway, her heels clacking against the polished floor.

"No different than during normal hours," she said. "Every room is closed from the inside and students are not allowed to move between rooms until the lockdown is ended. If there is an active shooter, the teachers are instructed to barricade the doors. We didn't feel this was the case today."

"It sounds like you've trained on this," I said.

"We have in-service training drills," she said. "I've also attended training in Sutherland for three years in a row. It's a very big deal, Deputy. We're hoping for better cooperation from Butte County when Reba Wiley is elected."

"Better?" I asked.

"Oh, yes, you're new. Sheriff Leonard was unwilling to participate in our drills and we've received less than a warm reception from *Acting* Sheriff Ellis." She emphasized the word *acting*. Great.

I raised my eyebrows. I couldn't imagine why either man would have turned down working with the schools, although as with most things, there was probably more behind the story she was presenting.

She led me down a wide set of stairs, through another hallway to a set of four tall doors. "This is the gymnasium," she said. "We'll have to go through here to get to the locker room. There's an entrance at the end of the hall but it's exit only."

I didn't hear a question, so I looked on as she rapped loudly on the tall wooden door.

"Who is it?" a woman's voice called from behind the door.

"Mandy," she answered. "I have a sheriff's deputy with me. Please open up."

"Uh, okay," the woman answered and pushed open the door.

"Biggs!" April pushed past the coach and was almost caught by Mandy Jones before she reached me.

"It's okay, Ms. Jones," I said. "I know April and her family."

"Doesn't seem very professional," the woman said, but she shrugged and backed off.

"I need to work, April. Can you go back with your friends?" I asked.

"I'm so glad you're here. It was horrible. That man from the forest tried to break in, but Janie shut the door on him ... but he grabbed it ... and then Sarah hit him with her math book ... and his hands let go ... but I think he got her book ... but she doesn't like math very much, so it's okay ... and then they got the door to close."

I'd been around April enough that I had some skill at deciphering her excited speech. There was something about the ten-year-old girl that connected their brain to their mouth in such a way as to create rapid-fire speech.

"Was anyone outside?" I asked, looking at the coach.

"All the girls are accounted for," the woman answered. "Mostly just scared. April's been telling stories of something she said happened at Sage Creek last weekend. Did that really happen?"

I felt Mandy Jones' eyes boring into me. "Not the right time for this conversation. I need to get a look at that locker room."

"Keep the door locked," she ordered. "I'll escort Deputy Biggston."

The coach nodded.

"Go with your coach, April," I said, peeling her arm out from around my waist.

She hesitantly let go. "Where's Diva?"

"In the Bronco." I followed the assistant principal.

"Wish she'd been here."

The locker room looked about how you might expect it would with a bunch of ten and eleven-year-old girls in the middle of getting changed.

"I need you to stand back," I said as I approached the door Ms. Jones pointed out.

"You're going out there?"

I placed a hand on my pistol and nodded. "Close it behind me," I said. "I'll knock and announce myself to get back in."

I pushed through the door into the bright late-afternoon sun. The locker room opened into a grassy area on the side of the school. I scanned the property and didn't see any evidence of the intruder beyond Sarah's math book lying forgotten in the mud.

Diva's frantic barking rang out in the distance. The sound was not her normal bark of excitement when she was locked in the truck and wanted out. She was angry. She was at war.

"Ms. Jones, do not open this door under any circumstance," I yelled at the door.

"What's going on?" she asked, a question I couldn't answer because I was running as hard as I could toward the end of the building.

15 / PISS AND VINEGAR

SPRINTING AT FULL SPEED, my lungs burned as I came around the front side of the school. Sitting next to my Bronco was Ellis's rig, but he was nowhere in sight. In the distance, I still heard Diva barking. She was angry and on the hunt, well north of my position. There was no way I'd catch her on foot with the lead she had. Decision made, I raced to my truck. My heart lurched when I saw that the rear driver's side door was open. Someone had let her out. I pushed the information down as I slammed it shut and climbed into my seat.

"Butte-Base, Butte-2 in pursuit," I called. "Diva is loose and north of the school." I dropped the radio onto the seat next to me and fired up the engine.

The Bronco roared to life. The old truck was far from a performance vehicle, but she was all I had. I dropped her into low and mashed the accelerator. With her massive engine and low gearing, she had lots of low-end torque which meant, for twenty yards, acceleration wasn't a problem. The Bronco had another feature for which she was well named. I jostled in my seat as she bucked over the sidewalk and bounced into a wide lawn that separated the school from the street. With wheels spinning, I slid sideways as I navigated down a small hill, back up over a sidewalk and onto the street.

Sirens blaring and lights flashing, I navigated in the direction I'd heard Diva barking. After ten blocks of faster-than-safe navigation, I slowed, having overrun what I imagined Diva's last position to be. With sirens blaring and the engine racing, I had no chance of hearing where she was now. I doused the lights and sirens and slowed to an idle, hoping to hear her. I didn't.

I turned the truck down a street and scanned the neighborhood. I had a decent sense of how far Diva could run and I was past that range. Luck was with me as a kid on a bike caught my attention. A girl about April's age waved me down from the sidewalk. I slowed to pull over and talk with her.

"Are you looking for your dog?" she asked. I didn't recognize her and wondered how she knew I had a dog.

"Yes, she's a German Shephard," I said.

"I saw her chasing a man." She pointed across an open lot that had been turned into a small park. "But he got in a car and drove away. I think he hurt her."

"What's your name?"

"Jilly Baker," she said.

"Thank you, Jilly Baker," I said. "Would you do me a favor and go straight home? I don't like the guy who was running around. He's not a very good driver."

She smiled at me with her innocent, freckled face. It worried me that she'd come into such close contact with such a dangerous man. She was blissfully unaware, however. "You're welcome. See yah, Mr. Policeman."

I put some distance between me and Jilly before I sped up and turned around the end of the block to get to where she'd seen Diva. Four blocks later, I found her jogging down the middle of the street, her tongue hanging from her mouth about as far as I'd ever seen. She turned at the sound of my truck and glanced at me. The light caught her shoulder just right and illuminated a tuft of fur lifted up and blood covering her leg.

I jumped from the Bronco and ran toward her. She gave a woof in the direction she'd been running and then jogged back to me. She hated giving up the hunt, but she was spent.

"What happened to your shoulder?" I asked, running my hand across her fur. She whined as I gently touched and probed the puncture wound. The trauma was localized and not too deep, with smooth edges. She'd been struck by a knife. I sighed with remorse. I hated it when she got hurt. "We'll get you all fixed up."

Diva barked and looked down the street again. It was clear she didn't feel I was moving with enough urgency.

"Always the hunter. Let's go," I urged and turned to the truck. Blood droplets splashed from her wound onto the pavement when she pawed at the back door of the truck. She was such a warrior and I hated myself for ignoring her wound, but we might not get another chance to track this guy. Diva barked percussively as I closed the door on her and climbed into the truck. There was no question what her vote on the matter was. I flipped the lights and sirens back on, put the Bronco in gear and raced forward.

"Butte-Base, this is Butte-2, I'm still in pursuit. Suspect is no longer on foot and is in a vehicle," I called. "I'm on Mears, north of the tracks, turning east onto Beaver Valley. Over."

"Copy Butte-2. Be advised that turns into gravel. Do you have eyes on the suspect? Over," Hollie asked.

"Negative," I said. "Witness saw suspect jump into vehicle near Boog Horse Park. Do not have a good description of vehicle. Over."

Indeed, it was the knowledge of gravel ahead that caused my decision to turn east. The weekend snow hadn't amounted to much in Wood Creek and as a result, the gravel roads were still dry. I was gambling on being able to see the plume of dust that announced any vehicle moving at speed. Sure enough, only half a mile from my position I saw clouds of dirt. If I was chasing the grey Impala, I liked my odds. My larger, lugged tires would eat up the gravel. Of course, it was entirely possible I was just chasing some random teen.

The sound of small engines in the distance announced our approach to Wood Creek's local motocross park. The park was just a wide-open field where a dirt track had been carved into all manner of suicidal hairpin turns and short, steep hills to provide maximum excitement for motocross riders. The sport was actually the sort of thing that would have appealed to me when I was younger.

Fortunately, the north wind helped blow the gravel dust away from the road, keeping visibility better than it could have been. Even so, I found myself in a cloud as I pulled even with the park. A male dressed in a white jumpsuit wearing a sporty motorcycle helmet ran through the dust and up onto the side of the road, waving his arms. I veered and jammed on my brakes. Due to the adverse conditions, I'd already slowed to 45 mph, but could have easily killed the guy if he'd continued into the road.

Undeterred by near death, the scraggly bearded man threw his helmet to the side as he raced toward me. Diva barked a warning and leapt at the window. I pushed the transmission into park and jumped out, hand on my pistol.

"Stop right there," I ordered, holding my left hand up.

"Some dude just took Jerry's bike." I put the wiry-framed man in his early twenties.

"Where?" I demanded.

"You gotta get him. He clocked Jerry with his rifle and took off across the field," he said, pointing into the cloud of dust that was settling. In the distance, I saw a figure racing across an unplowed field atop a high-performance motorcycle.

I reached back into the truck and grabbed my portable radio. "Butte-Base, suspect is headed south through open fields toward Highway 20. He's on an off-road motorcycle traveling at high speed. Suspect is armed. Over," I said.

"Copy that, Butte-2," Holly answered.

"I've got injured civilians. Over," I said.

"Emergency is on the way," she said. "Butte-1 is requesting status on pursuit."

I held down the mic transmit button to broadcast the conversation, holding it closer to the young man who stood next to me. "How much fuel does Jerry's bike have? How far can he go?"

"Maybe an hour," he said.

"How fast?"

"Oh heck, at least eighty on the open road," he said. "Be pretty squirrely, though. Knobby tires suck on asphalt."

I nodded, bringing the mic back up to my chest. "I don't have a clean shot, but I can try to intercept. I believe he's headed down to Highway 20. He probably only has sixty miles of range. Over."

"Break off, Biggs," Hollie said. "Butte-3 is two miles from your position. He'll take pursuit. You need to wait for emergency to arrive."

I gritted my teeth. I hated being stood down but given my position, it was a good call. It'd take me several minutes to backtrack and get around to the highway unless I blazed a trail across open fields, which held its own dangers in the form of holes and gullies.

"Copy that. Butte-2, out," I answered and turned back to Jerry's friend.

"You're not going after him?"

"We've got another unit on the highway and we'll alert state patrol," I said. "There's no way I'm getting around this field in time to catch up."

"You guys need motorcycles. Bigger towns have them," he grumbled.

"Get in and take me to Jerry," I said.

He jogged to where he'd dropped his helmet and came back around to climb into the truck. "He's in the parking lot." He pointed to a collection of pickup trucks, most of which had motorcycles sitting in their beds. I pulled into the parking lot and stopped behind the same gray Impala that had busted out of the barn after the shootout, the rear window having been blown out by my shotgun blast. "Sonnvabitch nearly wiped us out with his car. Then he jumps out all yelling like and took out Jerry. Happened so fast. I'd have stopped him, but he had a gun."

I nodded. Jerry sat in the bed of a pickup truck, drinking a beer, with his arm resting on a cooler next to him. He reeked of weed, but I didn't see any evidence of recent use in his eyes. He also sported a large gash across his cheek that was still bleeding onto the front of his jumpsuit.

"Put that back in the cooler," I ordered as I approached.

"Aww man, don't be such a buzzkill. Dude just totally stole my ride," he said. "Aren't you going after him?"

"We have officers in pursuit," I said. "Did you get a look at the suspect?"

"Duude, what the fuck do you think?" he asked. "The dude totally bashed me in the face with his gun."

"Can you give me a description?" I pulled out my notepad and wrote down his description, which was basically a tall, thin guy with a farmer's hat and a scruffy beard that could have been white or blonde or maybe both but definitely not brown or black. I bit back my irritation as I tried to glean more information from him but in the end, I wasn't overly successful. Fortunately, I was saved by the sounds of the EMT's approach.

"You're sure getting around today, Biggs," Stacie Morris, one of the regular EMTs from Wood Creek, called as he approached. I gave a friendly wave, hoping to finish with Jerry before the EMTs took over.

"Come to the station tomorrow to fill out a report. We'll need a VIN and description of the stolen property," I said. "You'll also want to call your insurance agent and let them know what happened."

"That's it? Some dude whacks me and takes off with my bike and you're just like *come down and fill out a report?*" Jerry asked derisively.

"When we recover your property, you'll be informed," I said. "He's all yours, Stacie."

"So, you think you'll get him?" Jerry asked.

I pulled out my radio. "Base, can you send a wrecker out to the north motocross parking lot? I've got an abandoned vehicle that we need to pull back to impound. Over." As much as possible we tried not to give too much information over the radio as it was monitored by more than a few local citizens.

"Copy that, Butte-2," Hollie answered. "Chief Ellis wants to know if the vehicle is the one we were looking for."

"That's affirmative. Ask him if he can get surveillance footage from the school. Over."

"Copy that, Butte-2. Base, out."

I pulled out my phone and dialed Faith. "Hey, there's something going on at the school," I said.

"April. Is she okay?" Faith's voice went from zero-to-sixty in one second.

"I saw her," I said. "She's fine. Someone tried to break into the girl's locker room. We missed him but we've got a unit in pursuit right now."

"Where are you?" she asked. "Are you sure April is okay? I'm going over there right now."

"That's probably smart," I said. The school would release kids directly to parents only. "April is perfect. I saw her in the gymnasium. The school went into lockdown. They have their crap together."

"Are you okay?" she asked. I heard her truck door close and the big engine fire up.

"I'm good," I said. "Diva got hurt, though, I need to get her taken care of."

"Diva? What happened to her?"

"I really don't know. I think the guy we were chasing let her out of the Bronco. I don't know if he was trying to take the truck or if he was messing with her."

"Epically stupid," she said.

I nodded even though she couldn't see me. I couldn't imagine anyone who would open a door on a trained German Shephard and think it would go well.

"I'll probably be late tonight," I said. "What are you going to do?"

"I'll bring April back to Hootskill," she said. It wasn't uncommon for April to sit in the office and watch TV or work on homework while Faith completed a shift. The room really looked more like a living room than an office and I'd spent a few quiet moments there with Faith. I was glad April wouldn't be at home with our suspect out running around.

"I'll check up on you when I can," I said.

"I meant what I said this morning. I wasn't just sleep-talking."

"Oh?" I froze in place.

"I love you, Henry Biggston."

Of all the things I was prepared for, this declaration wasn't on the list. "Um. Me too," I said.

The pause on the other end of the line worried me until I heard Faith laugh. "We've finally found something Henry Biggston is afraid of. Better get that story straight, Biggs." And then she hung up.

I sighed, knowing I'd blown the conversation. Pushing through my angst, I opened Diva's door and helped her to the ground. She whimpered, her bleeding shoulder giving her trouble. I poured her a bowl of water and she lapped at it greedily. As she drank, I located my first-aid kit and much like I had done with Dawdry, I made a quick compress bandage.

"So glad you can't talk," I said as I wrapped a bandage around her shoulder.

"Doesn't look too bad," Doc Peters said, tilting his head back so his reading glasses were in line with Diva's shoulder. Diva took the opportunity to test out his face for lunch remains which caused him to chuckle. "Oh, you're just a little opportunist, aren't you?" He took another moment to give her attention before turning back to the wound she was trying to keep him away from. The two had gotten a chance to know each other well over the last several months and while Diva loved the man, she wasn't overly impressed with the type of attention she always received from him. "Good spot, too. No cone of shame on this one. Knife wound?"

"I didn't see it," I admitted.

Doc Peters *hmphed* as he sprayed the wound with antiseptic. Diva was tolerant enough of pain that she would put up with a few stiches, especially with a topical. "Didn't get into the muscle too bad. Looks like a sharp blade. I think the blood on her muzzle probably isn't hers. Oh, lookie here." He redirected his attention to her mouth and dug a finger into the loose folds at the back of her jaw. "Looks like she got hold of something tender."

He started to hand me a piece of skin. "Hold on, Doc," I said and fished out a plastic baggie so he could drop it straight in. "That might be evidence."

"I don't suppose you know anything about the rumors flying around about a shooting up on Highway 20, do you? Maybe a fugitive running around? Heard something was going on over at the middle school too."

"Sounds like you might have a radio in that office," I said.

"Guilty," he shrugged. "I find it entertaining most days. Not against the law, is it?"

"Nope. I'd appreciate it if you'd keep what I'm about to tell you to yourself, at least until Friday," I said. He nodded so I continued. "I believe the suspect who did this has been injured. A veterinary clinic is a nice place to pick up medical supplies."

"I keep things pretty well locked up," he said and patted the holstered pistol at his waist. "My clinic has been the target of bad people more than once. That's why I listen to the radio, if you know what I mean."

I nodded. "Just be careful. This guy is dangerous," I said.

"Understood."

With Diva patched up and sleepy from a mild tranquilizer, I drove to Dawdry's apartment. I heard the puppy whining and yipping from the time I was ten feet from the front door and it wasn't a great smell that greeted me when I walked in. At some point during the day, the pup had broken through Bess's barricade and made more than a few messes.

"What are you doing, you little scamp?"

I sank to a knee and rubbed the pup's fat little belly as it rolled over and wiggled. The puppy was all tongue and needle-sharp teeth and seemed in very good shape. After taking the little guy out and playing with him for a few minutes, I took pity on Dawdry and scooped up the messes as best I could. I located an aerosol deodorant from the bathroom and knocked down the worst of the smell but with the house closed up, I was afraid the odors would only get worse until she returned. After locking up, I dumped the little pile of piss and vinegar onto the floorboard behind my seat so he couldn't get to the defenseless and drowsy Diva.

My next stop was fifteen miles away at the Hendricks' farm. I'd met Paul Hendricks at some point – although I couldn't recall when – and recognized him as he walked out from the barn when he heard my approach.

"Deputy Biggston, what brings you out this way?" he asked, approaching the truck.

"Caper of the missing puppy," I said, through my open window. I reached around for the puppy who was quite a bit more interested in the taste of my hand than letting me get a grip.

"You found him already?" he asked. "That's pretty good."

"Some days you get lucky," I said. "Is Norma around?"

He knit his eyebrows together in confusion as I handed the puppy to him. The man's hands were weathered and cracked from hard work. "Norma? Why, sure she is. What do you need with her? She's up in the house. She done something wrong?"

"I was hoping to get a description from her of the man who stole the puppy," I said.

"Said he was kind of a creepy guy. Maybe a foreigner." He walked with long strides toward the house. "Norma!" he shouted. Before we'd made it another ten feet, Norma appeared at a screen door.

"You found him?" She rushed over to grab the puppy away from her husband and was all smiles as the puppy licked and nibbled at her.

"Deputy Biggston has some questions for you," Paul said. "Needs a description of the fella that took your pup."

"Oh, that's not hard. He was tall. Dirty blonde hair and had a smell like he didn't bathe much. Also had a beard, probably four inches, hadn't trimmed it at all. Tanned face. Could have been a farmer. Had an accent, maybe Russian. I don't really know my accents. Definitely not German, though. That's where my family's from."

I worked furiously to write down her description. Apparently, she'd paid the man quite a lot of attention as she was able to describe his clothing all the way down to his worn combat boots.

"Anything else you can recall about him?"

She tipped her head to the side. "I was kind of counting on that money," she said.

"How much were you asking?"

"Two hundred," she said. "We normally have purebred border collies and they fetch quite a bit more. Neighbor's dog got out and knocked up my good bitch. He'd be a good dog, but nobody wants a Border-Lab mix. They're too soft to run stock."

"Would you take a hundred?" I asked, pulling out my wallet.

"I figured we'd lost him," Paul said, although Norma looked like she wasn't quite as happy with it. "Hundred sounds pretty good."

I peeled off five twenties and handed them to her.

"Care to stay for dinner?" Paul asked. "I was just about to take a break."

"Appreciate the offer," I said, accepting the puppy back from Norma. "Probably best if I keep rolling."

THE STATION WAS quiet late that evening when I finally hit *send* on my report about the incident at the middle school. I held up the bag containing the small piece of skin Diva had pulled from the suspect. Too small for me to get any sense of where it had been pulled from. I suspected she had latched onto a hand or arm, since the guy's legs would have been protected by jeans. I slipped the bag into an overnight envelope and set it on Hollie's desk for morning pickup.

Wiggling at my feet, Lucky was awake again. I'd brought both Diva and the pup up to the station, mostly because I wasn't sure why the suspect had broken into my Bronco with an angry Diva inside. Doped up, she wouldn't be able to defend herself if the guy doubled back and decided to take a second swing at her. She was in no mood for the puppy's ministrations and nipped at its nose. Lucky yelped but then ducked his head and snuggled into her neck.

Hollie had left two USB drives on my desk. The first was video from the drugstore's cameras for the day when Norma had set up her puppy display. The second was from the school. While I was happy to have the video, my frustration with Butte County's lack of video processing technology boiled up. At SPD, or even in the Rangers, we had special search and enhancement software that sped up the process by a significant margin. I had to rely on an ancient desktop computer and the native video player that came with the old operating system.

I opened the drugstore video first, which was supposed to contain five consecutive days. Everything about the footage was miserable. The pictures were very low quality. Plus, the camera had been mounted on the inside of the store to catch images of customers entering. The best chance I had to see people looking at the puppies was when the tinted front door opened and I got an unobstructed view of the entryway.

Initially, I was confused by the time references on the video. According to Norma, she'd set up at two in the afternoon and Lucky had been stolen around four. I dragged the bar underneath the video to the time range I was interested in. When I released, the sky outside the store was dark and Norma Hendricks was nowhere to be found. I checked the display. The date wasn't even the right year. I swiped the scrollbar and ran the video to the end, stopping a few times to note the date and time. Apparently, no one had bothered to set the date and time feature. I settled back into my chair. It was going to be a late night.

Twenty minutes later, after struggling with a horribly slow computer and equally ineffective software, Norma Hendricks finally came into view. I scrolled the video forward to where she disappeared from the scene and then started backing up. It was a laborious process, but I was finally getting somewhere.

The interaction between Norma and the suspect took only a few short minutes. During that time, not a single customer entered or exited the drugstore. Mostly what I was left with were dark, blurry images through tinted glass. On the positive, the clouds parted for just a moment, flooding the front of the store with bright sunlight. Unfortunately, our suspect appeared to be aware of the camera and kept his face turned away. Searching for other clues during the moments when the sunlight was maximizing the image, about all I had was a good view of his faded boots. Since we had a good boot print, the image might be useful for a later comparison. With my current equipment, that's all I could see, so I noted the time stamp information, attached the video to an email to ISD and sent it off. Immediately, I received an error that my file was too large to transmit. Irritated, I pulled the USB stick out and replaced it with the one from the school.

With a better timestamp, the school video was easier to scan. According to Hollie, the middle school only had a few cameras and none of them covered the backside of the school, making only relevant video from the front of the school. Just like with the drugstore video, the man was clearly aware of the camera as he ran into the frame and directly to my Bronco.

Holding up his arms defensively, he spoke to Diva before opening the door. I couldn't make out what he was saying, but Diva was barking furiously. She held her ground when the man opened the door but as soon as he reached in, she attacked, grabbing his outstretched arm. With speed I found hard to track, a knife appeared in the man's other hand and he jabbed at Diva, striking her in the shoulder. She yelped with pain and released his arm.

For a moment, the two locked in battle as he attempted to put the genie back in the bottle, keeping Diva inside by pushing against her with the door. She'd wedged her shoulders into the gap and was snapping at any part of him she could get to. He pushed and bounced against the door, trying to get her to back away. She yowled in pain but refused to give up. He changed tactics, looking around before turning, in a moment of brilliance, to grab a bicycle that was lying in the grass. He was on the bike in a flash before Diva could push the Bronco's door open and jump out. The two disappeared from the scene.

Replaying for the umpteenth time, I was startled when my phone rang. I hit pause and looked at the phone's display. It was Faith. "Hey," I said, suddenly more tired than I expected.

"Things are starting to slow down over here," she said. "You coming by?"

"April still there?" I had no idea where the time had gone. How was it eleven thirty already?

"She's asleep in the office. And before you ask, Jimmy and Reagan are both here too," she said. "Are you hungry? I saved you a sandwich and a salad."

I grinned. Salad wasn't something you could order at Hootskill. "Sure. Give me twenty minutes," I said, stretching in my chair. "I was just finishing up."

"Don't be too long. You have a shift tomorrow morning."

I cradled the phone on my arm and picked up the USB drives as I made my way over to Hollie's desk. I felt a soft squish under my heel and looked down only to realize I'd stepped in a small dog pile. I couldn't imagine where the chubby little guy stored it all, although I was starting to suspect his big life plan was to simply deposit poop wherever he landed.

"Are you sleeping at home tonight?" I asked.

I opened a storage cabinet next to Hollie's desk and rifled through, looking for USB drives. Fortunately, I found a couple as well as a container of wipes that we used for cleaning deposits of body fluids that were common in a sheriff's station.

"I'd like to," she said. "I don't think I'm sending April to school tomorrow."

"You mind if I leave Diva with April? She got banged up this afternoon and could use some downtime." The file transfer was ridiculously slow. I addressed another overnight envelope, planning to combine the USBs with the evidence bag already destined for Platte City.

"Sure. Are you sleeping at my house tonight?" she asked. "I'm leaving for home at midnight."

"If you're offering," I said. "Bad news is, I have that stolen puppy with me and he's definitely not house trained yet."

"Shouldn't be a problem," she said. "Worse case, we can keep it in the barn next to Reagan's goats."

"See you in about an hour," I said and hung up.

"You look like crap," Julio said when I walked into the station the next morning, half an hour late. "Hope you didn't eat breakfast yet, because I'm taking you to heaven this morning. And you're paying, boss."

I'd left Diva and Lucky at the Hudson ranch after helping Faith finish morning chores. I was working on five hours of sleep, which wouldn't have been horrible if not for the run of short nights I'd already strung together.

Ellis chose that moment to enter the station. "Do you have a report on the school for me yet?" he asked without a greeting, his face filled with tension as if he were expecting a fight.

I turned to Ellis, reciting to myself: *respect the position, if not the man.* "Sent them last night, Sheriff."

His flustered demeanor settled. "Good. We've got that town hall meeting tonight. Your attendance is mandatory and I expect you to wear a clean uniform shirt." He turned without waiting for an answer. "Hollie, call Game and Fish. Invite Ranger White. I don't suppose Dawdry is feeling well enough to be in attendance?"

"I can try to reach her at the hospital," Hollie answered. "Are you sure Game and Fish will let their rangers say anything?"

"For eff's sake, Hollie! I don't need them to talk," Ellis said. "I just need people to see that we're all on the same side here, trying to find a damn serial killer."

"Don't you get snippy with me, Gene Ellis," Holly fired back immediately. "You gave this case to ISD and you know as well as I do that Game and Fish doesn't like to get between departments."

"Fuck." Ellis slammed his insulated coffee thermos onto the table. "Just do it already, would you?"

I caught Julio's eye and pointed at the back entrance to the station. I plucked my copy of the blotter from Hollie's desk and followed Julio out of the station.

"Those guys always get into it like that?" Julio asked as we took the narrow stairs down to the small prisoner-processing area at the back of the building.

"Gene's keyed up about the election," I said. "He knows he's out on a limb with this town hall thing."

"Did you read the paper this morning?" he asked, pushing through the back door that led into the alley where my Bronco was parked.

"Didn't have time," I said. "Ellis said he was going to talk to them, though."

"Check it out," he said, handing me a folded paper as we slid into opposite sides of my truck. "Where's Diva?"

I unfolded the paper. At the top and in three-inch-high block lettering was the single word: MANHUNT. Beneath the headline was a professionally-taken picture of Ellis in his uniform. I shook my head as I scanned the copy. Ellis had told Morty and Denholm virtually the entire story about what had been found at the cabin in the forest, including how Dawdry and I had tracked a serial killer through a snowstorm in the dead of night. The story went on to describe how, on a tip from an undisclosed source, we'd come in contact with the suspect. He finally ended with a shorter description of the lockdown at the middle school, saying it was a developing situation and that he'd have more information at the town hall meeting.

I whistled, pulled out my phone and dialed Cropsie.

"State Patrol Investigative Services Division," a man answered. "May I direct your call?"

I had Cropsie's direct line, so was surprised at the redirection. "Deputy Biggston for Detective Cropsie."

"Transferring you now."

"Did you have anything to do with the article in the Wood Creek Sentinel?" The voice on the other end of the phone belonged to Captain Jack Arnold, not Cropsie. I wasn't overly surprised.

"Negative, Captain," I answered.

"I thought Ellis was leaving this investigation to us," she said, cluing me in to the fact that I was on a conference call.

"That's affirmative, Detective," I said.

"Is this bullshit about that election next week?" Arnold asked. Before I could answer, he continued. "Damnation, but I hate small town politics."

I knew this conversation well from my days in the Rangers. There was always some sort of bad news when tensions were high. I had no doubt Ellis both cared about the well-being of the citizens of Butte County and that he was using the situation to help himself in the election and was pretty sure everyone on the call understood that.

"I have video evidence I'm sending from the drugstore and from Wood Creek Middle School. It'll be in an overnight pouch that's going out this morning. Our equipment isn't very good, but I've noted various time logs that might help with identification. There's also a tissue sample that might be from our suspect," I said. "For some reason, the suspect attempted to break into my vehicle and my K-9, Diva, responded aggressively."

"Did you dust the locker room door for prints?" Cropsie asked.

I mentally face-palmed. Between chasing the guy and getting Diva medical attention, I'd completely spaced it. "Negative. I lost control of the scene when I went in pursuit. Although, in truth, I didn't think to return to the scene."

"That's a little sloppy, don't you think?" Arnold asked.

"Yes, sir," I answered.

"Wasn't your K-9 injured in that altercation?" Cropsie asked.

"Yes, ma'am," I answered. "No excuses though."

"Probably no use in going back now," Arnold said. "That scene has to be completely contaminated."

"Agreed," I answered.

"I understand you have a town meeting in Wood Creek tonight," Arnold pushed. "I assume Ellis arranged that."

"Roger that, Captain."

"Look Deputy, I know this is complicated and I'm not actually in your chain of command, but this meeting tonight is a big mistake.

The last thing we need is a bunch of ranchers and farmers all running around shooting at strangers."

"I understand," I said.

"Because that's exactly where we're headed."

"Sir, respectfully, don't you think this is a conversation better had with Sheriff Ellis?" I asked.

Arnold choked off a laugh. "Talked to him this morning. He threatened to rescind Butte County cooperation in the case, including your contract. I'm considering taking him up on his offer. Is that what you want?"

"No, sir. I don't think that is the best course of action."

"I know you copy Ellis on your case reports," he said. "I can't believe I'm saying this, but I need you to slow down your written reports. Do you read me?"

"Sheriff Ellis has expressed considerable interest in those reports," I said.

"But you do understand that the state has jurisdiction and you are creating those reports as part of the contract the state has with Butte County?" he stressed. "Let me make this easier on you. The state is formally requesting that all reporting be delivered orally."

"Are we any closer to identification of the bodies at Sage Creek?" I asked.

"We pushed them to the top of the coroner's list this morning," Cropsie said. "Should know more by the end of the day. Preliminary indications are female, late teens, early twenties."

"Is Game and Fish still excavating?" I asked.

"It's tough going. They're waiting on more equipment. Probably won't know anything for a few more days," she said. "What's your next move? Any sign of that stolen motorcycle?"

I scanned the blotter from the previous day. There were no new reports of suspicious activity. As far as I could tell, Raff had a very quiet night. "No motorcycle yet. We're still waiting for the owner to file a stolen vehicle report," I said. "I was going to process that Chevy Impala we recovered at the motocross."

"Unnecessary. We had the tow truck drop it at our garage. I'm going to have a couple of techs pull it apart. It'll probably take most of the weekend," Cropsie said. "Any other leads?"

I shook my head. "This guy is a Houdini," I said. "Every time I get close, he disappears."

"Keep the pressure up, Biggston," she said. "He's been driven from cover. As much as I hate to admit it, Ellis ratcheting up visibility will force his hand even more. Unfortunately, these guys tend to go down messy."

Arnold cleared his throat. "You should know, we've got our rapid-response team on standby if this thing breaks loose," Arnold said. "We have an air asset that can put them in Wood Creek in forty minutes."

"Copy that," I answered.

"Find this guy, Biggston," Cropsie said and then hung up.

"What was that all about?" Julio asked. "Sounded like you were getting your ass chewed."

"Not far off," I said. "I'm contracted with State Patrol's Investigative Services Division. Brass wasn't impressed with Wood Creek Sentinel's lead story."

He chuckled. "You're one loco dude, you know that? Why would you take a contract like that?"

He wasn't wrong. I was now stuck firmly between Ellis and the State Patrol.

———

A large part of being a deputy in Butte County was the constant driving. We responded to calls county-wide but for the last year, had scaled back our time through many of the remote areas. I didn't like the uneven coverage our current understaffing required. Most of our patrols focused on the three largest towns: Wood Creek, Crawford and Hemingford. Given our short staffing, we went where trouble demanded, which, depending on the time of day was often as not one of the county's sixteen legal drinking establishments.

While someone could reasonably argue that the larger population centers warranted more attention, there were sections of the county that hadn't seen a sheriff's vehicle in over a year. I was interested in resolving that disparity, but there was only so much a single officer could do.

While our destination was the community of Agate, at the extreme south and west edge of Butte County, we first needed to stop by the mechanics shop and retrieve the computer from my disabled truck, thus finishing the Bronco's transformation to a fully functioning patrol car.

"Did you tell Mia we were coming?" Julio's girlfriend lived in Agate and he'd been commuting from the small town since accepting the deputy position.

While I'd been through Agate a couple of times, it was small enough and difficult enough to get to that a patrol didn't happen very often. The small town was over half Hispanic, which by itself had little bearing on our duties. In practice, however, the mix played a big role in how we interacted with the residents. For as long as I'd been in the department, we'd never received a single call from Agate. It was clear that our department wasn't trusted within the community, something I hoped Julio would help us get past.

From the corner of my eye I saw a lopsided grin crawl up the side of Julio's face. "Don't tell me you're afraid of the brown," he said. The words were delivered as a joke, but I had no doubt it was a serious question. I decided to hit the issue head on.

"Four years ago, the Agate meat packing plant was raided by immigration," I said. "Fifty-two undocumented immigrants were captured and deported. Our department took part in that raid. We haven't received a single call from an Agate citizen since."

"Gee, I wonder why?" Julio said sarcastically.

"Our official policy is that we don't check immigration status unless there's a felony arrest," I said. "That policy was created after the raid on Agate Meats."

"I know why Ellis hired me," Julio said. "He thinks that by showing off a brown-skin deputy, he'll get their votes. It doesn't work that way."

"No?" I asked.

"Everybody wants the Hispanic vote. People in Agate know about Ellis. They talk about him, how he was part of that raid four years ago. People don't forget that kind of shit," he said. "Hiring me brought attention to the election, but it's not good attention for him."

"He probably didn't have a choice," I said. "He was part of the department."

"Maybe so," Julio said and pointed at a dilapidated single-pump gas station that badly needed fresh paint. "Restaurant is behind the station there."

I pulled off the asphalt street and into a gravel lot behind the station. At the back of the lot was a light-green travel trailer where the windows on one side had been modified to provide a walk-up concession window. Overhead, a faded, pink hand-lettered sign read *El Peppe's*. Temporary wooden poles with cement footings made a rectangular dining area in front of the trailer and supported strings of lights. Beneath the lights sat a handful of picnic tables with a mish-mash of lawn chairs pushed in around them.

Patrons, who up to this point had been enjoying their breakfast, turned to stare at Julio and me. I felt a pang of guilt as we exited the Bronco. Surreptitiously, three men stood and walked from their table toward a line of parked vehicles, careful to keep their eyes averted. Their actions stirred my chase instinct, but I fought to ignore the urge.

"Julio!" an older woman exclaimed, exiting the trailer and holding her arms wide. She spoke rapidly in Spanish even as her eyes drifted over Julio's shoulder to me. Her eyes narrowed but then she returned her attention to Julio.

"Mamasita," Julio said and continued in Spanish. He quickly

turned toward me and switched back to English. "This is Deputy Henry Biggston. He owes me breakfast, so I brought him here. Biggs, this is Mamasita Hernandez, Mia's mother."

I pulled my hat off and offered my hand. "Nice to meet you, Mrs. Hernandez. Julio said you serve the best food in the county."

The older woman tipped her head back and ignored my offered hand, giving me a defiant look. "Are you here to make trouble?" she asked with a thick accent.

I replaced my hat. "No, ma'am. Like Julio said, we're just looking for breakfast."

"Mama!" A young woman, who'd been watching from the concession window, exited and raced toward us. She was slightly taller than the older woman and wore a stained apron over jeans and a blouse. "Be nice! This is the man Julio was talking about last night."

The older woman tipped her head back, her eyes still fierce. She turned to her daughter, letting loose a string of rapid-fire Spanish. While I wasn't fluent in Spanish, between the vehemence and the words I did recognize, I could tell the old woman wasn't impressed with my presence. To accentuate, she left abruptly in a huff.

"I'm so sorry. Mama does not trust the police," she said. "I'm Mia."

I nodded and held out my hand. She ignored my offered hand and pulled me into a hug. I was taken off guard by her action and looked to Julio as I returned her embrace. Fortunately, she let me go quickly thereafter.

"I'm Biggs."

"I'm sorry. Normally, I'm not quite so forward, but Julio told me about the shooting. He said you really had his back," she said. "Thank you for keeping him safe."

"That was a two-way street," I said. "I'd have been in a lot of trouble if not for Julio."

"Well, I hope you're hungry," she said. "Don't worry about Mama. She'll warm up eventually. Just sit anywhere. I'll be right back."

I SAT BACK in the wobbly white lawn chair and took a long drink of hot coffee. My mouth was on fire and the coffee did nothing to help. I'd always enjoyed spicy food, but I suspected Mama – as Mia called her – hadn't held back on the peppers she put in my breakfast burrito. Fortunately, I enjoyed the heat, even if the burrito was somewhat over the top.

"Mia seems nice," I said, making idle conversation. Julio gave me a sidelong glance and I wondered if he was the jealous type. He looked over to the trailer where Mia worked alongside her mother. She must have sensed our eyes on her because she glanced at us and flashed a big smile.

"I hope this job works out," he said. "It's hard to get hired this far north if you have brown skin."

"I wish that wasn't true," I said, but Ellis's racist comments still burned through my head. "There are a lot of hard-working people around here who would be better served if they trusted us."

Julio knit his brows. "I can't figure you out, Biggs. Do you just talk a good line or do you mean that?"

"Do you mean, do I think the color of a person's skin or where they were born should dictate their chance at success and happiness?

No. Do I think that sneaking into any country and breaking their laws is okay? No. Do I really know what the fuck to do about it? No."

"And you wonder why people around here have trust issues."

"No, Julio. I don't wonder that at all," I said. "As deputies, we exercise discretion in every stop we make. Did you know that Ellis will throw out any speeding ticket for a license plate that starts with 69 if it's not for fifteen miles over or better?"

"Yeah, he actually mentioned that in my interview. What's that got to do with a department full of racists?"

"Buddy, you've got a chip on your shoulder the size of Kansas," I said, trying to cap the anger that was rising. "I don't disagree that Ellis isn't shooting you straight about this job, but you're painting with a wide brush. Besides, he's just the acting sheriff. He doesn't have the job yet."

"Look. You seem like a standup guy, Biggs," he said. "But you're surrounded by people who've systematically ignored twenty percent of the population because of the color of their skin or their immigration status. Are you supposed to serve and protect only the whites?"

"I told you, we don't even get the calls," I said, flustered. "We only have two patrolmen right now. That's all we do. We respond to calls."

"You boys playing nice?" I hadn't seen Mia's approach as I was so focused on Julio. He was hitting a sensitive topic and I didn't like how easily I was riled by the conversation.

"I just told my boss he's a racist," Julio said, wearing a strained grin.

Mia's eyebrows raised and she moved closer to Julio's chair. "Julio!" Her voice was a harsh whisper. "You shouldn't be making trouble. I'm sure Deputy Biggston is an honorable man."

"Like Butler?" Julio asked, his grin vanishing.

"You must stop, Julio," she said. "We have to live here."

Something on the back of my neck prickled. "What's Raff got to do with this?"

"Julio, no," Mia said. "You promised you wouldn't say anything."

"Biggs can keep a secret. Can't you?" Julio turned toward me, his eyes mere slits.

The atmosphere around our table cooled significantly as the once ebullient woman all but collapsed into herself.

"Did you know that Mia has no papers for working in the US?" Julio asked. Like lightning, Mia's hand reached out and slapped Julio across the face. She hadn't held back and her blow turned his head to the side.

He slowly brought his hand up to test the damage. Blinking a couple times, he whistled and grunted out a low cough then spit on the ground.

"You have no right!" Mia said.

"Hey, we need to slow things down here guys." I used my best calm voice. "Mia, I don't have anything to do with immigration. Unless you commit a felony, we don't even look at status. Even then, what happens is a judge's call. Julio is trying to make a point, although I'll admit it's lost on me."

Mia's eyes bored into Julio as he turned back. If the anger in her face was any indication, I wasn't sure their relationship was going to survive the morning.

"Did you know that Mia and Deputy Butler dated?" Julio said, straightening up, his eyes locked on his girlfriend.

"No, Julio," she said, her voice small and pleading.

"Oh, that's right, they didn't actually date," he said. "They just went out a few times."

Tears streamed down Mia's face. The woman was in anguish and I wanted to punch Julio for causing her so much pain.

"No, please," she whispered, frozen in place.

"I don't understand," I said, softly. "Did Deputy Butler hurt you, Mia?"

"No." Her breath shuddered.

"He said he would call immigration if she said anything. Said he would turn in her whole family," Julio said.

The once delicious burrito rolled in my stomach as the implications of the conversation washed over me. The information was secondhand, but I was hearing an allegation of rape against a woman who stood right in front of me. While Mia had lost the ability to voice a confirmation, I had absolutely no doubt of the veracity of the report. I did the only thing I could think of, which was to stand and wrap my arms around the quietly sobbing woman.

"I am sorry, Mia," I whispered. I no longer wondered where Julio's anger toward Butte County was coming from. I now shared his outrage. If anything, I wondered how he managed to keep it together.

"Please," she struggled to talk between shudders. "Please, say nothing. My family has no place in Mexico. It is too dangerous for us to return. We have a good life here."

"I will make this stop," I vowed, releasing her.

"Please, no," she said. "My family."

"If Raff did this to you, then he's done it to others," I said. "I can leave your name out of it, but I can't let the assault go."

<hr />

"Did you know about Raff's assault before you applied to Butte County?" I asked as we pulled away from El Peppe's.

Surprisingly, Mia had given Julio a hug and even a kiss on the cheek before we'd taken off. Mama's angry stare had followed me as we left and as far as I could tell, she blamed me for Mia's distress, even though she'd yet to talk to her daughter. I wasn't sure she was wrong. A woman was being sexually assaulted by one of my coworkers and the sheriff's department hadn't done anything to stop it.

"No," Julio said. "Did you mean what you told Mia?"

"That I'd make it stop?" I didn't wait for an answer. "There's a lot you don't know about Butte County. Raff Butler is April's father."

"Your girlfriend's daughter?"

"Faith, yes" I said, deciding to fill him in on some of the details.

"They were married. Raff hurt Faith, but she won't let me deal with him either."

Julio sighed. "When girls try to come to the US from Mexico, they're given birth control. Sexual assault and rape are widespread on that journey. Our women have come to expect abuse from powerful people."

"Bullshit," I said. "No woman expects to be abused."

"You saw Mia. She knows Butler will come back and she won't be able to do a thing about it."

"No wonder her mother is so angry," I said. "When's the last time Raff came here?"

"About a month ago," he said. "At least that's what I think. I was still in Texas. Mia was pretty upset. I'm just now putting things together. It wasn't until I came up for the interview that I got her to tell me about it."

"A population that lives outside the law is at risk," I said.

"So, because they fled poverty in Mexico, they should be raped?" he asked, getting hot again.

"Shit! Stop, Julio," I said.

"What? It's a popular opinion," he said. "For the simple crime of crossing a border without permission, we should stop caring what happens to these people?"

"Think like a cop already. Our job is to protect and serve and that extends to everyone in Butte County. We need to do better. We need to figure out how we can make our county safe for everyone."

"Now you're the white knight," he said sarcastically.

"Did you quit your job in Texas or were you fired?" I asked.

This caused him to laugh. "You gotta admit, I'm starting to grow on you."

I shook my head. "Not even a little."

"Butte-2, this is Butte-Base. Over," Holly's voice crackled to life on the radio.

"Go ahead, Base," I answered.

"We just got a call from a rancher up toward the South Dakota border, north of Rush over in Dawes County. According to the sheriff, they've recovered the motorcycle we had that BOLO out for. Chief Ellis wants you to go pick it up. Over," she said.

"Copy that," I answered. Apparently, Ellis was ignoring ISD's demand that he back off from the case. I didn't much care. I wanted to get a look at the bike. "We're ninety minutes out. I have the computer in my unit, go ahead and send the address. Butte-2, out."

Julio rotated the computer and started typing as I turned on my flashing lights. If I pushed the speed, I could shave our travel time. If I'm honest, however, I'd have to admit that a part of me always enjoyed driving fast, even if circumstances didn't entirely warrant it. Julio turned the display back to me, showing a route that would take us through Hillsville and out to a rural section of the state.

I handed my cell phone to Julio. "See if you can get Sheriff Kirst on the line. He's in my contacts." As a matter of course, I'd programmed emergency phone numbers for the sheriff's departments of all five counties that surrounded Butte.

Julio did as I asked and handed the phone back to me. "It's ringing," he said.

"Dawes Sheriff Department," a man's voice answered.

"This is Deputy Biggston from Butte County," I said. "My dispatch said you have a bike up in Hillsville we've been looking for. Is Sheriff Kirst available?"

"Just a minute," the man said.

"Deputy Biggston?" The background noise behind the voice suggested the speaker had been patched through via radio.

"That's right. Is this Sheriff Kirst?"

"Thought I might be getting a call from you," Kirst had a country drawl to his voice. An older man with bright white hair, I'd only met the man in passing, but he seemed friendly enough. "You coming this way?"

"I'm a little over an hour out," I said. "We appreciate you reaching out."

"Read the newspaper this morning," he answered. "Sounds like you guys are in the shit again. Anything we can do before you get here?"

From the background noise, I imagined Sheriff Kirst was either already on the scene or getting close. "Actually, I'll be passing through Hay Springs on the way and wondered if you fellas might have missed breakfast." By my nature, I didn't have great social skills. Pappi, however, had drilled into me that when someone, especially a cop, went out of their way to help, you recognized and appreciated the effort.

"Probably wouldn't turn that down," he said. "I'll take a poke around out here and we'll see you in an hour or so."

When I hung up, Julio turned to me. "What's in Hay Springs?"

"Best donuts for a couple hundred miles," I said, handing him my phone again. "One more call? Contacts, State Patrol."

"So now the brown guy is your secretary?" he asked.

I shook my head and kept my attention on the road. I was driving eighty-five on a single lane highway with a vehicle that on a good day didn't track straight. I wasn't about to stare at a phone screen and take a hand off the wheel.

"Geez, take everything so serious already," he said, handing my phone back to me.

"State Patrol." I'd called the office often enough to recognize Trooper Thompson's voice.

"Hey, Thompson. Can I talk to Detective Cropsie? This is Biggston from Butte County," I said.

"Hey, Biggs," he answered. "Here you go."

"Cropsie."

"Did you get notified that Dawes County recovered that stolen motorcycle? I'm headed out there right now," I said.

"They called Ellis?" she asked. "Dammit. That BOLO was issued by State Patrol."

"Ellis told me to bring it back to Wood Creek," I said.

"Shit. How far out are you?"

"An hour, give or take," I said.

"Don't load it up unless you hear from me."

"I'm going to have to rent a trailer," I said. "I don't have any way to carry it. We're probably going to get tied up for a couple hours. Kirst is at the scene."

"Not surprised he's on Ellis's side in this. Sheriffs all stick together," she said. "I'll have Patrol meet you out there, they'll take control of the bike and get it back to the lab."

"I need to call Ellis and let him know we talked," I said.

"That's not necessary," she said. "It'll just piss him off."

"Probably," I said and hung up.

"Call Ellis?" Julio asked as I handed my phone to him.

I nodded. "Might as well get it over with."

I had Gene's personal cell and he answered on the second ring. "Let me guess, your girlfriend at ISD doesn't want us to have the bike."

"Thought you should hear it from me," I said.

"After this investigation, I'm canceling your contract with State Patrol," he said. "I thought you were a team player. To be honest, if we weren't short-staffed, I'd be reviewing your employment with Butte County. As it is, I'll be shortening your leash."

"I understand." Truth was he was making a mess of things and looked to vent his irritation on me.

"Didn't have to go this way, Biggs."

"Gene, we need ISD to process the bike for evidence," I said flatly. I knew it'd send him over the edge, but I had a job to do.

"Don't you fucking tell me what we can and can't do. I've been a cop in this county since before you were in diapers," he said. "My job is to protect the citizens of Butte County and I don't need ISD getting in the way."

"Understood." He wanted to draw me into an argument, but I wasn't biting.

"You're a smug bastard, you know that?" Gene said and waited for me to respond. I allowed the dead air to become uncomfortable. In the Army, I'd gained some immunity to barking superiors. "Dammit," he finally said and hung up.

"That sounded intense," Julio said.

"He's under a lot of pressure," I said, setting the phone down. I'd been chewed out a lot in my life and it wasn't something I was particularly sensitive to.

For the next thirty minutes we drove in silence as I processed the conversation I'd had with Gene. He'd given away this case to ISD and now it seemed he regretted it. Moreover, when he'd been just a deputy, Gene hadn't ever been a particularly angry man. If anything, I'd thought he was too laid back, more prone to showing up late because of a morning fishing trip. I wondered if his sour attitude was because of the demands of managing a whole department, the upcoming election, or something else.

The whole *cops and donut shops* thing is something of a stereotype that most cops don't love. However, given my instinctive and enthusiastic detour to Beth Bowrey's home-based bakery, maybe there was a little truth to the stereotype. Of course, if pressed, I could point out that she was a great source of local information and that cultivating community contacts added value to the sheriff's department.

"Deputy Biggston. Who's that you have with you?" Bowrey smiled broadly, greeting us as we walked through the screen door and jogged up the half flight of stairs into her kitchen.

"Deputy Julio Ocampo," I said. "Second day on the force."

Julio stepped forward and pulled off his hat as he shook the chubby baker's hand. "Nice to meet you, ma'am."

"Where do they get you boys? Always *ma'am* and *missus*," Bowrey said. "So polite. I've got a batch of glazed cooling on the rack right now. You're headed up to Hay Spring then?"

Julio gave me a confused look and I gave him a half grin in return. "Ms. Bowrey has a police radio. Butte County isn't encrypting yet."

"I hope you never do," she said. "Otherwise, I'd never have anything to talk about."

I poured a cup of coffee. Bowrey had upped her coffee game and was still pricing it at fifty cents. For under two bucks, you could get a donut and a coffee, something I very much appreciated on my paltry deputy's salary.

"Who's got your vote for sheriff, Biggs?" Bowrey asked.

"Don't think that's something I should talk about," I said.

"Morty said you were keeping your opinions close to the vest," she said. "I can only think of one reason why that'd be the case."

"Oh?"

The coffee was scalding, but I drank some anyway.

"My guess is, you don't like either of the candidates. Still think you should have run," she said. "Are you tracking the fugitive right now? Is that why you're running out to Dawes? I mean, I know they recovered the motorcycle."

She'd managed to package a dozen donuts while pumping me for information. "Eight dollars, unless you're paying for your partner, then ten."

"It's on me," I said, pulling out a twenty and accepting a ten in return.

"Nice to meet you, Mrs. Bowrey," Julio said as we retreated down the stairs. "She seems nice," he mumbled, chewing around his donut.

"She is, but she's a talker, so be careful with what you say."

"You were right about the donuts," he said as he quickly finished a second. "I'm gonna get fat if we keep eating like this."

"Did Mia ever say if Ellis got mixed up with any girls – like Raff has?" I asked.

"I could ask," he said. "She really only mentioned Raff. I don't think she would have told me about him, except I pushed her."

"I thought you two were done this morning," I said. "She was mad."

"I've gotta figure out who my friends are," he said, shrugging.

"Not following."

"Tell me Ellis isn't going to fire me a few months after the election if he wins," he said.

"Why would you take the job if you already knew that?"

"Do you know something?"

I nodded. "Ellis said the mayor won't want to keep you."

"Because I'm Mexican?"

I nodded.

"Shit. Guess I called it right."

"What's that got to do with bringing up Raff in front of Mia?"

"I got *Captain America* to give her a hug," he said. "You're on Mia's side, now. I couldn't have played it better even if I'd known about the whole Faith thing."

"That's pretty conniving."

"You know us Mexicans. We're sneaky bastards."

I shook my head and kept driving. Julio was right. There was nothing I wouldn't do to protect Faith and now that I knew about Mia, there was no turning back.

THE AKRON RANCH was fifteen miles north of the small town of Rush. It was surprising how quickly the terrain changed from the steep hills and heavily treed groves of Sage Creek National Forest to the rolling green expanse of the sandhills. By its name, the sandhills sounded neither beautiful nor interesting, but I found them to be both. The sheer desolation of thousands of square miles of nothing but grassy hills and sand gullies was mesmerizing, if not particularly productive from a land-use perspective. About the only thing a person could do here was set livestock out to graze and only then if you had access to large swaths of land.

"Sure is a lot greener than Texas," Julio said. "I wasn't expecting so many rivers."

I nodded. I should have reminded him that we'd just left Hay Springs, aptly named for the source of water that fed the only crops that survived there. The springs filled the riverbeds he was looking at. I stayed quiet and let Julio enjoy the ride. We drove in silence, not seeing another vehicle, until we came over the top of a rise. My eyes were drawn to a homestead, sitting atop a low hill and surrounded by a smattering of weather-beaten barns. The stubborn old house stood proudly against the ever-present winds.

"You sure this is right?" Julio asked.

"Nope." Even as I said the words, a Dawes County sheriff's vehicle came into view.

"Somebody actually lives here? My cell phone doesn't have any signal," Julio said.

"I imagine they've been ranching since before that was a thing," I said as I slowed to a stop. Before exiting the Bronco, I pushed my hat onto my head, snugging it on good so it didn't get taken by the strong south wind. "Bring the donuts."

"Okay, boss." Julio's tone seemed to suggest he wasn't using boss as a term of affection.

Sheriff George Kirst had a quick smile, a full head of white hair and a deep tan that could only be earned by spending a lot of time in the outdoors. Dawes County, like Butte, was short on population and long on square miles, two factors which ordinarily equated to low crime rates. Kirst's tan suggested he was either an avid sportsman or more likely worked a small farm of his own in his downtime.

"Deputy Biggston," Kirst said, grinning broadly with his arm outstretched.

"Sheriff Kirst," I answered. "This is Julio Ocampo. New deputy."

"Nice to meet you," Kirst answered, offering a hand to Julio, his eyes drawn to the box of donuts. Julio didn't miss a beat and opened the top once Kirst had released his hand, careful to block the wind with his body. "Don't mind if I do." Kirst plucked a donut from the box.

I scanned the sandy gravel drive that joined the story-and-a-half home to the other buildings but found no one nearby.

"Where'd they find the bike?" I asked.

Kirst swallowed the chunk of donut he'd been working on. "Down by the river," he said. "Let's take your rig down."

With a glance at his newer SUV, which could easily handle the terrain, I chuckled. I respected his desire not to scratch up the paint.

"Have you heard from State Patrol yet?" I asked. "They'll be swinging out this afternoon."

Kirst raised an eyebrow and pulled open the Bronco's front passenger door. "How'd they hear about the bike already?" He swung himself into the front seat.

Having already been chewed out by Ellis, I chose not to answer. Julio bailed me out and pushed the box of donuts over the seat as he climbed in the back. "Another donut?" he asked. Kirst raised an eyebrow but obliged.

At Kirst's direction, which was reduced to mostly grunts and pointing due to the donut, I followed a sandy, heavily rutted path that pitched downhill. Unlike the grassy plains we'd seen for most of the last forty miles, the backside of the farm gave way to a line of trees at the bottom of a steep hill. It was a familiar pattern. Where there was water, there were trees.

"According to the paper, you boys got shot at a couple of days ago. How's that little ranger girl doing?" Kirst asked.

"Bess Dawdry. Took one to her thigh. It was a through and through. She'll recover. She's a tough lady. " I wasn't sure why I felt compelled to say the last part. Having spent time in the field with Dawdry, I didn't like his demeaning characterization.

Kirst nodded, holding onto the chicken-handle as we bumped down what wasn't much of a path.

"It's down there," Kirst said. I followed the line of his arm and just barely picked out the back wheel of a motorcycle leaning against a thick cottonwood.

"Did you get a look at it yet?" I asked.

"One of my deputies came out early and ran the VIN," he said. "Otherwise, we haven't touched a thing."

"Appreciate it," I said and parked the truck on a more-or-less level patch of ground. Before I got out, I reached around my seat and extracted a high-def camera from its bag, grateful that I'd finally remembered to pack it. "Julio, would you grab the evidence bag in the back?"

"Copy that," Julio said.

"I thought we were waiting for State Patrol," Kirst said.

"I'm contracted with them." I stopped to snap a wide-angle view of the scene.

"Ah," he said. "In that case, you probably don't need me to stick around."

I let the camera rest on its strap and looked up at the older man. Even with the slower pace of a rural county, he'd most likely processed thousands of crime scenes.

"Not sure why he'd bail here," I said, ignoring his comment.

"That part's not so hard," Kirst said. "Take a look at the front of the bike."

I continued down toward the river and paused as I got around the tree. The front tire was ruined. "Were the Akrons home at the time?" I took a couple more pictures. "These motocross bikes make a lot of noise."

"Wind was blowing pretty good last night. We're far enough from the homestead that the noise probably didn't make it back up the hill," Kirst said.

After slipping on a glove from the evidence bag Julio had lugged down, I twisted off the fuel cap and stuck my finger down into it. It was almost full. "Probably parked along this tree line and took off on foot to get gas," I pointed to a gas can twenty yards downstream along the wood line and then scanned the ground back along the edge of the water. "Is that where he wrecked, you think?" The muddy single-wheel track led to a handful of sandstone rocks that would have been hidden in the dark.

"That's about how I see it," Kirst agreed.

I walked back to the rocks. There were scrapings of steel where the wheel had fallen into a channel and snagged. After taking pictures, I scanned ahead of the wreck sight. He must have freed the wheel after that and tried to keep going only to realize the wheel was ruined beyond the point of being usable. That's when I located boot prints that pointed toward the house.

"Where are the Akrons?" My eyes followed the faint prints up the hill.

"What are you looking at?" Kirst asked as I crouched so I could zoom in on one of the prints. Without touching it, I traced an imaginary line around the boot print with my finger.

"Akrons," I repeated.

"They headed into town," he said.

"In what?"

"An old pickup," he said, concern raising the pitch of his voice. "Had a load of junk in the back."

"We need to locate them." I unclipped my holster and jogged back to the truck. "Julio, get in."

The race back up the hill was faster and considerably bumpier than our more controlled descent. As we drove, Kirst attempted to raise his dispatch with a portable radio but got nothing.

"I'll call it in," Kirst said, leaping from the truck as I skidded to a stop. While his portable radio might not have the range to reach his home base, no doubt the unit in his rig had more than enough power.

"State Patrol is here," Julio announced as a white cruiser turned from the highway onto the long gravel lane.

I flipped open the tailgate of the Bronco and pulled out my Benelli tactical shotgun. I chambered a round and stuffed a handful of bullets into my pants pocket.

"We'll clear the big barn first," I shouted to Kirst as Julio and I hustled over to the barn, weapons drawn.

I kicked open a back door and spun into the wide-open expanse of a tall barn that looked to be getting short on hay. Together, Julio and I moved quickly to shelter behind the doorframe until our eyes could fully adjust to the dim interior. I wished Diva was with me. Her capacity to quickly clear a large space far outmatched my own, but I was pleased with Julio's ability to keep up as the two of us searched the old barn. We found nothing.

"Where to, boss?" Julio asked as we exited. I scanned the other vehicles and found neither Kirst nor the State Patrol officer who'd just arrived. I could, however, hear them working together to clear the main residence.

"We'll take the other outbuildings," I said.

Thirty minutes later, we exited the last of the buildings and joined up with Kirst and the Patrol officer by Kirst's vehicle.

"Old man Akron and his wife were found on Highway 87 just north of Rush," he reported. "He's a little beat up, but he'll be okay. Suspect took their pickup. We just issued a BOLO."

"Which way did he go?"

"South into Rush," Kirst said. "He's at least two hours ahead of us, but we'll get him. I have four cruisers out looking."

I nodded. I didn't give them a chance in hell of finding the guy, but if it happened, I'd be happy just the same. "Good chance he'll switch vehicles," I said. "We'll want to pay attention to nearby stolen vehicle reports."

The patrol officer cleared his throat. "Detective Cropsie wants you to give her a call when you get back in cell range," he said. "I have a wrecker on the way. I've been instructed to process the scene and get the bike back to the lab."

"Thanks," I said. A flatbed truck was already rolling down the lane and the officer excused himself to talk to the driver.

"Appreciate your help today, Sheriff," I said, turning and shaking hands again with Kirst.

"Sure thing," he said. "Any chance I could get a donut for the road?"

I opened the back of the Bronco and handed the box to him. "I'll pass along your compliments to Beth next time I'm through there."

"You do that," he said, smiling. "And say, if things don't work out for you in Butte, give me a call, you hear?"

I nodded and swung up into the Bronco as Julio jumped into the passenger side.

"Now you're BFFs because of a box of donuts?" Julio asked, shaking his head as we started down the drive. I grinned but didn't respond. There was a lesson in there about treating people well. I'd been fortunate to have a good coach.

I finally picked up decent cell reception when we slowed at the T intersection for Highway 20. Immediately to the east was the small town of Rush and thirty minutes west was Wood Creek. In that I wasn't driving eighty-five, I felt comfortable dialing the phone on my own.

"State Patrol, Investigative Services Division," Thompson answered.

"Thompson. Biggston. Is Cropsie available?"

"Transferring." His words were cut off as he transferred me.

"Cropsie."

"Our guy took a truck and I think he's headed back to Wood Creek."

"Understood. Two things," she said. "I'll be at Ellis's meeting tonight. You should probably ignore me. It sounds like he and Captain Arnold got into it this morning. Arnold wanted me to pass along that if you want into the next class, you've got the job."

I chuckled. "What else?"

"Not sure how helpful it is, but we got a positive ID on one of the girls' remains," she said. "Morena Arrabal. Mexican national. She'd have been eighteen in July."

"Dammit."

"There's more," she said. "She was picked up for prostitution last year just south of you guys on the interstate. She was remanded to her mother because of her status as a minor."

"What about the other girl?"

"Hispanic, in her mid-to-late teens also. Nothing in the computers. Both bodies show signs of severe abuse, likely torture," she said.

My tongue thickened in my mouth as I considered the implications. This animal had been preying on girls who had little protection and doing unspeakable things to them. To make it even worse, he was playing a cat and mouse game with me as he tried to get closer to April. I flipped on the lights and stomped on the accelerator as my mind ran through all the worst things I could imagine as if they were happening right now to April.

"Anything else?" I wanted nothing more than to get off the phone.

"Just play it cool tonight. You understand?" she asked.

"Sure. Got it." I hung up.

"What's going on, boss?" Julio asked.

"I've got a bad feeling about this," I said. I ignored the fact that I was flying down the road as I punched in Gene Ellis' phone number.

"What is it, Biggs?" he answered. He didn't sound near as angry as he had this morning.

"Our guy stole a truck up by Rush," I said. "Check the BOLOs in the last hour."

"You sure you can tell me this?" he asked, irritated.

"No," I said. "Suspect stole the truck from an elderly rancher and his wife. I think he used them to get off the property while Sheriff Kirst was there. According to them, he continued south on 87 after dumping them out."

"He's coming back," he said flatly. "Where are April and Faith?"

"Julio and I are just a few miles from the Hudson ranch," I said.

"Good. Have you heard from Raff today?" he asked.

"No, but we don't talk that much."

"I don't suppose. I'm not sure he did his shift last night," he said. "We didn't have a single call on the blotter."

"Did you check the GPS log on his cruiser?" I asked.

"Shit, Biggs, I don't know how to do that," he said.

"Have Hollie get the log for you," I said. "It's updated every fifteen minutes and should have details for last night."

"I might need you to work this weekend if I can't find him," he said.

"You should put Julio in a cruiser on his own," I said. "He did plenty of patrol in Texas."

"I could. No speeding tickets under twenty over, though," he said. "We got Schroeder's rig back. I was going to put Julio in that next week anyway."

"Twenty?" I asked. He knew I didn't like his lax speed enforcement and for me, allowing twenty miles per hour over the limit felt criminal.

"Fine. Fifteen," he said.

"You need to stand up for him if the mayor pressures you," I said. "You're better than that."

"Dammit, Biggs. I'm your boss," he growled.

"You know I'm right."

"Why didn't you endorse me?" He sounded more hurt than angry.

"You're a good cop, Gene," I said.

"But what?"

"But nothing," I said.

"But you don't think I can hack the top job?" he asked.

"I'm surprised you want it."

"Not sure I do anymore. I'm tired of fighting with everyone."

"I would be too."

"Tell Ocampo he's got weekend graveyard, starting tonight. I need him to pull a double," he said.

"He's sitting right here. I'll pass it along."

"I need you at the meeting tonight, Biggs," he said, sounding tired.

"See you there," I hung up. For all of Gene's previous bluster, it felt like some of the air had been let out of his tires. I wondered if the attitude change had anything to do with his talk with Captain Arnold. While, technically, State Patrol couldn't give orders to a sheriff, Arnold could cause Gene no end of trouble.

"You guys kiss and make up?" Julio asked.

I shook my head and focused on the highway. "Gene says he needs you to pull a double today. You up for that?"

"How's that going to work? Are you picking up a double, too?"

"You'll be driving solo," I said.

I slowed at the drive that led up to the Hudson Ranch. I searched for and found Faith's truck sitting dutifully in front of the barn. I could also see our mutual friend Jimmy's sedan parked next to it. I'd been out of cell range for much of the afternoon and had no idea what their plans were. My pulse slowed as Faith's lean frame appeared on the back porch. Hearing my vehicle, she turned and waved.

"Da-yum. That's your girlfriend?" Julio said. "And she was married to Butler?"

"I wouldn't bring that up," I said as I parked the Bronco.

He snickered. "No shit."

I jumped out of the truck and caught up with Faith. She was still in her winter bartending uniform, which amounted to tight jeans and a collared shirt she tied in a knot above her stomach. She smelled like a spring breeze and I relished the momentary peace I felt when we hugged.

"What are you doing here?" she asked. "And this must be Julio."

"He talked about me?" Julio asked. I didn't remember mentioning it but the past couple of days had been hectic. "Did he mention how heroic I am?"

"Oh, absolutely," Faith said, grinning. Faith's sister Reagan chose that moment to exit the house and Julio's eyes nearly bugged out their sockets. Aside from a few years difference in age, the two women were nearly identical.

"Biggs!" April said, pushing out from behind Reagan, carrying the puppy, Lucky. Close on April's heels was Diva, who barked joyfully at the reunion. Jimmy appeared in the doorway but decided not to join us.

"What would you say if I kept April with me tonight? I'm about to go off shift," I said. "After Gene's town hall, I was going to hang out with my folks."

Faith narrowed her eyes. "What's going on, Biggs?" she asked.

"Jimmy, come out and meet Julio Ocampo," I said, avoiding Faith's eyes. "He's a new deputy."

Julio looked at Reagan. "Jimmy's your husband?"

Reagan laughed. "Feels like it some days," she said. "We spend enough time together."

"Jimmy is security at Hootskill," I said as Jimmy walked down the stairs. While he wasn't an overly muscular guy, he was good at de-escalation, which made him perfect for the job. He was also capable of giving as good as he received if the situation demanded it. "You'll end up getting to know each other since Hootskill gets pretty active on the weekends."

While the two men greeted each other, I turned to Faith. "Some stuff's going on," I said. "I'd just like to keep an eye on her."

"Can I, Mom?" April asked. "That way, Jimmy can work at the bar tonight."

"I don't love the thought of her going to that meeting," Faith said. "There will be a lot of angry people there. What if her name comes up?"

"Pappi will be there," I said. "He'll take her into the hall if things get out of the control."

"Geez, Mom, I'll bring my headphones. Like I want to hear a bunch of old people talking," April said, her voice shifting to baby talk. "But what about Lucky? He's the cutest little demon you've ever seen, but he's a piss and poop factory."

"April, *words*," Faith admonished.

"Sorry, April. Lucky's babysitting was temporary duty. Deputy Ocampo is taking the puppy tonight," I said.

Julio abruptly halted his conversation with Jimmy and turned in my direction. "I am?"

"I don't get to keep him?" April asked. I'd told her as much when I left Lucky with her.

"I can't keep a puppy," Julio said. "I barely have a place to sleep as it is."

"It's a border-lab mix." I extracted the puppy from April's arms and pushed it into Julio's. Reluctantly, he accepted it. "Maybe you'll come up with someone who needs him."

"Wait, wasn't the dog who got killed at Folsum's farm a border collie?" he asked. I raised my eyebrows. After a moment, Julio smiled and then nodded. "Yeah. I bet Mildred would like that. You think she has any more of that pie?"

AFTER DROPPING Julio at the station, I breathed a sigh of relief. I didn't mind having a partner, but that man was a talker.

"Why are we going to Pappi's?" April asked. "I haven't had dinner yet. Can't we get burgers? Or maybe pizza?" Inwardly, I groaned. Julio had nothing on April.

"Pearl texted that she has dinner," I said. "I have to pick up Pappi for the meeting tonight."

April shrugged. She seemed to enjoy hanging out with my grandparents, although I think the hundred-inch television screen and high-tech sound system in the theatre room might have also been a draw.

"Why don't I just stay with Nanna then?" she asked. For some reason, Pearl didn't like April calling her by her first name and was training her to use Nanna.

"Maybe not tonight," I said, hoping she wouldn't push the issue.

Of course, she instantly recognized my weakness.

"Why?" she pushed back. "Is that bad guy back in town? Jilly Baker said that he stole Jerry Lake's motorcycle and rode it to California."

"You know Jilly Baker?" I asked.

"Of course. She's in my grade," April said. "Did you know she saw that guy? She's been saying that she helped you find him, but you let him go. I told her she better shut up or I'd kick her ass."

"Don't do that," I said.

"Kick her ass?"

"Right. Jilly did help me. Maybe she was scared," I said.

"She better be scared," April said. "I'll kick any townie's ass if they're talking crap about my family."

I sucked in air. I needed to get my shit together and figure out my relationship with Faith. First with the *L word* being dropped and now April thinking of me as family. I'd never been the settle-down type.

"Be nice," I said, trying to sound forceful, which was hard with April.

"What the heck is that?" April exclaimed, causing Diva to bark as she pointed over the Bronco's dash. We'd just crested the final hill on the way to Pappi and Pearl's and April's sharp eyes had picked out something I'd missed. Sitting in the driveway was a massive, shiny new motorhome.

"Looks like we have visitors." I had a pretty good idea whose RV we were looking at.

"Who?"

"With everything going on, I forgot my buddy, Snert, and Mel were coming out," I said.

"Mel. You mean Melinda? As in *your last girlfriend*?" April asked. If I wasn't mistaken, I heard jealousy in her voice.

"Where'd you hear that?" I asked.

"I overheard Mom talking to Aunt Lexi," she said.

"Oh? What'd she say?" It wasn't fair to use April to spy on Faith, but since she'd brought it up, I was in safe territory.

"That you had the hots for this *Melinda*, but she dumped you because you're too quiet."

I sighed. April hit pretty close to the mark and I was surprised how much it stung. It wasn't as if I still wanted to go out with Mel, but having my failure so plainly exposed was disconcerting.

"That so?" I said noncommittally, hoping to escape the conversation. But April was like a TV defense attorney and she jumped on what she felt was weakness.

"Did you have the hots for Melinda Garcia? Is she prettier than Mom?" April asked.

Comparing women wasn't something I did. Mel was short and curvy with a smile that lit up a room and a personality to match. Faith was tall and lean and followed more closely to what media considered beauty. "They aren't the same."

"That's not an answer," April pressed, no doubt trying to interpret my *deer in the headlights* look. "If you have to think about it, you're making something up. Are you gonna dump Mom for this Melinda?"

"No," I said, shaking my head. "Mel and Snert are together."

I pulled into the drive and approached the bus-sized RV. Aside from some dust from a long trip, it sparkled as if it was brand new.

"Oooh," April said. "So, you're like not interested in her then?"

I laughed. "Right. Just a friend. Like Snert."

April pushed the door open. "Snert's a weird name. Why do you call him that?"

I was saved by Pearl's high-pitched squeal of excitement as she appeared on the front porch. Diva barked with excitement. I hurried to let her out before she hurt herself attempting to get into the front seat and out April's open door. April was gone, sprinting toward Pearl for an enthusiastic greeting and a big hug. After locking up the Bronco, I followed, watching to make sure Diva didn't leave any landmines on Pappi's perfectly maintained front yard.

"Who's this?" I heard Mel before I saw her. I felt a small tug of something like jealousy when I spotted her. As beautiful as ever, she wore a flattering blue dress and was smiling broadly as Pearl introduced her to April. I caught Snert's eye as he appeared behind Mel. He looked good and if I'd had to guess, I'd have bet Mel had taken over his wardrobe.

"Hey, buddy," I said, accepting a hug from him. "When'd you get the rig? It's huge."

"That was the surprise I was telling you about," he said. "Mel and I are doing the whole full-timer thing."

"Biggs!" Mel said, switching from her conversation and pulling me into a hug.

"Hey, Mel," I said.

"You didn't tell me April was so pretty," Mel said. "I guess, how could she not be, given what you've said about Faith."

April smiled as she tipped her head back in pride. "Biggs says she's the prettiest woman he knows."

Mel didn't skip a beat. "You mean other than you." She raised an eyebrow and gave April a mischievous grin.

April giggled, clearly done sizing Mel up. "Can we go in your bus?"

Mel held her hand out to April. "There's a bunkbed in the back. Do you think you can climb it?"

"I climb in the rafters of our smelly old hay barn. I can climb anything," April said.

"Dinner in fifteen minutes," Pearl called after the girls as they ran to the camper.

"Okay, Nanna," April called over her shoulder without looking back.

"How's that going?" Snert asked.

"April?" I asked.

"Yeah. Built-in family," he said. "That's a big change from your normal *date 'em and stop returning their calls* routine."

"Harsh," I said.

"Accurate."

"April is Faith's world. They're a package deal," I said. "She's like the tough little sister I never had. Last fall, she broke a finger working her horse and barely even cried."

"You want to see the coach?" he asked.

"As long as we can do it in under fifteen minutes," I said.

Snert chuckled. "I have three different antennae systems and sat-phone capable link-up. But you don't want to use satellite if you can avoid it, because it's super expensive. We're always on wi-fi. The coach is short on lab equipment space, but I'm adjusting. I'm not sure how I'm going to set up a useable workspace since I have to store a lot of my stuff in the basement."

No surprise that the first thing he talked about was the nerdy-techie part of his new rig. "Basement of your building in Sutherland? I thought you sold that."

"I did. No, *basement* in a coach is all the compartments under the living space. If I didn't need to tow the Tesla, I'd pull a trailer with my gear," he said.

"What'd you do with your Sprinter?" I asked. His last portable workshop had been a fully customized Mercedes Sprinter van and I had a hard time imagining him giving that up.

"In storage back in Sutherland," he said, opening the door. "I might have a service drive it out here, but we need to talk first."

We climbed the steps and entered the RV. The first thing I noticed was that the interior finishes rivaled Pappi and Pearl's home. Everything was highly polished wood, granite or leather. I whistled as I took it all in. "This must have cost you a mint."

"Do you want to know how much – or will it make you feel bad?" Snert asked. I smiled. Same old Snert, always awkward. I loved his completely honest outlook on life.

I grinned. "I'll never feel bad about you doing well, Snert. Ball-park me."

"Ballpark is an expensive home in Sutherland," he said. "Which, really it is, if you think about it."

We heard giggles from down the hallway. "Come find me, Biggs," April's muffled voice called.

The only clutter in the main room was on a narrow, sleek dining table. Instead of soldering irons and diagnostic equipment, Snert had a laptop with a large secondary monitor set up. Next to the laptop was an unlabeled box full of electronic components and fancy blinking lights. I'd ask him about that project later.

I followed Snert to the back of the bus, passing a kitchen with stone counter tops and every possible amenity. Entering the master bedroom, we found Mel sitting on a king-sized bed, leaning back with a huge grin on her face.

"Where's April?" I asked, playing along.

"I'm not sure," Mel said.

A giggle from behind a wall panel gave away April's hiding place. The giggle was followed by the thump of something solid closing. I pushed at the wall panel and it sprung back at my touch. Clothing hung on hangers but there was no April. There were, however, shoes that had been pushed to one side and I could see a recessed handle in the floor that obviously pulled on a hatch to Snert's basement.

"You missed me!" April's shout came from outside and was followed by the sound of the front door opening.

"This is nice," I said. "Feels huge in here."

"We're going to tour the country, maybe go up into Canada," Mel said. "I've always wanted to travel. As long as Alan has his keyboard time, he doesn't mind at all."

"It's a lot of vehicle to drive," I said. "I'm surprised Snert would get something this big, considering how he doesn't like driving his Sprinter."

Mel laughed as April jumped up on the bed, kicked her legs out and made a show of going to sleep. "So comfy," she said.

"Melinda does most of the driving," Snert said.

"We should head inside. Pearl is holding dinner for us," Mel said. "Alan, be a dear and grab that package we have for Pearl and Lester, would you?"

"Sure," he answered and changed subjects. "I'm glad you're wearing body armor, Henry. I read your local paper. It sounds like you are once again in danger. Chasing some criminal away from school kids ..."

I glanced back at April and watched a dark pall settle over her face. The once ebullient ten-year-old stilled and became sullen. Mel also saw the change and wrapped an arm around April's shoulders.

I knew Snert well enough to know I couldn't be subtle if I wanted to stop that conversation. "The paper isn't wrong," I cut in. "April was in the school when the guy tried to break in, so it's probably best if we leave it alone for now."

"Ah, geez," Snert said, his face falling. "I'm sorry. I saw the report about the school. I just didn't know."

April pushed around us and ran from the bus.

"Biggs, I'm sorry," Snert said. "I had no idea."

Mel started after April but I raised a hand. "Hold on, Mel. She'll be okay. You couldn't have known, Snert," I said. "There's more, though."

Mel looked anxiously at the door where April had disappeared. "More?" she asked.

"This guy got a good look at April last weekend. I think the reason he was at the school was to try to grab her," I said.

"You're kidding," Snert said. "The paper said there were bodies recovered in Sage Creek Forest. This guy is dangerous."

"That's right," I said. "You guys need to be careful."

"My security system isn't commercially available," Snert said. "Nothing is getting past it."

"Passive or active?" I asked.

Mel reached over and pulled a purse from a drawer in the nightstand. "Passive," she said, lifting out the handle of what I suspected was a Ruger. "I'm the active component. I'll talk with April."

"Should I say something to April?" Snert asked.

I shook my head, knowing from experience that Snert would focus on this until I gave him something else. "Would you look at Pappi's security setup? Make sure he's got it dialed in? I feel like there might be a blind spot on the back of the garage and there's a window."

"Let me grab my laptop."

"We better get in for dinner," I said. "Don't forget that package Mel asked for."

"Ooh. Thanks," he said, handing me his laptop bag.

The smell inside the house made my stomach growl and I realized I hadn't eaten since breakfast in Agate.

"Get washed up, Henry. I've got dinner on the table," Pearl called from the kitchen.

"This way." I pointed Snert to a bathroom just off the main entrance as I unloaded my equipment belt and weapon into their designated spots.

When we entered the formal dining room, I flashed back to the last time I'd sat down to a meal in this room. The owner of the house at that time had been Sheriff Leonard and he'd poisoned my drink. Subconsciously, my eyes lit on the window that looked out over the back yard and the forested hills beyond. Thinking fast, knowing my life was in danger, I'd turned the tables on Leonard by tackling him and sending us both through that window. We'd landed on the soft ground below, with no more damage than a few cuts and bruises.

"Oh, that's so nice!" Pearl's acceptance of an elaborate music box from Mel pulled me from the dark place my mind had drifted to.

"You okay?" Pappi asked, quietly. "Thought we lost you there for a minute."

I nodded and smiled as I took in the feast Pearl had brought together: fresh rolls, steaming vegetables, salad and a huge slab of roast beef covered with a brown gravy. It seemed to me, given the amount of food, that Pearl had known Mel and Snert were coming for dinner.

"What would you think about staying back here with April tonight?" I said quietly to Pappi. "I'd like to take Snert by the station after the meeting."

"April is always welcome," he said. April must have heard her name because she gave me a private little grin, her way of letting me know she was good. I thought back to Snert's comment about instant family. I wasn't exactly sure how she'd wormed her way so thoroughly around my heart, but I was all in. There was nothing I wouldn't do for that little girl.

"Lester, would you say grace?" Pearl asked, setting the music box on the table.

Pearl always insisted that we join hands as Pappi prayed. Ours had been a Christian home and I found comfort in the grounding Pappi's blessing brought.

"Henry, when is your meeting tonight?" Pearl asked after we all sat.

"I have about half an hour," I said. Her face registered disappointment, but she'd lived with a cop and knew the job. "April, if it's okay with your mom, would you like to stay here instead of going into town?"

"Is Mel staying?" she asked. If I didn't know Mel better, I might have been shocked at how quickly April had moved her from the *potential enemies* list to the *shiny new friend* list.

I looked at Mel. "I'd like to take Snert by the station after the meeting. We shouldn't be too late."

Mel had military service and even more importantly had been in the shit with me before. Knowing that April was a target had brought her protective instincts to the fore and unlike Snert, she easily picked up on cues.

"I was just planning on relaxing tonight. It was a long drive," Mel said. "Maybe we could have a slumber party, watch TV and eat popcorn in the camper."

"Hells, yeah!" April exclaimed and then guiltily looked at Pearl. "Sorry, Nanna. No bad words."

"It's okay, dear. Remember, a young woman chooses her words for her situation," Pearl said.

"I remember," April said and sat up a little straighter.

I pulled my phone from my pocket and dialed Faith as I stepped from the room.

"Heya, sexy." She had to shout to be heard over the noise of the bar. Friday nights were always crazy at Hootskill, but it sounded more like eleven than six-fifteen.

"Hey. Are you okay if April stays at Pappi's tonight instead of going with me? Mel and Snert showed up early. I think it'd be a better environment for her," I said.

"Sure, babe," Faith said, muting the phone. She was in her

element and having a good time. "Thanks for freeing up Jimmy. We've already had a couple of fights. People are really spun up about that newspaper article. You might have a wild meeting tonight."

"That so?" I asked.

"Lots of talk about manhunting parties and the like," she shouted back. "Hey, I gotta go. Where are you going to be after my shift?"

"I'll come by," I said.

"Sweet," she said, laughing. "See you then."

I hung up the phone. It was nice to hear Faith laugh.

"What'd she say?" April asked as I sat back at the table.

"You're in," I said, scooping food onto my plate.

My phone buzzed at my hip and earned a glare from Pearl when I pulled it out. She hated phones at the table. The caller was Ellis.

"Sorry," I apologized and got up from the table again. I accepted the call but held my hand over the microphone and looked back to the table. "Snert, we probably better get going." I avoided Pearl's eyes which were likely shooting laser beams at me.

"Biggston," I announced as I placed the phone next to my ear.

"Biggs, where are you?" Ellis asked.

"My folks," I said.

"Meeting is starting in forty-five minutes. You need to get in here," he said. "Have you heard from Raff yet?"

"No Raff, and I'll take off in five," I said.

"Fine, just get here. Cropsie is showing up with three troopers," he said. "You sure you know who you work for?"

"I'm a Butte County Deputy," I said. "No question in my mind."

Instead of heading back to the table, I went out to the foyer where I changed my t-shirt for one from the stack Pearl kept next to the gun safe.

"I wish you would stay." I hadn't heard Pearl approach. When I turned, she held a bag that I knew held dinner.

"Gene's worked up about the meeting," I said. "I've got to get going."

"There's enough dinner in here for both you and Alan. Will you be late?" she asked.

"I'll have Snert drop me at Hootskill so I can spend some time with Faith," I said.

"I'm not driving that Bronco," Snert said, joining us. "I'll get the Tesla off the dolly. Bring my backpack."

"Sorry, beautiful," I said, leaning over to kiss Pearl on the forehead. "Duty calls."

"I'll put up with you missing dinner if you promise to be safe," she said, handing me the sack of dinner.

"Deal."

THE PARKING LOT at Wood Creek High School was already full when Snert pulled in. His year-old Tesla felt like a veritable space-ship compared to my old Bronco. For a moment, I felt a twinge of jealousy as we silently cruised through the lot.

"Back in next to that Butte County Sheriff's vehicle," I said, pointing out Ellis's rig. As a matter of course, we always parked so we couldn't be pinned in. "How is it you aren't out of charge?"

"I made a slow charger," he said. "As long as either the main motor or generator on the motor home are running, the car is charging."

I grinned. Classic Snert to solve problems elegantly. "So, you sold that piece of software you were working on, liquidated everything, and took to the road?"

"Mel has family in Texas and Arizona," he said. "And I have you."

"Won't you miss your repair business?"

Snert took his hands off the wheel after lining up his parking and allowed the car to back in by itself. "I was going to talk to you about that. We were thinking about buying a parcel of land and building a barn to store the Sprinter. Mel thought I should talk to you about the farm you inherited."

"You want to buy the Quinn farm?" While the paperwork wasn't quite finished, Pearl and Pappi were in the process of turning over both the Quinn farm and ranch to me. Located next to each other, they covered half a section of rough pasture and farmland on the west side of the forest.

The car slowed to a stop. "No. I'd like to rent the barn and some of the utilities," he said.

"That barn is not in good shape, Snert," I said. "The septic tank probably needs replacing, the electrical service is ancient and the well is partially dry."

"My rent could go toward improvements." he said. "Look, I'll be straight. The improvements I'm interested in will cost forty thousand give or take. I'm willing to invest that so we have a place to dock while we're here. I also want to bring my Sprinter out so I can set up my lab. I'm hoping that if we get things going out there, you might consider working on the old farmhouse. We'd like to see you when we're in town."

"There's no town out there," I said. I caught sight of Ellis at the gymnasium door. He was stalking angrily toward us. "There's my boss. Let's talk about this after."

"Okay," he said.

I stepped out of the vehicle and surprised Ellis as I stood up. "Diva, out," I called and snapped a leash onto her harness when she stepped onto the grass.

"Whose car is this?" Ellis asked, giving Snert a once-over.

"Sheriff Ellis, meet Alan Snerdly," I said. "Alan's the one who got us access to the GPS data when George Lynch was killed."

"Oh," Ellis said, drawing back. "I ... I guess I thought you lived in Sutherland."

"Yes, sir," Snert answered. "I'm visiting."

"Have you seen Raff?" Ellis asked. I was tiring of the question. I shook my head and about to answer when he continued. "Mr. Snerdly, do you think you could help us gather some GPS data like you did last time?"

"It would be my pleasure," Snert said. "I've already signed your confidentiality agreements. Has anyone changed the passwords since last time I worked on the system?"

I just shrugged when Ellis looked to me. "You'll have to talk to our office manager, Hollie Wilder. Biggs has her number."

"Deputy Biggston, Acting Sheriff Ellis." A cheerful voice interrupted our impromptu meeting as Reba Wiley briskly approached. "I sure hope you have some good news for us tonight."

"I'll be sure to fill you in at the meeting just like everyone else, Ms. Wiley," Ellis said, stiffening.

I grabbed the brim of my hat and nodded. "Ms. Wiley."

"Deputy Biggston. I understand you've had a busy week. Thank you for keeping the streets safe." She extended a hand to me and I instinctively accepted it, which earned me a glare from Ellis. "And who is this fine young man?" Reba pushed between Ellis and me so she stood in front of Snert.

"Alan Snerdly, ma'am. I'm a friend of Henry's," he said, looking at me with concern and then back at the enigmatic woman.

"So you are," she said, shaking hands.

"He's not a registered voter in Butte County, Reba," Ellis growled. "You can lay off already."

"Now, Gene. That's hardly called for." She turned back to Alan. "Alan, I hope you don't mind me calling you that. Are you in town long?"

"Maybe a week or two," he said. "We're staying at the Ploughman ranch."

"Close friends, then," she smiled. "It was nice meeting you. I guess I'll see all you boys in there."

With a sharp nod, she turned and was off again, heading for the gymnasium doors.

"I despise that woman," Ellis confided when he was sure she was out of earshot.

"Do you need help with anything?" I asked, redirecting the conversation that was sure to turn into a diatribe about what he thought of Wiley.

"I got a call from Cropsie. She's wants me to reserve spots for her and three troopers at the front. I need you to get a rope or something and help with that," he said.

I nodded, following him through the back doors and into the gym. The gym looked like every other high school gymnasium I'd ever been in with bleacher seats that extended out on each side of a wood-planked basketball court. Only the *home* side was extended tonight, and at the center circle, a portable wooden lectern stood ready for the sheriff to address the expected crowd. A student tapped on the microphone and his amplified voice announced, "Test test test."

"Can you keep Diva with you?" I asked Snert. There were only a few people I trusted to handle Diva. Snert was top of that list. The two had a special connection.

"Where do you want me to sit?" he asked.

"Maybe take her for a walk, she might need to relieve herself," I said. "Don't go too far, though." Snert nodded and accepted Diva's leash.

As it turned out, Ellis had several last-minute preparations he needed my help with. As it closed in on seven thirty, he became more agitated.

"Sheriff Ellis," Cropsie announced in her clipped, professional voice. She exuded authority, something people generally missed at first glance because she was not a tall woman, nor was she particularly fit looking. Cropsie had something one of my commanders had always referred to as *command presence*. Wiley had it also, but Gene Ellis, not so much.

"Trooper Cropsie," Ellis said, extending his hand, although his face made it clear he was not pleased to see her.

"Detective." She raised an eyebrow, refusing the handshake. The clack, clack, clack of heels announced Reba Wiley's approach. Cropsie turned slightly, acknowledging the woman. "Captain Arnold asked me to personally reinforce State Patrol's position. If you insist on sharing further details of the Sage Creek investigation, you will risk charges of obstruction. The last thing we need are mobs of angry townsfolk running around with torches and pitchforks."

"Reba Wiley," Wiley chose that moment to offer her hand to Cropsie. Cropsie blinked and accepted it. "I'm Gene's opposition for Butte County Sheriff."

"I know who you are," Cropsie answered, looking back to Ellis.

"Are we clear?" Cropsie stared at Ellis who looked like he might burst into flames at any moment.

"Um ..." Ellis started what I was afraid would be a blistering response.

Surprisingly, Wiley came to his defense. "If there is a murderer running around Butte County, our citizens have a right to know what's going on so they can adequately defend themselves."

The gymnasium, which was almost full by this point, quieted. Somehow, Wiley had managed to successfully position herself close enough to the podium that her voice carried over the public address.

"This matter does not concern you," Cropsie said, turning to Wiley.

"This matter is a concern to all of us," Wiley answered. "And I, for one, expect some answers."

"Deputy Biggston, would you escort Mrs. Wiley to her chair so we can get started?" Ellis said, recovering.

Wiley smiled as I nodded toward the bleachers. I walked her back to the front row center seat she'd claimed with her jacket.

"You're dangerous," I said, under my breath.

"I believe *underestimated* is the word you're looking for," she said, wrapping an arm around mine so it looked like we were old friends, for the entirety of Butte County to see.

"If I could have your attention," Ellis called over the PA as I deposited Wiley at her seat. He thumped the microphone, making a popping sound which quieted the gymnasium. "Deputy Biggston, if you and your K-9 would join me up here, we'll get started."

I scanned the crowd and found Snert standing near the back door, leaning against the padded wall which kept overly enthusiastic basketball players from injuring themselves. Diva sat alert, tugging against her harness.

With all eyes on me, I jogged to Snert and retrieved Diva. "Heel," I ordered and jogged her to center court. I took a position behind Ellis, a yard back and to the side. "Setzen." Diva complied and sat dutifully next to me.

"Thank you, Deputy Biggston," he said into the microphone. "We have an hour. I'll keep things short to make sure we have enough time for questions at the end. First off, I'd like to thank Detective Roseland Cropsie and the State Patrol for being in attendance."

I'd reserved a position left of center in the front row for the troopers, several feet down and across the aisle from where Wiley sat. While I'd been fetching Diva, Mortimer and Denholm had snuck in and taken a seat next to Wiley. Denholm smiled as he noticed my eyes on him.

In my opinion, the entire assembly was a political maneuver on Ellis's part. With the election next week, he wanted to make sure people knew his name and voted for him. I wasn't much of a politician, but it might work. Who would want to change sheriffs when they were in the middle of a critical investigation? Wiley had come out swinging with the stunt at the microphone and sitting next to Morty and Denholm, but it was now Ellis's turn.

"As you likely read in the newspaper, Butte County and the State Patrol are engaged in a countywide – and even statewide – manhunt for an unknown subject," he said. "Disturbing evidence was found atop Bald Hill in Sage Creek. This evidence has been turned over to the State Patrol for processing. As such, we've turned that investigation over to the state's Investigative Services Division."

"If that was all that we were up against, I'd have no reason for newspaper articles or town meetings. As it is, we are independently investigating several other individual crimes that may or may not be related to the suspect we first ran into in Sage Creek Forest.

"Deputies Biggston and Ocampo, along with State Ranger Bess Dawdry, who couldn't be here tonight for obvious reasons, were acting on intelligence gathered during what originally appeared to be an unrelated burglary when they came under fire. Ranger Dawdry was injured in the exchange of gunfire, but I've been told she'll make a full recovery."

He paused for applause. I had to give it to him. He was making sense and seemed to have the crowd's attention.

"After that, we came into contact with the subject after he attempted a break into Wood Creek Middle School. I'd like to thank the school's administrators for their quick thinking in executing lock-down procedures that were developed in coordination with the Sheriff's Department."

He paused again for applause. I flicked my eyes over to the middle school Assistant Vice-Principal Mandy Jones. Her face was red with anger and I was pretty sure Gene was in for a nasty conversation later.

Ellis continued and I found myself tuning him out. He was conflating relatively innocuous events with the investigation, including reported, but not confirmed, burglaries and even a few traffic stops.

"Deputy Biggston?" The room went quiet and I felt all eyes on me.

I turned to Ellis and gave him my attention. "The microphone. Can you hand it to people so they can ask questions? Folks, if you'd form a line near center court along the foul line, we'll keep things nice and orderly."

"Diva, stay." The order was mostly unnecessary as Diva was lying on the floor, having long ago lost interest. I retrieved a corded microphone from the table and walked to the quickly forming line suppressing a grin as Reba Wiley jumped up to be first.

"Go ahead," Ellis said, sounding dejected.

"Reba Wiley of Hemmingsford," Wiley said. "If you didn't know, I'm running against Gene for Sheriff of Butte County."

"Reba, this isn't the place for political statements. Do you have a question?" Ellis asked.

"The budget for Butte County is five patrol deputies in addition to the resources used to operate the county jail and man the courthouse," she said. "Why is it that we only have three deputies, one of which was hired just this week?"

"What's that got to do with anything?" Ellis asked, angrily.

"Butte County occupies an area more than twice the size of the state of Rhode Island," she said. "I'd argue that by allowing staff size to shrink to such a low number, you've endangered our county by sheer negligence."

An angry murmur surged through the crowd.

"We just hired Julio Ocampo," he said. "And we'll be posting a new opening next week. Next person, please."

I reached for the microphone, but Wiley wasn't quite ready to give it up. "There are rumors Deputy Butler has gone AWOL. Is it possible he is in danger? Can you tell us anything about that?"

"Where did you hear that?" Ellis asked angrily. "Raff isn't missing. He just missed a shift. He probably just had the schedule wrong."

"Two shifts," Wiley pushed. "You only have two deputies working? That's the number of deputies you had the entire winter while that crazy was up in the hills killing people. We all know Biggston's a helluva deputy, but don't we deserve more?"

"Dammit, Wiley! You're out of line," Ellis spat. "Biggston, get that microphone away from her."

"Do your job, Ellis. And stop showboating. Butte County deserves better," Wiley said and handed me the microphone. Instead of sitting down, she stalked across the gymnasium and slammed open the back door, letting herself out as the assembly descended into chaos.

It took Ellis several minutes to calm the crowd. "Sorry about that, folks. I guess Ms. Wiley had in mind to do some electioneering tonight. Let's get back to the topic at hand," he said. "Deputy, if you'd give the microphone to the next gentleman in line. Say your name and your question, please."

"My name is Bob Linsey. I thought Wiley asked a good question.

Are we really that short-staffed? Is that why I never see a sheriff's car on the road?" he asked. "How are you expecting to catch this guy if there's only two of you?"

"Quiet, quiet," Ellis said, trying to calm the crowd. "We have three active deputies and we're working to fill the other positions. Butte County is only assisting State Patrol in this investigation. Next?"

"What do you need us to do, Gene?" an older man in cowboy boots asked. "I'll get some boys rounded up and we'll start doing patrols. I bet there's enough of us that we could get twenty trucks out running the county. We'll find this fucker."

"No, Joe, you can't be doing that," Gene said.

"You said it yourself," Joe argued. "You're short-staffed. Can't you deputize us or something? Bunch of us have military backgrounds. We know how to handle ourselves."

Movement from my left startled me as Roseland Cropsie stood up and approached. She looked at Joe with pursed lips and held out her hand. "May I?" she asked, her eyebrows raised.

"Oh, hell. You're a scary little thing, aren't you?" Joe said, handing the microphone to her all the same. His comments earned him a tense laugh from some of the assembled crowd. It wasn't hard to tell that Cropsie meant business, especially since all four of the patrolmen who'd accompanied her were also standing.

"Joe. Take your seat. All of you, take your seats," she said, pointing at the people who'd lined up to ask questions. "To supplement patrols, the State Patrol has assigned the officers you see standing behind me directly to Butte County for the duration of the investigation of the matter at Sage Creek. Butte County Sheriff's Department has been relieved of all duties pertaining to this investigation. As such, this meeting is closed. On a go-forward basis, we will strictly enforce all traffic and gun-safety laws."

She looked at Joe who, instead of sitting, had simply backed away. "Joe, do you have a conceal permit for the weapon on your ankle?"

"What?" he asked. "We're under attack, lady. You can't do me like that."

"One-time *get out of jail free card*, Joe," she said. "Next time you come into contact with law enforcement, you can bet it'll go differently."

"Come *on!*" Joe complained. "I have a right to defend myself."

"Yes, you do. *If* someone breaks into your home and threatens your life or that of your family, I'll be first in line to say you did the right thing," she said. "I take the law seriously and so should you. If I so much as see two men in a truck driving suspiciously, you'll be stopped and your vehicle searched. Do not turn Butte County into a war zone. Now, if you do see something suspicious, we've set up a hotline that will be manned twenty-four hours a day. We want your calls, but please folks, if you send us on wild goose chases, it'll take us that much longer to get this guy."

She unplugged the microphone from the long wire that connected it and walked back to where Ellis stood, looking shell-shocked.

"Dismiss the meeting, Sheriff Ellis," she said.

"I quit," Gene said, looking me square in the eyes, pulling his badge off his shirt and handing it to me.

It had taken twenty minutes for the gym to empty and the janitorial staff to lock the back door. A few stragglers stood talking in the parking lot but mostly people had cleared out. Snert shifted uncomfortably, not quite sure what to make of the events that had transpired.

"Don't do this, Gene," I said.

"I'm the laughingstock of Wood Creek now. Cropsie completely cut my balls off. Her and Wiley both did," he said. "What are women even doing in law enforcement? I knew a time when we only hired one just to say we did."

"You don't mean that," I said. "Detective Cropsie treated us fairly when Sheriff Leonard blew up."

"I *do* mean that, Biggs," he said. "I'm going to lose the election and Wiley is going to be sheriff. Why the hell didn't you at least run? I could have handled losing to you. There's no way I can work for that red-haired demon."

I held the badge out to him. "Don't go out like this."

Instead of taking it, he pulled the sidearm from his holster and then the keys from his belt, holding them both out to me. "It's done. I'll inform the county commissioner in the morning. As First Deputy, you're officially sheriff of Butte County. Of course, since you're not on the ballot, Wiley will run unopposed and you'll lose your job next week. Thirty years of service and I'm being put out to pasture like a broke old racehorse."

"Your keys and badge will be at the station," I said. "Pick them up in the morning."

"Whatever," he said and walked off. Not sure what else to do, Snert and I watched him go. As Gene neared his truck, he unbuttoned his uniform shirt and pulled it off, tossing it to the ground.

"Biggs?" Hollie Wilder asked as she opened the front door of her well-kempt brick ranch on the eastern edge of Wood Creek. She wore dark-blue velour sweats with a matching zip-up top. The clothes and the sound of TV in the background suggested I'd interrupted a quiet evening.

"Hey, Hollie," I said. "Could I bother you for a couple of minutes?"

She looked over my shoulder at Snert and back to me, then pushed open a security screen door. "Where are my manners? Of course, come in."

"You remember Alan Snerdly? He worked on the GPS data for the Quinn case," I said.

"I don't believe we've actually met, but we talked on the phone," she said. "Very nice to meet you in person."

"You too, Mrs. Wilder," he said.

"Herb, turn that TV down," Hollie called. "Can I make you boys some coffee?"

"We won't be staying long," I said, holding my hat in my hand.

"How did Gene's meeting go tonight?" she asked. "He tried to order me to come, but I just couldn't do it."

I pulled the sheriff's badge from my pocket and showed it to her. "Gene just resigned to me in the parking lot of the school."

"Now, why would he go and do a dumb thing like that?" she asked.

"State Patrol shut down his meeting," I said. "He was upset."

"What are you doing about it?" she asked.

"I told him to pick up his badge in the morning," I said.

"But ..."

"He's not coming back," I said. "Thing is, I'm not sure what the next step is."

"I see," she said. "There's not much you can do about it this weekend. I'll call Mark Halberg first thing on Monday morning. He'll have separation papers for Gene and then you'll need to be sworn in. I'll let dispatch know Gene's unavailable this weekend and to call you."

"Have you heard from Raff?" I asked, changing subjects.

"No," she said, shaking her head. "But he did this before when he was working for Leonard."

"Understood," I said. "Thank you, Hollie."

I pushed my hat back on and turned to leave. "Do the right thing, Henry Biggston. There are a lot of people depending on you."

I allowed the screen to close behind us as Snert and I walked back to his car. I felt Hollie's eyes on my back, just as I felt the weight of responsibility settling on my shoulders. The sheriff's office was in shambles. No sheriff, a missing deputy suspected of rape, and a new hire of less than a week. We were chasing a possible serial killer who had too many reasons to stick close to Wood Creek. All the responsibility was now on me. How in the hell had we come to this point?

"Where to?" Snert asked, noticing I hadn't said anything after loading into his car.

"We take the low-hanging fruit first," I said, deciding. The strategy was something I'd learned in the Rangers. If a problem seemed unsolvable, it simply needed to be broken down into smaller, solvable chunks. I had no leads on the serial killer, but I could probably find Raff. "Let's head to the station."

"What's the fruit?" Snert asked, confused. I ignored him as he navigated the short distance from Hollie's to the station where I had him park in back.

"Raff Butler is into some bad stuff," I said. "I've got nothing on the serial killer and I can't solve my staffing problems. What I *can* do is track down Raff."

"If you're the sheriff, can't you deputize?" he asked.

"Not sure," I said, leading him through the darkened station. "Do you think you can track Raff's GPS?"

I gestured to the ancient desktop computer on my desk. Snert chuckled derisively and set his laptop bag down. "That ruggedized tablet I got you has more processing power than ten of those machines. Seriously, Henry, why would you even consider using that old thing?"

"It's how I log in," I said.

Snert rolled his eyes as he extracted his ultrathin computer. "Your GPS data provider is a service. It has nothing to do with these computers." He unclipped a cable from the back of my computer and stuffed it into the side of his laptop. "Hmm. Your internet connection isn't horrible. You should have asked Hollie if they changed the password since I was in last time ... Oh, never mind, I'm in. That's a really bad practice, Henry. If you're in charge, you need to adopt modern IT policies to secure your data."

I bit my tongue. We were chasing murders and rapists. Data security would not be the first problem I solved as sheriff.

"I think I still have that old program. What's Raff's designation?"

"Butte-3."

"I'll load the last three days," he said. "It'll take a minute. It's more data than you'd expect."

A map of the western side of the state appeared on his screen and an outline of Butte County soon showed up. Snert zoomed in so only Butte County was showing.

"That's weird," he said after a few minutes. "The signal is stationary. We're getting data, but it's all from the same location." Snert pinched in the display and we zoomed in to Wood Creek. The GPS was pinpointing Bard's Auto.

"Can you tell when the vehicle designation was last changed?" I asked.

"About a year ago, looks like."

"Try Butte-4," I said.

Lines appeared on the map and Snert zoomed out so all of Butte County showed on the screen.

"What's down here?" Snert asked, zooming out even further as several lines dipped outside the county. He continued to zoom out until all the recorded locations fit on the screen.

"I-80," I answered. "Can you tell when he was down there?"

"Give me a sec," Snert said and the picture disappeared. I grunted in irritation as I tried to make sense of the spaghetti-like jumble of Raff's travel. A moment later, the map reappeared, only the lines had been replaced by a vector icon that crawled across the screen in slow motion, leaving a fading worm trail behind it.

"A little faster?" I asked.

Snert stood, relinquishing his chair. "Right arrow key speeds it up and left slows it down. Space bar starts and stops the display."

I tapped the right arrow a few times and watched the worm zip along faster. I'd traveled the roads in Butte County enough that I had no problem keeping up with Raff's travels. I slapped the spacebar when I recognized one of the locations.

"That's Raff picking me up after Dawdry got shot." I hit the spacebar and watched the worm zip across Highway 20 and into town. I'd kicked the speed up so fast that I barely had time to register when Raff had dropped me in town.

"I'll look up that address," Snert said, pulling out a tablet from his computer case.

"No need," I said. "That's his house."

The trail moved on quickly from Raff's house, turned south and continued directly to the interstate. Once there, I slowed the speed. "What are you doing, Raff?" I mused as his cruiser slid through the parking lots of truck stops and restaurants. Apparently not finding what he was looking for, he got onto the interstate and drove west, only to take the next exit and repeat the process.

"He's looking for someone," Snert said.

"He was angry," I said. "He was pissed that the Sage Creek suspect would go after April."

"Seems like he thought he could find him along the interstate," Snert said.

The two of us watched as Raff's trail repeated the same search pattern over several hours.

"What time is it for him?" I asked.

Snert pushed my hands from the keyboard. Once again, the map disappeared and was replaced by a screen full of computer code. Minutes later, Snert restored the map only now a time and date hovered next to the head of the worm trail.

"Looks like he fell asleep," Snert said, when the worm stopped moving at midnight. The next morning, around six o'clock, Raff's cruiser started moving again. He repeated his search pattern a few times, stopped for breakfast and then seemed to give up, heading north.

"Why would he be going to Agate? " I said. "That's *this* morning. Julio and I had breakfast there, but we didn't tell anyone that was our destination."

"Is there a restaurant in Agate?" Snert asked.

"Behind an old gas station," I said. "A friend of Julio's – her family, really – has a kitchen set up in an old camper. It's better than I'm making it sound, though."

"Maybe that's where Raff went," Snert said. "I take it you didn't see him there."

I shook my head. Snert zoomed in on the small town. It took me a few moments to locate the gas station on the map. I searched my recollection. I was pretty sure we'd arrived around ten in the morning. It was eerie to watch Raff's cruiser approach the station and then veer off, shortly after ten. He'd probably seen my Bronco. Instead of leaving, however, he circled around and parked on the street. I racked my brain, trying to recall the buildings down the gravel alley and across the street.

"That's a church," Snert said. I vaguely remembered a large white structure, but I certainly hadn't seen his patrol car in the street. He must have parked beyond our line of sight and walked up through the landscape and buildings to watch us.

"Shit," I said and pulled out my phone. I dialed Julio's number.

"Can't talk right now," Julio said, his voice tight.

"Call me back."

He hung up.

"Can you get me a location on all vehicles, right now?" I asked.

Snert took command of the keyboard and four dots showed up: my truck at the mechanic's, Gene's Yukon in back of the station, Raff's truck back down at the interstate, and Julio's out at Hootskill.

"Any way you could load this onto my tablet like you did last time?" I asked.

"It wouldn't be real-time," he said. "But I could load what we're looking at here. Where's your tablet?"

"Back at Pappi's." I'd forgotten I'd left it there.

He grabbed his tablet. "We'll use this. Just be warned, it doesn't have a steel frame or any type of shock absorption. Please don't drop it or spill beer or blood on it."

I smiled. It was interesting to hear what Snert thought of my environment. I reached for the tablet, but he slapped my hand away and fished a cord from his laptop bag. "Give me a minute."

Fortunately, my phone rang. "Biggs," I answered.

Expecting Julio, I was surprised when Faith's mother, Darlene, started talking. "Is there a reason Gene Ellis is drowning himself in expensive bourbon?"

"Is he being belligerent?" I asked.

"Gene belligerent? No. I've known him for years and he's always been a little sweet on me. I've just never seen him drink more than two or three," she said. "He's getting pretty clingy and I think he needs a ride home."

In the background, I could hear a steady stream of pop music. Unlike the country-music-only Hootskill Bar, Press Box, the Hudson family's second bar, catered to the local college crowd and apparently, my ex-boss.

"How could he be drunk already? I just saw him at the school," I said.

"He's been here for almost three hours," she said. "It's midnight, Biggs."

I looked at my phone in disbelief. Snert and I had been working on the GPS logs longer than I thought. My phone beeped. This time it was Julio.

"I gotta hang up, Darlene," I said. "I'll swing out in a few minutes and run Gene home."

"That'd be great. Thanks, Biggs," she said and hung up.

"When did you last talk with Mia?" I asked Julio.

"Nine thirty," he said. "They opened the trailer at six in the morning, so they have to go to bed early."

"But you talked to her? She's fine?" I asked.

"Yes, I talked to her. What's going on?"

"Probably nothing. Aren't you about done with your shift?"

"Hey, did you know someone left the lights on in the station?" he asked.

"That's me," I said.

"*Lucy*, I'm home." Julio's voice carried across the station from the door that led to our small holding cell.

I waved and hung up my phone. "What are you doing here?"

"I was going to catch some z's," he said. "I've been sleeping on Mia's couch, but Mama doesn't like it when I come in late."

"How'd your shift go tonight?"

"Did you know your town has a serious drinking problem?" he asked.

"Nobody's in the drunk tank," I said.

"Well, let's just say there was a lot of deputy-suggested ride sharing tonight," he said, dropping a fistful of car keys onto the desk. "Explain again why you were asking about Mia?"

"We tracked Raff back to Agate this morning. I think he was watching us at breakfast," I said.

"Did you know that most serial killers are white? You people are so messed up," he said.

"That statistic is misleading," Snert piped in. "Violence in Mexico is grossly underreported. The incidences of serial murder and rape are rampant amongst drug cartels."

Julio gave a half smile. "Who's the new guy?" I knew he wasn't serious about his racial comment but was equally not surprised that Snert couldn't let it go.

"Snert, meet Julio Ocampo," I said. "My friend is a high-tech wiz. We've been tracking Raff's vehicle for the last couple of days."

Julio nodded as he pulled out his phone and placed it against his ear. He spoke in Spanish and I recognized enough words to realize he was both apologizing for waking Mia as well as talking a little suggestively. After a bit, he hung up.

"Hablas español?" he asked, with an eyebrow raised.

"Un poco," I answered.

"Diva's handler and a close Ranger friend of Biggs' was named Angel Hernandez," Snert explained as he handed his tablet to me. "Biggs understands better than he's letting on. Although, I think you might need to cuss more."

"Good info. Thanks, Snert," Julio said. "So boss, is it okay if I get some rack time in the cell?"

"Snert and I were just getting out of here," I said. "I'm going to need you for a shift tomorrow. Could you take the six pm to two am shift?"

"Let me guess," he said. "New guy gets all the graveyards."

"Only on the weekends," I said.

"I'll be here."

—

"He's over there." Darlene Hudson didn't look like any grandmother I'd ever seen. Like her daughters, she wore a knotted shirt and tight jeans when working behind the bar. It was half past midnight by the time I got to Press Box and Gene was passed out in a booth where she could keep an eye on him.

"He cause you any trouble?" I asked.

"Nothing I couldn't handle. I've been doing this a while," she said. "To be honest, I'm more worried about you."

Her statement took me off guard. I shouldn't be on anyone's radar. "Me?"

"Gene's not exactly a quiet drunk, if you know what I mean," she said. "And if I know you, you're taking on the weight of the world. You've got to take care of yourself, Biggs. You're not getting enough sleep and I bet you aren't eating."

My thoughts flitted to the dinner I'd left in Snert's car, which was now headed home to Pappi and Pearl's. Darlene tipped her head sideways as she read my mind.

"What did Gene say?" I asked.

"He said that you're the new sheriff and that I should be proud Faith picked such a stand-up guy," she said. "That ... and how he wished we'd been closer. He claims, now that he has time on his hands, he is going to court me until I give in."

"You and Gene?" I asked. I didn't think Gene was anywhere near Darlene's league.

She chuckled. "I have a great life," she said. "I don't need a man to mess all that up."

"Biggs," Gene's eyes fluttered open. "What are you doing here? Darlene, did you know Biggs is here?" The smell of alcohol assaulted my nose as he slurred his words. "He's going to be the new sheriff, at least until that bitch, Wiley takes over."

"I'll get him home," I said, cajoling and lifting Gene to his feet.

"He should be fine. I was mixing quite a lot of water into his drinks toward the end," she said and then raised her voice. "Gene, honey, you need to go home with Biggs now. Drink water when you get there, otherwise you're going to have a big headache in the morning."

It was a struggle to get the one-hundred-eighty-pound man through the front door and into what used to be his vehicle. I moved Diva to the front passenger seat so Gene could sprawl out across the bench in the back. The Yukon smelled like it had never been christened by a drunk. That statistic was likely about to change.

It was after one thirty when I finally pulled into the Hootskill parking lot. All but the most hard-core drinkers had already left for the night as last call was only thirty minutes away.

"Biggs!" Lexi Hudson greeted me as I walked across the hardwood plank floors and slid onto a stool at the bar, Diva curling up quietly at my feet. Without asking, she slid a bottle of my favorite light beer in front of me.

I had a thing about being seen drinking with my uniform shirt on. Fortunately, I'd thought ahead and left the shirt and my gun safely locked in my rig. I set my hat on the bar upside down and tipped back the beer, closing my eyes as carbonation burned down my throat.

As I drank, hands slipped around my stomach and Faith's cheek came to rest next to my own. I turned into her and she planted a quick kiss on my lips. I stood so that I could hold her. Diva was so tired, she didn't even bother to get up.

"Aww," Lexi said, only partially sarcastic.

"I heard you had a tough night," Faith whispered as she wrapped her arms loosely around my neck and pulled me in for another kiss. She was swaying with the music and I closed my eyes and enjoyed the moment. I'd learned to take life as it came, not focusing too much on how I felt about my circumstances. At that moment, however, I felt perfectly centered. The universe and its troubles slipped away and for a few minutes, only the two of us existed.

"Not anymore," I said.

"Did I freak you out by telling you I love you?" she asked. I opened my eyes and found her staring back at me. I thought we'd gotten through the conversation but apparently it was on her mind.

"I'm not good with words, Faith. I just know that I feel whole when I'm with you," Tears puddled in her eyes. "Shit, I'm making it worse."

A tear escaped the puddle and ran down her cheek. Suddenly, she pulled on my neck and fiercely kissed me. I closed my eyes and enjoyed the moment.

"You're not making it worse," she said when she finally pulled away. "That's the most romantic thing I've ever heard. You don't have to say you love me if that's weird for you."

"But I do love you," I said. "Should I have said that?"

She smiled. "When you said you didn't date a lot, you weren't kidding, were you?"

I shrugged. "I've always been pretty busy. Snert says I had a lot of first dates but not many seconds."

"April says Melinda is very pretty. You didn't tell me that," she said, pecking a kiss on my lips. "And Snert is a little odd."

"Both are true," I said.

"Could we sleep at your place tonight?"

"Sage and Rosemary?" I asked.

"Yeah."

"Sure. Between Pappi and Mel, April couldn't be safer," I said.

"Melinda?"

"Her dad owns a gun store and she's seen combat," I said. "She's also earned expert in marksmanship in both pistol and rifle."

"You sound like a proud dad," Faith chuckled. "Dance with me." We continued to sway together until Lexi turned the lights to full bright, announcing the closing of the bar. There was a general groan from the holdouts, but everyone knew the drill.

―――

"Biggs, your phone is ringing," Faith said, shaking me.

I blinked at the bright light streaming in through the windows on the west side of my loft apartment atop the Sage and Rosemary Inn. Faith's arm lay across my naked chest and I was surprised to find she only wore a thin lacy bra. Curious, I allowed my hand to stray down her back, where I found she was wearing matching lace panties I'd only briefly seen the night before. Now that I was awake, I really wanted a better look.

"Phone," she reminded me, kissing my chest. I was pretty sure she had no idea the effect she was having on me. I had no trouble being patient, but certain rules needed to be observed. She was playing with fire.

"What time is it?" I asked as I fished around for the stupid phone.

"Ten thirty," she answered. I quickly did the calculation, trying to recall the events from the night before. Faith had insisted we both take showers before hopping into bed. We'd been kissing and I recalled being a little handsy – then there was nothing.

"Did I fall asleep on you last night?" I asked, my hand finally contacting my phone, which had stopped ringing.

"Nope, you definitely got lucky," she said, grinning impishly as she sat up. Between her tousled hair, the matching sheer bra and panties and her athletic body, I couldn't imagine a more beautiful woman. "Why? Don't you remember?"

My phone started ringing again. "You're such a liar," I said, answering the phone. "Biggston."

"Biggs, its Julio. I need you to come over to Agate," he said. "Something bad happened. A girl got hurt last night. She needs to go to the hospital, but she's afraid."

"Hurt?" I asked, sitting up and allowing my legs to hang off the side of the bed. "How?"

"She was beaten. There's a lot of blood," he said. "It's bad, Biggs."

"Are you with her now?" I asked.

"Si."

"Get her to the hospital and stay with her, Julio," I said.

"She won't go. She says it was one of us."

"I'm coming," I said.

"Okay." Julio hung up.

"What's going on, Biggs?" Faith asked, running a hand down my back and scooting in next to me.

"A woman's been hurt," I said. "I've gotta go."

"Hold on," Faith called as she jumped out of Gene's Yukon and ran over to her old dually F350. I'd taken her back to Hootskill, which wasn't on my way to Agate, and she could sense my impatience. A moment later she returned with two bottles of flavored sports drink and a protein bar. She leaned into the truck and we kissed.

"Berry flavored? You're the best," I said. "Where will you be today?"

"Taking April back to the ranch," she said. "Jimmy's going to meet us out there. Mom and Reagan are headed down to Platte City for a shopping trip. We might go with them. Don't know yet."

"Text me," I said.

Faith closed the passenger door and I waited for her to get into her truck and start the engine before I flipped on my light bar and pulled away. The drive to Agate would take seventy-five minutes at normal speeds. I planned to make it in under an hour.

"Butte-Base, this is Butte-2. Over," I called, picking up the handset in Gene's truck.

"Go ahead, Butte-2," Shelby Cantrell, our weekend dispatcher, answered.

"Shelby, I need you to patch me through to Alan Snerdly. He's in your rolo. Over." We still referred to the computer database containing phone numbers and names of people we shared as contacts across the department as a rolodex. The reference, while antiquated, was efficient.

"Copy that, Butte-2," Shelby answered.

The value of the radio was considerable. Cell phone coverage in Butte County was at best, spotty and I knew I was headed for a long stretch of dead air if I used my phone. Fortunately, the county had spent money in the eighties to construct a number of radio-repeater towers for emergency vehicles. While there were still plenty of dead spots in coverage for the radio, the highways were covered.

I waited in silence as I sped down Highway 20. It was springtime and I would need to be careful to avoid farm equipment and wildlife.

"Butte-2, I'm connecting your call. Over," Shelby finally answered.

"Hello, Biggs?" Snert sounded unsure.

"Good morning, Alan. We're on an open line," I said. I figured using his first name would put him on guard as much as anything. "This is Deputy Biggston of Butte County."

"Okay. I ... uh ... okay," he said.

"Alan, I need you to access that information we reviewed yesterday," I said. "I need to pay attention to a time period between ten last night and four this morning."

"I understand, Deputy Biggston," Alan answered somberly. "Will you have access to your data tablet?"

"That's affirmative," I answered.

"Turn it on. It will establish a connection when available," he said. "I'll send updates."

"Copy that. Appreciate the help," I said and hung up.

Almost as an afterthought, I'd tossed Snert's ruggedized electronic tablet into my backpack before leaving that morning. I hung up the microphone, teased the tablet out of the pack and turned it on.

My stomach growled at the sight of the protein bar. The last thing I'd eaten was a donut and that had been over twenty-four hours ago. Diva whined as I tore open the wrapper with my teeth.

"Sorry, girl. It's all I have." I bit off half the bar and tossed the other half to her.

One of the hardest things about law enforcement in a rural county is often the distance required to simply get on scene. Driving at high speed takes concentration and I was glad I had the Yukon. Ellis's rig was easier to handle and capable of significantly higher speeds than my old Bronco. I was within a few minutes of Agate when my tablet finally established a network connection. It started sounding off with multiple beeps I recognized as new messages.

I slowed as I entered the small town, reaching up to wake the computer mounted to the dash. As expected, Julio had been in contact with the dispatcher and the address was waiting for me in an information window. Using the maps function, I located the address and pulled in behind his cruiser, dousing the Yukon's flashing lights.

My phone had service, so I stuffed it in my front pocket, then used the fingerprint reader to unlock the screen of Snert's tablet. A prompt asked if I was willing to install a new piece of software. I accepted. A download progress bar appeared so I pushed the tablet into my backpack and jumped out of the truck.

Diva whined and pushed at the back door. We'd blasted out of the loft quickly that morning and it wouldn't be fair for me to leave her trapped in the truck. I hated to make the victim wait, but I had a responsibility. Fortunately, Diva took care of business and while she complained, hopped back into the truck, giving me a baleful look.

The address I'd been given was for an old home in bad need of repair. A knot of Hispanic men milled around on the front porch and grumbled angrily as I approached. When I attempted to make eye contact, none would look at me. They did, however, part as I approached the front door and knocked.

"We don't need you, gringo." The words were quiet, but distinctive. I looked to who I thought was the likely speaker, but the man continued to stare at the ground.

"Are we going to have a problem?" I asked.

Apparently, my words got his attention. "There's never a problem in Agate," he said, stepping in close to me. His accent was thick, but I understood him well enough. "Especially when the policía visit."

I frowned at his invasion of my space. The mood of the four men on the porch darkened as they focused on me. Four-to-one odds were not good and a physical response, while warranted, was not likely to achieve what I needed.

"Don't make this worse." I took a half step toward them so there was only a hair's breadth between us. I was a head taller and glowered down.

A well-timed shriek came through the screen door. "Basta, Hector! Cállate!"

Turning my attention from Hector, I cautiously looked over my shoulder to identify the female speaker. it was Mia's mother, who I simply knew as Mama. Her angry face looked especially weathered today and her hair messy, the long gray strands flying behind her as she moved through the front room. There was no stopping her and no translation needed. She was pissed. She pushed through the screen and jammed an angry finger into Hector's face.

Hector wasn't quite done and let loose a stream of angry Spanish, only the naughty words of which I recognized. I was certain his venom was targeted at me, but Mama wasn't having any of it. Her hand lashed out faster than I thought possible and slapped his face. I intercepted Hector's arm as he angrily attempted to retaliate. Twisting his arm, I spun him around, being careful to protect myself by putting my back against the wall of the house.

Two of the remaining three men closed in on us, ready to fight. I pushed Hector into the largest man and dropped my hand to my sidearm. In actuality, I had no intention of drawing my weapon; we were simply too close for the effective use of a gun. If I had to defend myself, it would be a slugfest until I could break away and get enough distance for the pistol to come out. Fortunately, the threat of deadly force was sufficient. Hector's buddies held their hands up and backed away.

"You men need to leave," I ordered.

Hector shook his head defiantly, but Mama gave him a piece of her mind. That she didn't use any curse words, or at least none I recognized, made it nearly impossible for me to follow the rant, but Hector and his boys had no such difficulty.

"We have a problem?" Julio stepped through the screen door, holding an already extended telescoping steel baton.

"No problem, Julio," I said, taking my hand off the pistol. "Just a simple misunderstanding. Right, Hector?"

"I understand fine." Hector turned and stalked off.

"What was that about?" Julio asked, looking from me to Mama.

"Hector keeps peace for our people," Mama said.

"Where is the girl?" I asked.

"Back here," Julio said. "She is resting."

As we walked through the house, I noticed overturned furniture in the living room. Even though the home was in poor repair, the contents were otherwise tidy, apart from that.

"What's her name?" I asked.

Mia and an older woman sat on either side of a double bed. Beneath the covers, a woman who was possibly in her late twenties lay propped up against a stack of pillows. The right side of her face was puffed up such that she couldn't open her eye and her lip was split and still oozing blood. I didn't see any other injuries, but the rest of her body was hidden under the white coverlet.

"Marta Collazo," Julio whispered.

My throat burned as I took in the damage a severe beating had inflicted. Marta's cheek was broken, if not her orbital socket as well. Her one good eye tracked me suspiciously as I came further into the room.

I walked next to the bed on her good side, holding my hat in my hand. "I'm sorry, Ms. Collazo. Please tell me who did this to you."

Mia didn't look at me but spoke in Spanish, apparently trans-lating my words.

"Policía," Marta said, lifting an arm above the covers to point at my chest. I looked down. She was pointing at my badge.

I looked to Mia.

"Nombre?" I asked, using the Spanish word for name.

Marta shook her head. "No lo vi." Mia started to translate, but I already knew she was denying knowledge of her attacker.

I pulled Gene's sheriff's badge from my pocket and lifted Marta's hand, then pressed the badge in her palm. "You are in no trouble," I said. "Today, I am sheriff. You have my word that you will be safe. No men will come take you, but you must go to the hospital."

She shook her head more vigorously and repeated the words for *no hospital* a few times.

Julio stepped up next to me. "What do you mean, *you're* the sheriff?"

"Gene resigned last night," I said, not taking my eyes from Marta. I needed to make a connection with the woman.

"Seriously? What happened?" he asked.

"I'll tell you, but not now." I tipped my head toward the young woman. As a ranger, I'd had advanced combat medical training and every move, every word Marta spoke let me know she was in a world of hurt and her condition was degrading. If she didn't get help soon, I didn't like her odds of survival. "Marta, was it Raff Butler who hurt you?"

She recoiled at the name and a tear streamed onto her cheek as she sobbed quietly. The sound of a far-off siren filtered into the room. On the drive over, I'd made a decision to call EMS. If the woman wouldn't go to the hospital, at least she could be seen by competent technicians.

Mia spit. "Do not say his name!"

"I need to know." I looked back at Mia. "He has to be stopped."

Mama spoke rapidly in Spanish, speaking first to Mia and then to Marta. Whatever she said had the desired impact, because Marta reached for my arm. I thought she was looking for comfort, but instead she pressed Gene's badge back into my hand. "Yes. Butler," she said, in a harsh whisper.

"You are very brave, Marta," I said. Even as I spoke, the siren grew closer and louder. "I need you to be brave one more time. You're hurt very badly. EMS is coming and they will help you. You must go to the hospital."

"No," she said, her eyes pleading.

"You must. Raff left evidence on you, inside you. The hospital will collect that evidence and we will use it to stop him." I hated myself for how I spoke to her. I didn't believe Marta would go to the hospital to save herself, but she might go to save others. "He won't be able to hurt other women."

The siren outside suddenly stopped. I needed her to allow the paramedics to take her to the hospital.

She grabbed my wrist with strength I hadn't expected. "Please."

Loud knocking at the front door echoed through the quiet house.

"I need your help." I still refused to break eye contact with her. "Deputy Ocampo will stay with you the entire time. He won't leave your side." I tried to sweeten the pot, but I was fighting a losing battle. In Agate, amongst Mexican immigrants, the Butte County badge might as well have been a white hood or burning cross. It was only because of the color of Julio's skin and his connection to Mia that we even stood in the house.

"Butte County Emergency Services," a woman's voice called out.

"Si," Marta said in the smallest possible voice.

I held Marta's hand for a moment and gave it a reassuring squeeze. "I'll do right by you, Ms. Collazo. I will stop Raff."

I didn't realize that Julio had slipped from the room until I heard him talking with the EMS crew. There were only a few paramedics who worked the area and I had recognized the woman's voice. We'd worked numerous traffic accidents together and I nodded at her as she entered the room.

"Mia, we should clear the room," I said. "Give the paramedics room to work."

"Her mama," Mia urged, looking at the woman who sat quietly on the other side of Marta's bed.

"She should go with Marta to the hospital," I said. "I promise. No one will make trouble for them. Julio, you hear me, right? Nobody in that room except family. No State Patrol. No lawyers. Just doctors and nurses."

I wasn't really speaking to Julio as much as I was to Marta and her mother. State Patrol would have no reason to care about the woman's immigration status, especially given the situation. I needed Marta to hear the orders.

"Are you really sheriff?" Julio asked as we exited the bedroom.

"Acting sheriff," I said. "At least until Gene sobers up and takes it back."

"Meeting at the school must have been a train wreck," he said.

I nodded. "It wasn't good."

"You want me to put out a BOLO for Raff?" he asked.

"Not yet. Help me process this scene and get some pictures before they take Marta."

"Why not?" Julio stopped, suspicious.

"I can find him," I said. "And I don't want him to know I'm coming."

"You gonna mess him up?" Julio asked.

"Justice for Raff will be prison," I said.

Julio was right to ask, though. I wanted nothing more than to deal with Raff myself. When I'd first seen Marta, my mind had flashed to what Faith must have looked like when Raff had beaten her. Faith told me Raff had tried to kill April while she was still in the womb and caused her to be delivered early. That was the reason I'd found Raff's agitated response to a possible serial killer's fixation on April so confusing. He'd literally gone dark in order to protect a daughter he didn't want in the first place. What did he know that I didn't? Why was he searching the truck stops? Why had he suspended his search to attack Marta? The pieces spun in my head and a few ideas started coming together, mostly too insidious for me to fully consider.

⊏━━━⊐

I looked around the living room and sighed. Manhunts and crime scenes were just about as contrary to each other as two things can be. Critical evidence in Marta's attack would be lost if I didn't carefully collect and catalog evidence. I desperately wanted to take action, but if Raff got off on a technicality due to my sloppy work, I'd hate myself.

"Deputy Biggston," Mia's voice surprised me. I thought everyone else who'd been in the house had gone to the hospital with Marta. From the front porch, Diva barked, apparently also surprised by Mia's sudden appearance.

"You must be getting hungry," she said, holding out a paper-wrapped burrito. My stomach immediately flopped in anticipation.

"I thought you went to Wood Creek with Julio," I said.

She shook her head. "I have work tonight. People depend on us," she said. "Julio will tell me what is happening."

I accepted the burrito and opened it. "What's up?" I asked. "I get the sense that you didn't just come over to feed me."

Mia smiled. "Not only," she admitted. "Marta won't go to court."

I nodded. "If the rape kit shows Raff did what she says, the District Attorney might not need her to testify."

"Julio says you are a good man."

I carefully packed up the evidence I'd collected before biting into the burrito. The food wasn't overly warm inside, but it might as well have been steak for as hungry as I was.

"Would you testify?" I asked.

"I don't know," she said. "But I will talk to your attorney. I will tell him what has happened to me, even if I am deported."

"I respect that. Tell me something," I said. "Have you heard of

Mexican girls disappearing from the truck stops down on the interstate?"

"Whores?"

I nodded.

"Mexican girls go missing. People do not care," she said.

"Is that a yes?"

It was her turn to nod.

"When?"

She shrugged. "It happens more than you would expect. It is a dangerous life. It is hard to know, though. Sometimes girls disappear because they catch a ride."

I pulled out my paper notebook and flipped back to the conversation I'd had with Detective Cropsie. I seemed to recall that ISD had identified one of the girls whose remains were found in Sage Creek. My eyes fell on the name. "What about Morena Arrabal?" I asked.

Mia's face seemed to melt. She hadn't seemed perturbed when speaking in generalities, even expressing a certain disdain for the women in question. I could tell she both recognized the name and understood why I was asking.

"Morena was such a beautiful girl," she said, her eyes downcast. "Everyone loved her. Why do you bring up her name?"

"I think you already know."

Mia looked up at me. "Was it quick?"

I struggled with how to answer that question. The honest answer was simple: Morena Arrabal had been tortured over a period of days and then killed.

"Did Raff Butler know her?" I asked, dreading the answer.

"Si."

DIVA HAPPILY MUNCHED on the remainder of Mia's burrito as I packed equipment back into Gene's truck. I watched jealously as she enjoyed the moment, greedily lapping at her water bowl. My thoughts were much darker. I'd known Raff was capable of abuse, but some part of me had hoped his offenses had ended with Faith. Thinking an abuser would stop was a fantasy and I mentally kicked myself for not looking closer for other evidence of that behavior.

A nagging question tugged at my mind as I pulled out Snert's tablet. I truly believed Raff was out hunting our killer, but found it odd that he'd gone lone wolf. He was generally antisocial, but I'd never considered bravery to be one of his attributes. He'd helped me take down Sheriff Leonard, but if I was honest, he'd simply chosen the right side in helping me instead of the sheriff. No, Raff going off on his own was born out of self-preservation. I didn't believe for a moment he was acting to protect April, the girl he'd once tried to kill while she grew within Faith.

I scrolled through my notifications. Snert had gained control of the device, installed a new program and uploaded data. I opened the map application. Three vehicles showed on the map: the Yukon I now sat in, Julio's older cruiser, and Raff's. Snert had gone beyond my request. The timeline started a week back and continued to almost real time.

I fought against my desire to skip to the end and locate Raff. I was making assumptions about his involvement based on a witness statement. I believed Marta, but the case would be much stronger if I could put him in Agate when she was attacked.

I set the timeline on Snert's mapping application to midnight the previous night. Unsurprisingly, Julio's vehicle and the Yukon I was using were at the station and Raff's was at the interstate, unmoving. I zoomed in on Raff's vehicle and thumbed the timeline forward. He wasn't moving. My pulse quickened as I questioned what I thought I knew. At three o'clock, Raff's vehicle headed north. A small part of me wished the timeline was something I had control of, that I could warn Marta Collazo to leave her home because danger was coming. Of course, I knew I couldn't.

It was hard to watch as Raff pulled to a stop only a block away from Marta's house just after four. I hadn't been able to gather a complete timeline from Marta, but I knew every moment Raff's vehicle didn't move, bad things were happening in her home. She might never fully recover from what Raff had done. Hell, she might not recover at all. As I watched the time tick away, my pulse quickened and outrage boiled within me. What gave Raff the right to invade the sanctity of this woman's home?

Time passed. Four thirty turned into five o'clock, then five thirty. Raff was cocky beyond reason. As a general rule, cowards who committed rape knew better than to stick around. Did he really believe he wouldn't get caught? Did he ever think that his vehicle would be recognized and tied to the crime? Mia wholeheartedly believed she couldn't step forward and others obviously thought the same. That widespread fear said a lot about Raff's depraved indifference over the years. A quiet voice in my head whispered that there had to be more going on.

At nine o'clock, Julio's vehicle rolled into my zoomed view and I stared at Raff's still stationary cruiser. What was he doing? Had he abandoned his vehicle? I scrolled forward. At eleven fifteen, my Yukon arrived on the scene. Ten minutes later, Raff's vehicle started moving. In my mind's eye, I saw him hiding and watching while Hector and his friends confronted me. There had to be no doubt in Raff's mind that I would be on to him – and soon.

I scrolled further, almost to real time. Raff's vehicle drove south. I assumed he was headed back to the interstate. A chill grabbed my chest as he turned east. I dropped the tablet and quickly dialed Faith's number.

"You've got Faith," her recorded voice answered. I hung up and dialed again with the same results. I quickly switched to April's number. Nothing. I composed a text to Faith, telling her to call me immediately. I racked my brain and recalled that Jimmy would be out at the ranch. I had his number and punched it up. Nothing. My heart raced. I was an hour away at the highest possible speed.

I switched gears and dialed Pappi.

"Henry?" Pappi answered on the third ring.

"Are April and Faith with you?" I asked.

"No. They went back to their ranch to do chores," he said. "Is there trouble?"

"I don't know. Hang on," I said. My hands trembled as I picked up the tablet and scrolled all the way to the right. Raff's cruiser had stopped half a mile from Hudson's ranch. "Shit. Yes. Raff Butler is packing trouble and I think he's taking it out to Hudson ranch. I need to get off the phone and call in the State Patrol."

"I'm going over," he said.

"Pappi, no. Raff is dangerous and he's heavily armed."

"He's a cop," Pappi answered.

"Don't go, Pappi," I said.

"Like it or not, Faith and April are *my* family now," he said. "I'll be careful."

"Mel has body armor in her RV." I hung up. It would do me no good to argue.

"Diva, kennel!" I barked, jumping out of the truck. She yipped at my outburst but jumped right in. I closed the door behind her and scooped up her water bowl.

I mentally chastised myself. If only I'd watched the GPS data through to the end when I'd first pulled up, I'd have seen that Raff was still in the area and could have given chase. Even as I thought it, I knew better. It was likely that Snert's program hadn't been loaded when I'd arrived. But what if it had? I snipped off the useless thread. I could analyze later. I started the Yukon and punched Gene's number as I accelerated away from Marta's home. I was already an hour behind. I needed help.

"I told you I quit, Biggs," Gene answered, his voice thick with sleep.

"No time for that, Gene," I said. "Raff raped a woman in Agate this morning. His car is at Hudson ranch. I can't raise anyone out there."

"Shit," he said. "I'm going now."

I hung up and tossed the phone onto the seat beside me. Agate was in the middle of nowhere and the tall hills neatly blocked all cell phone reception within a few short miles of town.

"Butte-Base, this is Butte-2," I said. "I need you to patch me through to Detective Cropsie, State Patrol HQ in Platte City."

"Copy that, Butte-2," he said.

The hills were both steep and curved around Agate and I had difficulty get much past eighty miles an hour. There wasn't much traffic but with limited visibility, I was already over-driving the road. I flipped on both lights and sirens. They weren't a great deal of help because by the time the drivers became aware of me, I was already right on them. Fortunately, after ten minutes of terrifying the local traffic, the topography flattened out and I pushed my speed past a hundred.

"Butte-2, I have Detective Cropsie for you. Patching you through now," he said.

"Detective, you're on radio," I said.

"I understand, Deputy Biggston. What can I do for you?" she asked.

"I need you to send your closest units to Hudson ranch," I said. "There'll be three plain clothes deputies on site. POI is Raff Butler."

I hated putting his name out on the radio. First, if he was listening in his car, he'd know we were coming. Second, if he was somehow innocent, there would be no coming back. I didn't care. Faith and April's safety were paramount.

"Three plain clothes?" Cropsie asked. I wasn't sure that Mel would go with Pappi, but I thought it likely.

"Sheriff Ellis and two others," I said.

"We should have a unit there in twenty minutes," she said. "Are you requesting Arnold's contingency?"

She was asking me if I wanted to put a team of SWAT officers into an airplane and send them to Hudson ranch. I desperately wanted to say yes. The fact was, I'd arrive well before them in the best of circumstances.

"I'll be on scene in thirty minutes," I said. "Will advise then."

"I'll get them warmed up," she said. "It'll take at least thirty to assemble the team."

"Copy that. Butte-2, out."

I continued at high speed, my mind awash with possibilities. I'd be twenty minutes behind Pappi and Gene. It was a lifetime if there was trouble.

"Butte-2, you have an incoming call from Butte-1. Over," Shelby Cantrell announced over my radio when I was within ten minutes of the ranch.

"Go ahead, Base."

"Biggs, we're pinned down," Gene said. "We've got a shooter in the hills and wounded we can't reach."

"Who's hit?" I asked.

"Not sure. Looks like one of the Hudson girls," he said.

Someone I cared about was hurt. I felt a familiar rush of energy as hard-earned combat discipline settled around me like an iron mantle.

I'd learned long ago that losing your shit when bullets were flying was a quick way out of the fight.

"Have you called in EMS?" I asked.

"Roger. EMS is on the way, but they won't be able to get in here. It's too hot," he said. "There's something else. Your grandad's been hit."

"I'm fine, Henry," Pappi's muted voice came over the radio.

"Did you get a look at the shooter?" I asked.

"Don't think it was Butler," he said.

I'd already turned onto the gravel, recognizing the sense of floating one gets when traveling too fast on the stuff. I was close when my eyes fell on Raff's cruiser in the ditch. Wanting nothing more than to race past, I slammed on the brakes, engaging the Yukon's advanced anti-skid technology. I'd have landed in the ditch next to Raff if not for the computer's braking, but I stopped only twenty feet beyond. I slammed the truck into reverse and raced backward.

I jumped out of the vehicle only to be yanked back by the microphone's cord. Somehow, I'd forgotten I still held it. I released Diva from the back seat and she bounded across the road and into the ditch, easily beating me to Raff's vehicle.

As the dust settled, my eyes fell on a bright red line across the interior of Raff's windshield. I didn't need the coppery smell to confirm that I was looking at arterial spray. Diva barked excitedly and jumped at the open driver's side window. I grabbed at the passenger door handle and pulled, but the door refused to open, I withdrew a pointed glass-breaking tool from my belt and shattered the window.

Raff sat behind the steering wheel, his right hand on his neck and his left pressed against his thigh. Through cloudy eyes, he looked over at me. "Fuck you, Biggston," he gurgled.

For some reason, at that moment, everything fell into place. "Vuk Servy cleaned up your messes, didn't he?" It was almost a rhetorical question.

"Not take Faith ..." he rasped, spitting blood. The movement caused a fresh gush of blood from his neck. "EMS."

"Did you give Morena Arrabal to Servy?" I asked.

"She was just a whore."

There are moments in my life that I revisit when I'm particularly low. I call the recollections my *shithead reel*. The images are typically actions I can't take back, ones I'm ashamed of, where I lost my composure or reacted hastily and hurt someone. I added to that reel without hesitation as I smashed my fist into the side of Raff's face. The blow was so fast and so hard that he slumped, his hand falling from his neck. In and of itself, the blow wasn't where I crossed the line. What I would replay later was that I made no move to staunch the bleeding and simply slipped back out of the vehicle without a second thought.

Gunfire from a high-powered rifle echoed in the hills not far from my position. "Diva, come!" I turned to the Yukon. Diva's ears perked at the shot. It was in these moments, I saw exactly how intelligent she was. She tilted her head for just a second and then raced ahead of me, leaping easily into the back of the Yukon.

The vehicle's four wheels took turns grabbing at the gravel and throwing it behind us as I rocketed toward the gunfire. My truck slid on the rock as I pulled into Hudson's lane. Two vehicles sat across the long lane leading to the Hudson's house. On one side was Gene's civilian car, an old Civic, and across from it was Snert's Tesla. I could just make out Pappi, Gene and Mel hunkered down behind the vehicles. Mel was holding her AR and as I got closer, she popped up and fired three shots in quick succession.

My eyes traced along the drive and up to the house. Faith's inert form lay draped across the small wooden back porch. I didn't need to talk to Pappi to understand that he'd been shot trying to retrieve her. I guided the Yukon off the lane and through a barb wired fence. One of my front tires popped, and a pressure warning illuminated on the dash. I ignored it as I plowed through the pasture and around the assembled blockade.

Diva barked and jumped into the front seat just after a slug ripped through the door behind me. The shot had come from eight hundred meters and high on the hill. It was a helluva shot. I pushed forward and skidded sideways, placing the Yukon between the hill and Faith's body.

A second slug tore through door, barely skimming the top of my thigh. The shots were the kind of warning a person didn't want more than two of. I lunged across the seat and opened the passenger door, spilling out onto the ground beneath me just before a third slug plowed into the truck's passenger compartment.

I scrabbled to the porch with Diva close on my heels. Faith's face was covered in a mask of blood that oozed from a head wound. I swallowed and pushed my feelings into a dark corner of my mind. If we were to survive, I had to act with efficiency. Emotions could get us both killed. I pushed her sandy-blonde hair from her face as I searched her body for other wounds. So far, all she had a nasty gash on her head which bled profusely. It was bad, but I knew better than to get distracted. Triage was all about making quick decisions on which injury was most critical.

"April," she groaned as my hands expertly searched her body for damage. I found a deep cut along her thigh. Unkindly, I inspected the wound. A blade's path had crossed through muscle but had missed the femoral artery. She'd have a scar, but the laceration wouldn't kill her. I tore at her bloody t-shirt, knowing I'd have more success than trying to tear up my uniform shirt. We were well past the point of worrying about modesty. She was weak from blood loss and the blood flow from her head wound needed to be staunched.

"What about April?" I wrapped a long strip of t-shirt around her head. I winced as I tugged bloody hair from beneath the flap of skin so it would lay flat.

"He took April. Has Vegas," Faith struggled to talk. Vegas was Faith's Paint. The older working horse knew the tall hills of Sage Creek Forest better than any person.

"Hold on," For the second time that day, I heard the far-off cry of an ambulance.

I pushed an arm beneath Faith's legs and one behind her back. I lifted her so she was cradled in front of me and wasted no time as I put the house between us and the shooter on the hill. Faith pushed away from me, trying to straighten her back. "No. April. Drop me," she argued.

"Stop fighting," I said. "I'm going after April, but I need to get you to safety."

"No!" she growled.

I clamped her firmly to my chest as she attempted to buck away. Ordinarily, Faith was a strong woman, but her struggles were pitiful. I ran into the pasture I'd driven the Yukon through and when I got close to where Gene, Mel and Pappi were hunkered down, Mel popped out and fired three quick shots into the lower part of the hillside. She clearly had no intention of connecting with the shooter, but she knew it would be much harder for the sniper to aim if someone was returning fire.

"I need your rifle," I said to Mel. "How much ammo did you bring?"

"Two boxes." She set the AR on the ground, crawled over to the Tesla's door and cracked it open.

I set Faith next to Pappi and gave him a once-over. "I'm fine," he said. "Gonna walk with a limp for a couple of weeks. Never going to hear the end of it from Pearl, though."

He was right. Pearl was not going to be happy that Pappi had been in the line of fire, once again. I unclipped my portable radio. "Butte-Base, this is Butte-2," I said. "I need you to patch me through to Lieutenant Cropsie of State Patrol."

"Copy that, Butte-2. She's on standby. Connecting you now," he answered.

"Go ahead, Biggston," Cropsie answered a moment later.

"We have a shooter in the hills behind Hudson Ranch. Suspect has a hostage and a horse. I believe suspect is fleeing into Sage Creek Forest. Suspect is heavily armed and we have wounded. Over," I said.

"Transmission received," she answered. "Be advised Patrol is expecting arrival at scene in ninety minutes. You are ordered to stand down. You do not have sufficient assets to apprehend suspect."

I slipped the radio onto my belt. It was a stupid conversation. I turned to Gene. "Raff Butler is in his patrol unit a thousand yards south and in the ditch." I pulled his sheriff's badge from my pocket and handed it to him. "I need you to be sheriff today."

Gene accepted the badge and opened the pin that would hold the badge to his shirt. Instead of pinning on his own shirt, however, he reached over and removed my deputy badge and replaced it. "Get this guy, Sheriff. We'll take care of things here."

"WE HAVEN'T HAD return fire since you blocked Faith," Mel said, pushing a backpack at me. "That's my go-bag. There're two liters water and basic supplies. You have a hundred rounds of ammo in the bag and six remaining in the magazine."

The wail of the approaching siren was about as good a distraction as I'd get, so I slung Mel's backpack over my shoulder, grabbed her AR and ran off in a diagonal toward the barn, jogging to one side or the other to make it difficult for the shooter. The sixty-yard sprint to the barn was one of the longest in my life. I was wide open and even though hitting a runner at eight hundred yards was beyond difficult, our shooter was an expert.

The sound of an angry bumblebee was my first and only real warning that I was still alive and hadn't been hit. A moment later, the report of the gunshot marked the shooter's location. I noted his position as best as I could, knowing full well that once I was in the trees everything would look different. Even the prominent rock outcroppings would seem to change shape as I came closer to them.

I breathed heavily upon reaching the relative safety of the barn's shadow. I slowed my pace and fumbled with the old latch holding the tall sliding door closed, then hooked a hand around the end of the door to slide it open. I was greeted by nervous nickers and annoyed neighs. While the remaining horses all had access to exterior runs, they'd come inside at the sound of gunshots.

I scanned the horses. While I ordinarily rode El Chubby, I couldn't afford his sure-footed slowness. Vuk had taken Vegas, arguably the best horse to make a run with. Vegas still had the stamina of a younger horse and was also seasoned in the terrain. My eyes fell on Hermione, April's fiery young chestnut Appaloosa. I'd only been on Hermione once and while she'd tolerated me, we were far from friends.

"Hey there, girl." I approached her stall after setting my rifle on the ground. Like the other horses in the barn, she was fired up. Initially, she approached the end of the stall but then a wild look entered her eyes and she bolted out through the opening in the side of the barn, racing down her short runout.

I turned from her stall and made my way to the tack room where the bridles, saddles and other equipment were stored. A part of me demanded that I simply jump on the back of the horse and give chase, but I knew better.

Not unexpectedly, the tack room was in disarray. I searched through the equipment that had been pulled off the walls, setting a worn bridle and blanket atop Faith's saddle along with an older saddlebag. Say what you want, a saddle is unwieldy, especially if you're in any sort of a hurry.

By the time I was back at Hermione's stall, she'd returned and was nodding her head up and down at me. "Hey there," I whispered as I opened the stall door and walked in, holding only the bridle. Horses pick up on the energy of the animals around them. No doubt the agitation of the other animals and me busting into the barn had riled her up. My calm attitude was starting to reassure her and she allowed me to touch her neck. I had her. "Yeah. That bad man took your girl. What do you say we go hunt him down?"

I don't know if Hermione was responding to my attitude or if she actually understood what I was saying. The normally irascible horse settled and gave me no trouble as I slipped the bridle over her head and fastened the buckle. She behaved as if she was looking forward to her afternoon workout and I quickly laid the blanket on her back and cinched the saddle in place.

Looking around, I realized I didn't have a rifle scabbard. I considered going back into the tack room, but I didn't believe I'd have any luck finding one. Instead, I stuffed Mel's backpack into one side of the saddle bag and slipped the strap of the AR over my chest.

"Good girl," I encouraged as I stepped into a stirrup and swung my leg over the back of the saddle. Settling into place, I gave a short chop with my legs and a tap of the reigns. "Giddyap."

We blasted through the open doors at the front of the barn and a gust of wind blew a swirl of dust into our faces and threatened to rip my hat off. I grabbed for my hat and at the same time pushed my knee into Hermione's side, urging her to canter. The technique was something of a gamble. She was a barrel racer and responded as much to body position and knee pressure as she did the reins.

Diva barked as she gave chase. While Hermione and Diva weren't exactly buddies, they'd come to an understanding of sorts. Diva was allowed to bark as long as she didn't come close to Hermione's kick zone, a lesson Diva learned with a single application.

Racing past the barn, we chewed up the yard, accelerating at a ridiculous pace. I'd only ridden Hermione within the confines of the fenced dirt arena. I knew she was powerful, but there was only so much room for her to show off in the ring. Now, unconfined, I wondered if I'd made a terrible mistake. She was a lot to handle and we were headed straight for the barbed wire fence at the back of the property.

I pulled back on the reins. "Whoa, girl." Apparently, the actions were taken as more of a suggestion than an actual command.

Hermione seemed to slow for a moment, before kicking it into high gear. Let's be clear. I'd never jumped a horse over anything larger than a small log and all I knew was that I needed to give her free rein.

"Oh, crap!" I exhaled, standing in my stirrups to lean forward as Hermione pushed off with her powerful hind legs and leapt. It was exhilarating to fly through the air atop a thousand pounds of muscle. The landing, however, left a lot to be desired as I jammed forward into the saddle horn and struggled to maintain my seat. Hermione must have been testing me, because once we were on the other side, she slowed.

That I hadn't been fired upon suggested that either Vuk was waiting for me to get closer or he'd taken off. While there were dozens of smaller paths leading up the hill from the back of the Hudson's property, they coalesced into a few main trails. Initially, I urged Hermione across the bottom of the hill, having marked the most likely route Vuk and April had climbed. Turning west and into the hill, we started our ascent.

I marveled at Hermione's strength as we raced up the side of the mountain. I was merely a passenger as her familiarity with the trails meant she had no interest in taking my suggestions. Even so, I felt she was on the right track.

"Whoa!" I ordered as the trail flattened out several hundred yards up the hill. I'd caught sight of something pink. Fortunately, Hermione had burned off some of her wild energy and acquiesced to my demand.

I swung my leg off and settled onto the ground. I picked up the item and recognized April's glove. I looked around. We stood in a natural clearing and had a good view of the valley below, including the collection of buildings that made up the Hudson ranch. An ambulance had arrived, but I couldn't make out exactly what was going on. A pang of concern shuddered through me as I worried about Faith. Brass glittered on the ground and I picked up a spent casing. A .308 Winchester. A powerful hunting round and roughly equivalent to the heavy 7.62mm rounds I was used to in the Army. I wondered how many bullets Vuk had left.

Diva panted as she padded over to me. I'd lost track of her on the way up, but knew she'd find me eventually. "We need to find April," I said, holding the glove out for her to sniff. She barked in response. She hardly needed the glove to recognize April's scent. Still, I needed her to understand who we were looking for. "Hunt her up!" I said enthusiastically.

Diva barked, spun in a circle and raced off up the hill, staying right on the path. I jumped onto Hermione's back and we gave chase. Despite the effort it was taking, we'd really only made it halfway up the closest hill to the ranch. Generally, the hills within Sage Creek had anywhere from five to fifteen hundred feet of elevation change. While we weren't in the Rockies, the hills were relentless and steep.

Apparently, we weren't moving fast enough for Diva. She raced back down the trail, barked to get my attention, turned around excitedly and raced off again. She wasn't a young dog and I hated seeing her burn her energy so freely. I had no idea how long we'd be in these hills chasing Vuk and April. What I did know was that I couldn't slow down or let up. Vuk couldn't be allowed free time with April where he didn't feel the pressure of being hunted. I wouldn't be able to live with myself if she came to harm on my watch. I'd already failed Faith. I couldn't fail April, too.

Forty-five minutes later, we crested the final rise in the series of false summits on what most people informally referred to as Hudson Trail. I adjusted my hat as the sun caught my face for the first time since we'd started. I could just make out Diva fifty yards up the rocky trail. Sweat glistened off Hermione's back and I urged her forward, keeping her pace to a slow trot. She'd burned a ton of energy racing up the side of the hill and even a young horse had limits.

My radio crackled to life. "Butte-2, this is Base. Do you copy?" Atop the hill, I'd have good reception for at least another mile. After that, I'd be in a low spot and radio calls would be iffy.

"Go ahead, Base."

"Biggs, we need your twenty. Over," Cropsie said.

"Two miles west on Hudson Trail," I said. "We're tracking the suspect."

"I called State Game and Fish. They're bringing four-wheelers, but they say you're in a hard area to access. Over," she said.

"Roger that, Cropsie." I pulled up short as the tree line gave way to a high meadow.

A chill settled along my spine and I had the feeling someone was looking at me. The terrain was set up perfectly for a sniper, the meadow way too open. I started to pull Hermione around when the radio leapt from my hand and my shoulder zinged with pain. The sound of a rifle shot followed, causing Hermione to startle and rear up. I reached out to steady myself but somehow, I'd lost track of the reins. All I knew was that I was falling. My fingers scraped across the leather of the saddle and a moment later, I was thrown free.

A second shot rang out and Hermione screamed. I knew immediately that her cry was one of both pain and fear. The sound was as horrible as it was gut wrenching. Without hesitation, she bolted back onto the trail, making a critical mistake. Wildly, she ran into the meadow. Twenty yards in, a third shot sounded and she fell over. I watched in horror as the beautiful Paint writhed on her side.

The world around me became deathly quiet. At first, the only noises were Hermione's grunts. Then, floating along with the breeze, came the sound of April's mournful wail. Her lifetime friend had just been gunned down in front of her. I wish I could say that I didn't know the feeling but unfortunately, I knew that kind of shock and sorrow all too well.

The analytical part of my brain took over. My ability to compartmentalize emotion in the heat of battle had kept me alive on more than a few occasions. This time, mental toughness and discipline were required to save a little girl who had begun to mean the world to me.

I raced across the hillside, staying hidden behind the tree line. I slid down the hillside a few feet so the horizon would cut off Vuk's line of sight and scrabbled along the rocky slope, taking a course roughly parallel to the trail.

Slowing as I came even with the sounds of Hermione's struggle, I became aware of a persistent pain in my shoulder. I reached for my arm and my hand came away bloody. Something sharp was stuck in my shoulder. Brutally, I extracted a piece of plastic that had once belonged to the radio.

I pulled a knife from my belt, caught the tip near the shoulder seam and ripped the sleeve away from the shirt. I now had access to the wound and a long strip of material that would serve as a makeshift bandage.

A familiar whine announced Diva's approach and I watched as she commando-crawled across the ground to my side. In some animals, the move might be considered subservience, but Diva was simply using her training and showing her understanding that we were under fire. Smart dog.

"Stay," I ordered as I crawled up the side of the hill. Like Diva, I kept as low as possible as I attempted to judge whether or not Vuk had line of sight on me. I determined he didn't but kept low regardless. When I reached Hermione, she had stopped thrashing, her large lungs pumping great volumes of air as she vocalized her pain.

I'd like to say the reason I crawled up to Hermione was to offer aid. The fact was, I was in no position to help the downed horse. My target was Mel's go-bag contents. Unfortunately, as I crawled closer, the reality of the pain Hermione felt pulled at me. I knew her, not just as an animal, but through April's eyes as a beloved friend.

Sensing my presence, Hermione thrashed, kicking out her powerful back legs. I dared a quick look and my heart sank into my stomach. Vuk's bullet had torn a path high into Hermione's chest, just behind her front leg. How he'd missed her heart, I wasn't sure, but the wet sounds that accompanied her breathing told of a pierced lung and worse. Hermione was dying.

To delay what I knew to be right was not within my nature. I withdrew my 1911 and slid up behind her. Either from weakness or because she recognized my scent, Hermione stilled, rolling her head over so one eye could gaze at me.

"I'm sorry it had to go this way," I said. "Your girl needed you and you were brave."

Before I could lose my nerve, I fired a single shot and ended her misery.

"Noooo!" April cried out, before an uneasy quiet settled in the high meadow. I swiveled my head to orient on her voice, marking the location before ducking behind Hermione's quivering corpse.

I bit down and swallowed back the bile that filled my throat. How could April ever look at me the same again? I despised the loss of her innocence. Anger filled me as I tugged Mel's pack out of the saddlebag that had fallen beside the horse.

"If you keep coming, I'll kill her." Vuk's voice floated across the meadow.

I'd already crawled halfway to safety, back down the side of the hill. His statement stopped me. "Let her go, Vuk," I yelled back, hoping my voice wouldn't be lost. "You can get away."

"I won't hurt her," he said. "I would never hurt my Una."

I continued to crawl until I was completely out of his line of fire, then removed a water bottle from Mel's pack, took a long drink and cupped my hands so Diva could also have some. Talking with Vuk would bring no end to our struggle. I unslung my rifle and settled the backpack in place, adjusting the straps. Ejecting the magazine, I withdrew bullets from my pocket and filled the magazine.

"Are you listening to me?" he followed up.

"Heel," I whispered harshly and started across the slope toward the tree line on the opposite side of the meadow.

April's scream echoed against the rocks and filled me with fear. I knew Vuk was trying to elicit a response from me, but he was doing it with someone I loved. I wanted to yell back with horrifying threats, but it would do no good.

I pulled back the bolt on Mel's rifle and verified I had a round in the chamber. Her AR had an amber lens for a sight instead of a scope like Vuk had on the .308 hunting rifle he'd stolen from Faith's home. The sight was a relatively expensive module, given it had no magnification. Mel was all about home defense and as such, she preferred target acquisition over long-distance accuracy. The firearm wasn't exactly what I was used to, but it would do the job.

I felt a bit of relief when Diva and I gained the tree line, Vuk and April were only a few hundred yards north of my position. If I got lucky, I could catch him unaware. It wasn't a great plan, but I couldn't stand to have that sicko's hands on April any longer.

I worked through scenarios as Diva and I ran through the pine forest. In a direct confrontation, Vuk would certainly turn his gun on April and require me to drop my weapon. It was a horrible position to be in, as he seemed to have little regard for life – his or April's. I would avoid that confrontation as long as possible. What of Faith's horse, Vegas? Had it become injured? A mountain horse would be a significant advantage over a man on foot. Dark thoughts entered my mind as I considered shooting Vegas if the opportunity presented itself.

Options were taken away when I heard Vegas' heavy footfalls echoing through the trees. I would likely ruin my relationship with both April and Faith if I took the shot I was considering, but at least then I would be on an even footing with Vuk. A trade I was willing to make.

I settled the rifle against my shoulder and raced toward the noise. Through the trees, I glimpsed movement, stopped in my tracks and rested my cheek on the rifle's stock. Looking through the amber site, I swung the red dot toward the target. Trees flashed past as I tracked the horse and attempted to gain a sight picture. I flicked off the safety, brought my finger off the trigger guard and rested it on the trigger. Instinctively, I calculated the bullet's drop and how much I would need to lead Vegas.

Diva, recognizing her opportunity, took off through the trees. I couldn't have stopped her if I wanted to. I worked to slow my breathing. I was choosing to shoot in the direction of someone I loved. My shot had to be perfect. I cleared everything from my mind as I flicked my eyes forward, looking for an opening in the horse's path. There was a small one, but it would do.

A black ball of fur erupted from the ground at exactly the moment Vegas entered the small clearing. I fired.

I PUSHED the barrel of the rifle down. I'd missed, but it had been on purpose. In the moment between deciding to squeeze the trigger and my finger moving, I'd redirected the shot to miss Diva as she lunged at Vuk. In that short time, I'd calculated that Diva's body would deflect the bullet enough so the round wouldn't penetrate Vegas sufficiently to stop him. It would later weigh heavily on me that I had considered the damage to Diva as acceptable.

"Shit," I grumbled as I ran after them.

Driving a horse with two passengers through a forest is no easy feat, especially with an angry dog nipping at you. Unfortunately, Diva's assault spurred Vegas on and earned her a hoof to her side, or so I imagined was the genesis of her yelp.

For a while, I was able to keep Vegas' flight within earshot. Having crested the initial range, we raced down into a shadowed valley. At six in the evening we had an hour before full sunset; the valley below would be dark well before that. Exertion from the frantic chase had brought me to a full sweat, but the low forties I was likely to face through the night would soon become dangerous.

I needed to end this now.

The thought burned in me as I picked up the pace even though my legs ached. A familiar yip greeted me as Diva came jogging into view.

"What's up, girl?" I asked, mostly looking to encourage her. She looked up and came over toward me, swinging around to trot in front of me. I almost tripped a couple of times as she slowed, keeping her body just ahead of my feet so I couldn't go any faster. I realized she was pacing me.

"Find April," I ordered, trying to get her moving. She gave me a sidelong glance but continued along the path without changing her stride.

In truth, the slower pace was welcome. My breath had become ragged with exertion and while I didn't want to admit it, the small part of my brain which had remained rational knew I couldn't maintain that pace. How Diva understood this, I wasn't completely sure.

Over the next hour, we continued to slow as the sun set and I finally settled into what one old Army drill sergeant had called *survival speed*. It was his assertion that any grunt could jog for an infinite duration at that speed. I latched onto that idea and pushed forward.

After what seemed like forever, we reached the bottom of the hill, which I only recognized due to the stream that ran across the path. Diva lapped greedily at the water and I stopped and pulled out my phone to check the time. Nine thirty. I hadn't heard any four-wheeler engines and suspected Game and Fish hadn't been successful in getting them into the back country. Nightfall would make traversing the hills even more difficult.

Having stopped jogging, I knew I would not be able to start again without a small rest so I sat next to the path and carefully set down my rifle. I had no idea how far ahead Vuk and April were. I felt confident we were on the right path given the fresh signs in the dirt and trample marks through the overgrown foliage.

Even though I was exhausted, I was careful to set myself into a rocky nook along the creek's bank. Vuk had already shown he was adept at lying in wait and the stream was an obvious point for us to

256 / JAMIE MCFARLANE

stop. My suspicions were almost immediately confirmed when I heard rustling up the hill. I knew it wasn't Diva because she had wandered off along the streambed in the opposite direction, looking to relieve herself.

"You shouldn't have followed me." Vuk Servy called.

"Biggs, run!" April screamed.

I dove to the side as a shot buried itself in the soft bank two yards from my position. For a shot in the dark, it was impressive. Turns out, close doesn't count with bullets. The muzzle flash momentarily illuminated his position and I instinctively dove across the stream, leaving the AR rifle behind. Unlike Servy, I couldn't afford to fire and miss.

April screamed and Vuk must have struck her because I heard an *oopfh* sound. Knowing April, I imagined she had taken some type of action like jumping on the man, only to be swatted off. I'd lost track of Diva, but I heard her paws slap against the wet mud and she loosed a low-throated growl. I turned uphill and moved silently through the trees.

Rifle against dog is generally a losing recipe for the dog. While the dark evened things up slightly, I would not lose the opportunity created by ninety pounds of angry German Shephard. In a heartbeat, I'd trade Diva's life for April's. So would Diva.

I acted without thinking and raced after her as a second shot echoed through the valley. Diva's angry barking sent a surge of adrenaline through my body, pushing energy into my rubbery legs. Instinctive to dogs is the call to fight as a pack. No canine walks away while the pack is going at it. I might not be the first pack member on the scene, but I wasn't far behind.

The moon dully illuminated the scene in front of me. April had been thrown to the ground when Diva jumped at Servy. Quick thinking, Servy used his rifle to block Diva's charge. It was in her programming to bite at the first thing in her path and she grabbed at the rifle's stock. He was smart enough to allow Diva to pull the gun from his hands instead of being knocked over by her momentum. I subconsciously assessed the audacity and grace of Vuk's movements. He was obviously a man who was confident facing predators.

I caught the glint of moonlight on steel as Servy withdrew a massive knife. Quicker than lightning, he grabbed April by her hair and dragged her up next to him, working to keep her between himself and Diva. I was ready and had my pistol in hand a second later.

"Let her go, Vuk," I said.

"I am not disappointed you know my name. It is a good thing for men to face each other in battle. But you must call off your dog or I will cut this girl's throat. I would have one last joy before the darkness holds me forever," he said.

It was about the most perfect, bat-shit-crazy thing he could have said. He was anticipating his own death and made it sound like he'd be happy to take April with him.

"Biggs, don't let him take me. He's been touching me. It's so icky."

"What?" Servy turned and slammed the back of his hand into her face without letting go of her hair with his other hand. Even with the distraction, I was unable to gain a safe sight picture. Diva jumped, but Servy turned and pushed April toward the movement, holding her off. "I would never! It is your papa who used those girls."

"I don't have a dad!" April screamed back at him.

Chaos reigned as the three danced and spun out of control.

"Diva! Heel!" I ordered. I had to repeat myself, which was unusual, but she finally broke off.

"Rafferty Butler is your papa. How could you not know this?" he asked.

"You're an asshole," April cried.

"Yes. It was Rafferty Butler who broke those girls and used me to clean up his messes. Just like he broke your mama," he taunted.

"Leave the girl alone, Servy," I said, trying to drag his attention away from April.

"They all become whores," he growled. "They take your money for sex and leave you with nothing."

"April is innocent," I argued. "Let her go. and I'll stop tracking you. You can take the horse and be gone."

"You would do that for her?" he asked, using his long knife to lift a lock of hair that had fallen over her face. "Why? Do you give your money to her mother for sex?"

I tried to drill in on his face with my aim. He was moving around, jostling with April. The risk of hitting her was too high.

"We're both soldiers, Vuk," I said. "Natasa said you were one of the best."

"Oh? You talked with Natasa? Did she tell you she killed our daughter?"

"She said you cut the brake lines."

I angled around and kept my pistol pointed at him. He smoothly turned so that I had no shot.

"It did not happen that way," he said. "She was high with heroine, yet she blamed me. I have killed many, but not my Una."

"Let April go," I said. "You have my word that I will not chase you tonight."

"Are you an honorable man, Henry Biggston?"

"Honor is about a man's actions," I said, sensing he wouldn't accept my word.

"Put your gun down and kick it away. We will fight as men," he said. "We will let nature decide."

"You still have a knife," I said.

"I am an honorable man, Henry Biggston," he said. "I will toss it aside once you are free of your gun. Besides, you have your dog. Make your decision quickly. She smells good enough to eat."

He had released April's hair and quickly wrapped the arm around her neck, leaning in to sniff her hair.

"Dogs aren't the only ones who bite!" April yelled. Servy leaned forward, anticipating April's movement, but instead, she snapped her head back in a quick motion, the top of her skull contacting the bridge of his nose.

He yowled in pain and reeled back, his knife slashing through the air at her. It was a risky shot, but I had to take it. I calmed myself as much as possible and squeezed a single shot off. His face was turned away from April as he recoiled and my bullet caught his upper jaw, just behind his nose. Had I used a smaller round, there would have been some potential of the shot only wounding Servy, but I was packing .45 ACP hollow points. The soft lead spread upon contact, damaging him beyond recognition.

April screamed as chunks of viscera pelted her with enough force that, I suspected, she feared she'd been hit. Diva, sensing opportunity, joined the fray and before Vuk Servy's body hit the ground, was on him.

I holstered my weapon and raced to April, pulling her to me, holding her small head in my hand. She wrapped her arms around my waist and cried as the emotions of the last several hours washed over her.

"Is he dead?" April finally asked, through shuddering sobs.

"He's gone," I said. "You were very brave."

"You killed Hermione," she said, but didn't release her hold on me. I wondered what she was thinking. Did she hate me now that I'd killed her horse?

"I did."

I brushed at the gore in her hair. If she understood what I was doing, she made no mention of it. I hated what she'd been forced to endure and worried at the residual impact.

"Can I look at him?" she asked.

"You shouldn't," I said, knowing she was talking about Servy.

"I need to know he's dead."

Diva had already given up her attack on Servy's corpse but paced pensively, alert for danger.

"Don't turn around for a minute." I reached down and pulled Servy onto his stomach, so his ruined face was turned into the ground. From the back side and in the wan moonlight, it wasn't overly obvious that he'd had his face blown off. "You can look now."

April turned and stared at Vuk Servy. "He's really dead?" Her voice was small and I wondered if I'd done the right thing in letting her see him.

"He's dead," I said. "Where's Vegas?"

"Shit," she said.

"Language," I warned. Even in the midst of all the chaos and death, she quirked a smile at me.

"He's tied to a tree, up the hill. All this shooting, he might have bolted," she said.

"Let's go see," I said.

Together, we trudged up the hill. Sure enough, after thirty yards, we could hear Vegas snorting his irritation at our approach.

I lifted April into the saddle. She'd been holding it together, but I knew when the adrenaline wore off, she'd be in trouble.

"I was brave, wasn't I?" she asked as we started down the hill.

"Couldn't have done it without you."

"I knew you'd come for me, Biggs," she said.

My throat burned and I found it difficult to talk. Fortunately, I wasn't much of a talker. "I'm glad," I managed.

"He hurt Mom," she said. "Is she gonna be okay?"

"She is."

"He killed Jimmy, didn't he."

"I don't know," I said. "You want to make camp or try to walk out?"

"We don't have a tent," she said.

I brought her down to the stream where I'd left Mel's pack and rifle. Looking through the pack, I found a space blanket, a few hundred feet of paracord, a flashlight and a handful of Clif Bars. I tore the top off one of the bars and held it up to April along with the half-empty water bottle.

"Eat this even if you're not hungry. I'll be back in a couple of minutes," I said.

"Don't leave me by myself," she said.

"Diva, stay," I ordered. It was mostly unnecessary as Diva was already lying on the path but out of range of Vegas' hooves.

It took a few minutes to wrap the top part of Servy's body with the space blanket and paracord, but I managed. It was grisly work, but I couldn't leave his body to the coyotes. Slinging him over my shoulder, I grunted him back to where April still sat atop Vegas.

"Hold Vegas still," I said.

"What are you doing?" she asked, skeptically.

"He needs to ride behind you. I can't carry him all the way back," I said. "That is, if you're okay with it."

"Kinda icky, but if he doesn't touch me, I suppose it's okay."

We reached the meadow where Servy had shot Hermione a little after four.

"Why are you stopping?" April asked groggily. She'd somehow figured out how to sleep while slumped against Vegas' neck, something impossible for anyone without the rubber spine of a ten-year-old. I held my hands up and she dismounted into my arms. "I'm cold."

I'd decided to wait for daylight before descending the steep hillside that led to Hudson ranch. I, for one, was exhausted and not sure I could navigate the treacherous path with April asleep atop Vegas.

I unloaded Servy's body and pulled Vegas's saddle off. I wasn't worried about him wandering off as he knew this country better than I did. Placing the saddle blanket on the ground, I helped April lie down and called Diva over to rest next to her. She fell asleep almost immediately, which gave me time to retrieve the saddle blanket from Hermione. The dead horse was a grim reminder of the toll we'd paid.

With a blanket underneath me, I turned and propped an arm under my head, draping my other arm over April and Diva to keep them warm. I would have placed a hefty bet that I hadn't fallen asleep when I sat up, hearing the *thwup, thwup, thwup* of a helicopter beating the air high overhead. I blinked at early morning sun and willed myself awake.

Apparently, State Patrol had sent their helicopter from Pawnee City. I grabbed at Mel's go-bag and dumped the contents onto the ground, hoping to find a mirror. I found something better: two smoke flares. I struck one and stood, holding it downwind of my position.

The helicopter turned back and settled into the meadow forty yards from our makeshift camp. Movement caught my eye and I saw Vegas race toward the cover of the trees, spooked by the noisy machine. He was headed toward Hudson Ranch and would likely beat us home.

April awoke to Diva vacillating between licking her face and barking excitedly. I winced as I inspected the little girl. Her hair was matted with grass, blood and parts of Servy's skull. I plucked my hat from the ground and set it atop her head.

"Don't take that off until you're in the shower," I said.

She grimaced. As a kid growing up on a ranch, she'd been exposed to a lot, but this was different. Fortunately, she seemed to understand – or maybe she just liked the feel of my hat on her head. She lifted it so it didn't cover her eyes. "I feel stuff in my hair," she said plainly.

"Don't mess with it," I said. "We'll make it go away."

I guided her toward the landing helicopter. First on the ground was Detective Cropsie, who was followed by Darlene Hudson, April's grandmother. Darlene raced across the field and stopped in front of us. I could only imagine what she thought as she took in the dried blood covering April's once bright blue coat.

"April, sweetie, are you okay?" she asked, scooping the girl into her arms. She fell to her knees, cradling April in her lap and caring little that she knocked the hat off.

"It was scary," she said. "Hermione is dead. Biggs shot her."

I swallowed as Darlene looked at me. Oddly, there was no condemnation in her face. "Oh? Why did he do that?" she asked, unwilling to release April even for a moment.

"She was hurt real bad," April said, her voice once again shuddering. "The bad man shot her. She was crying and rolling on the ground. It was horrible."

Cropsie cleared her throat, her eyes looking across the meadow to where a silver blanket was wrapped around the top part of Vuk Servy. "That him?" she asked as quietly as she could manage.

I nodded and withdrew my 1911, first ejecting the chambered bullet and then removing the magazine. Cropsie pulled out a plastic bag and allowed me to place the weapon inside. "I've processed that gun before," she said. "Maybe you should think about retiring it."

"Probably not," I said.

"You two need to be checked out at the hospital," she said. "Looks like you've got a bleeder on your shoulder. I'll have the heli take you over while we process the scene."

"This wasn't the scene," I said. "We got into it about twenty yards past Soldier Creek."

"How far is that?" Cropsie asked.

Ranger Jasper White, who I hadn't realized was on the helicopter, stepped into view. "Are you talking about where the stream crosses the trail?" he asked.

"That's right," I answered.

"That's some rough terrain. Did you make it back here in the dark?"

"I tied a marker onto a tree near where Vuk fell. There should be plenty of blood evidence. My shell casings are fifteen yards down the hill."

"We'll find it," he said and turned to Cropsie. "Location he's talking about is roughly six miles west of here. There's a clearing half a mile away where we could land a helicopter."

⊏⊐

Three days later, I found myself back in that same meadow armed with nothing more than a shovel and a pickaxe. El Chubby pawed at the dirt, nibbling at the wild grasses which grew in the bolder-strewn field. Initially, he'd been skittish at the smell of Hermione's corpse but had settled over the course of the morning.

I'd received various offers of help in digging Hermione's grave, but I'd turned them all down. I needed to deal with my unresolved feelings of guilt at how things had gone down for April and Faith. I'd been pulled away from them at a critical moment and they'd paid a heavy price – a price they'd be paying for a long time to come.

The meadow was thick with rocks and the work was back breaking. As with all tasks, however, eventually even the most difficult are accomplished. It was well after noon when I drained the last of my water bottle and looked into the hole.

Moving a animal corpse isn't a pleasant task but with a rope and El Chubby's help, it wasn't as difficult as it was grisly. Two hours later, I'd finished packing the loose dirt and rocks atop Hermione and found myself sitting on the ground, watching the sun head toward the western horizon.

The slow clip-clop of a horse barely preceded Diva barreling into me. I'd been lost in thought and hadn't seen her approach, but gladly gave her neck a good scrubbing. With Hermione's body buried, peace had been restored to the meadow. I picked up my hat and stood, turning toward Faith and April who approached, sitting atop Vegas. I didn't find it surprising that neither made direct eye contact. The last day had been filled with a lot of heavy emotions.

"Hop off, April." Faith said plainly. My eyes searched for and found the large bandage hiding the gash across her scalp. She'd tried to hide it beneath her hat, but there was only so much that could be done. A chill swept down my spine as I once again considered how close she'd come to falling to Servy's knife.

April swung a leg off the back of Vegas and slid to the ground. Gingerly, Faith followed, extracting a large bundle of flowers and wheat stalks from a saddle bag.

"Smells bad," April observed, crossing her arms in front of her chest.

I was at a loss. There was no getting around that I'd shot her horse, her friend. The fact that I'd done it because Hermione was suffering didn't seem much of a defense, especially now that we stood next to the large mound of rocks which marked the grave.

"Do you want to say something, April?" Faith asked, handing her the bundle of flowers and grain.

"Why'd you have to do it, Biggs?" April asked, tears streaming down her face.

"April, that's not fair. You know why," Faith said.

I caught Faith's eye and shook my head. This was my burden to bear. I knelt in front of April and used my thumbs to push the tears from her cheeks. Her small body shook as she quietly cried.

"Hermione was hurt," I said. "I couldn't let her suffer. It wasn't fair to her."

"You shouldn't have brought her up the hill," she said. "If you hadn't, she'd be alive."

Faith started to talk, but I held up my hand.

"That's my fault, April," I said. "I had to make a terrible choice. The man who took you was dangerous. I was scared. I needed the bravest, fastest horse."

Even as she cried, her eyebrows knit together. "You were scared?" Her chest shuddered as she tried to breath.

"Yes. If something bad happened to you, I couldn't live with myself. I'd like to believe that Hermione felt the same way," I said, remembering the abandon with which the valiant horse had raced up the hill. "She came for you."

Abruptly, April wrapped her arms around my neck. "The bad man was so angry. Vegas was tired, but he beat him to keep him moving. We ran, but you kept coming. He said you were a devil. I knew you'd save me."

I looked over April's shoulder at Faith, who stood with her frame backlit by the afternoon sun. She was a strong, beautiful woman and looked at me with a kindness in her eyes that I did not deserve and had difficulty accepting. I held April for several minutes until she finally released me.

I stood and pushed my hat, which had been knocked off in the exchange, back onto my head.

"What was Raff's part in this?" Faith asked. While she looked at my face, she still couldn't look me in the eyes.

"I'm not ..." I looked at April. I didn't want to add to the girl's burden.

"We both need to hear it, Biggs," she said. "We've lived in fear for so long. I know he was found in the ditch by our ranch and I overheard Cropsie talk about a separate investigation. She mentioned your name. Did you do something to Raff?"

I nodded. I would not hide my actions from Faith. As I started to speak, April's small hand snaked into my own. I had to bite back the thick emotion I felt at her simple show of trust.

"As part of another investigation, I discovered Raff was abusing female undocumented Mexican immigrants. He was abusive toward them, both physically and sexually. At some point last fall, he came into contact with the man who took April, Vuk Servy. It's not clear how the two communicated, but Raff gave the girls he hurt to Servy."

"Raff killed those girls?" Faith asked.

"It's not clear who actually killed the girls. ISD is still investigating. You need to know something, though," I said.

"What?" Faith asked.

"I talked to Raff as he was dying," I said. "He knew the end was coming."

"Was he sorry?" Faith asked.

I shook my head. "Raff said something that made me believe he held only contempt for those girls. It made me angry and I hit him. Knocked him out. He bled out and I did nothing to stop it."

"Why?" Faith asked.

I shook my head. "It was wrong. He was defenseless and I made a choice."

"Why are you telling me this?" Faith asked.

"You need to know the man you're getting involved with, Faith," I said. "I hit him because I was angry. I walked away and let him die. I'm not sure I would do it differently."

Faith's eyes finally met mine as she stepped into me and rested her lips against my own. "I'm glad he's dead," she said, her voice small. "I love you with every part of me. We'll work through this together."

"ISD could make something out of it."

She tipped her head and laid her cheek against my shoulder, kissing my neck and holding me tight. "We'll face it together, Biggs."

April walked away, placing the flower and grain bouquet atop Hermione's grave. I couldn't quite make out what she whispered, but I didn't need to hear the words to understand her sentiment.

The three of us stood in silence for a while as a gentle breeze blew across the meadow. "I want to ride back with Biggs," April said, after a while.

"Yeah, we should get going. Pappi said they're doing a bonfire out at Quinn Farm tonight," Faith said. "Pearl said we should come out."

I stepped into El Chubby's stirrup and swung myself up. Reaching down, I lifted April up behind me. She scooted in close and wrapped her arms around my waist. A weight lifted from my shoulders as she buried her head into my back.

"You up for it?" I asked.

"Yes!" April said. "Pappi said he was bringing out his four-wheeler and that I could ride it."

Faith and I exchanged a look at April's sudden change in mood. It was in that moment that I knew we'd be all right.

It was dark when we turned off Sage Creek road on the far western edge of the forest and onto the fresh gravel which covered the lane leading to the old Quinn farmhouse. Ownership of the Quinn farm had reverted to Pearl when she had become the sole, living heir. The farm was three hundred acres of poor, relatively dry farmland that sat adjacent to another three hundred acres of even drier ranchland she already owned. She'd already added my name to the trust in which both pieces of land were titled, so technically, I now co-owned the land with her and Pappi.

"That's a huge bonfire!" April unclipped her seatbelt and dropped her arms over the back of the Bronco's front seat. Diva pushed up next to April and took advantage of the girl's preoccupation to sneak in an exploratory face lick.

She was right. A fire that reached twenty feet in the air burned brightly, right over the spot where one of the old sheds had stood. Hanna Quinn and her boys had raised both cattle and hogs for a long time. As a result, the few remaining sheds were so polluted they no longer had any value. Burning the shed was a good start, but only the beginning of the work required to clean up the farm.

Not far from the fire, Snert and Mel's large RV was parked with its awning rolled out. Someone had strung festive lights beneath the outside edges of the material and looped the lights across to temporary posts, creating a sort of courtyard where they'd set up camping chairs and folding tables. As we got closer, we could hear the thumping of music.

"There have to be thirty people up there," Faith said as I pulled the Bronco up next to one of the dozen vehicles parked in the lawn.

"I see Reagan!" April jumped out of the Bronco before I'd completely come to a halt. Diva barked happily and followed her out the door.

I looked at Faith quizzically. "Any idea what this is all about?"

"No idea. Is that Reba Wiley?" Faith asked, pointing at the enigmatic red-haired woman who would soon be my boss.

"Morty and Denholm too," I said, opening my door and hopping out.

Pappi caught our approach, walked away from where everyone was gathered and met us halfway. Over the music, I heard muted laughter and felt disconnected. People had died. Celebrating seemed out of place. I pushed back against the depression, knowing the feelings were temporary and nothing new for me after experiencing violence of some sort. Coming back from the war in Afghanistan, I'd often wondered how people simply got on with their lives.

"Faith, I'm glad you talked him into coming." Pappi wore a friendly smile.

"More people than we were expecting," Faith said. Her voice wasn't exactly accusatory, but it held an edge.

Pappi raised his eyebrows and nodded. "Yeah, sorry about that. Things kind of blew up at the last minute. There's a lot of people who care about you guys," he said. He held out a pair of brown beer bottles, condensation dripping from them in the cool night air. "Are you hungry? There's barbequed beef on the table."

Faith looped an arm into mine as we accepted Pappi's peace offering and started walking again. Reba Wiley must have been watching because she intercepted us before we made it to the main group.

"Mind if I talk to Biggs? I won't be but a minute," she said, looking directly at Faith.

Faith looked at me questioningly. I answered with a nod. "Find me when you're done," she said.

"Quite a woman you have there," Wiley said, watching as Faith picked up Pappi's arm and walked with him.

"I'm a little surprised to see you out here," I said.

"You're not really one for small talk are you, Mr. Biggston?"

"Not really," I agreed.

"Not sure you heard, but there was a big election today." Reba Wiley smiled as she crossed her arms. She wore an off-white lacey sundress that did her justice.

"Couldn't have been that big," I said. "Way I heard it, the challenger was unopposed."

She grinned and gave me a wrinkled-nosed questioning look. "Are you telling me you didn't read the Wood Creek Sentinel this morning?"

I shook my head. "No. Can't say I did. I've had a busy couple of days."

She nodded. "Not a lot of guile behind those pretty blues. Makes it easy to underestimate you, Mr. Biggston."

Despite my exhaustion, I grinned. In Reba's universe, that was likely about the highest praise a person could receive. "Just trying to do the right thing."

"Oh, for the love of God, stop!" she said.

"Feel like you're trying to say something," I said. "What's on your mind, Ms. Wiley?"

She closed her eyes and I could tell she was trying to center herself. Something I'd said or done was driving her nuts and I suspected I was just about to find out what.

"Were you aware that the Wood Creek Sentinel called for a write-in campaign?" she asked.

I shrugged. While I hadn't read it, I'd had a couple of people mention to me that Morty and Denholm wanted people to write my name in for sheriff. I hadn't put much stock in it.

"That's just talk," I said.

"No, my dear sweet man, it is not. As of three hours ago, the polls closed. I have it on good authority that the election committee has counted votes from a majority of the precincts," she said.

My head swam with the implications of the conversation. "You're serious?" I asked, even though neither of us had vocalized those implications.

"As a heart attack," she said and stuck out her hand. "Congratulations, Sheriff."

"How about that?" Shocked, I automatically shook her hand. Looking past her, I noticed most of the people gathered were surreptitiously tossing glances our way.

"I'm not sure what I find more annoying," she said, with a lopsided grin on her face. "That I lost or that you weren't even trying."

"Didn't even know that was a possibility," I said.

"Just as well. You'd have driven me nuts with all that understated macho shit," she said. "Although between you and me it is sexy as hell."

I smiled and shook my head. I figured a change of subject was in order. "Can't imagine this'll slow you down much. What's next on your list?"

"Wood Creek Mayoral election is in six months," she said.

"Poor Herb," I said, which earned me a smile.

"Get your department squared away, Biggston. Don't make me try to find money in the budget for a local Police Department. Wood Creek can't afford it," she said.

"For what it's worth, I think you'd have made a great sheriff," I said.

"Thanks, Biggs," she said. "I'm sure we'll be talking soon enough."

But of course, that's another story entirely.

ABOUT THE AUTHOR

Jamie McFarlane is happily married, the father of three and lives in Lincoln, Nebraska. He spends his days engaged in a hi-tech career and his nights and weekends writing works of fiction.

Word-of-mouth is crucial for any author to succeed. If you enjoyed this book, please consider leaving a review, even if it's only a line or two; it would make all the difference and would be very much appreciated.

FREE DOWNLOAD

If you'd like to receive automatic email when Jamie's next book is available, please visit http://fickledragon.com. Your email address will never be shared and you can unsubscribe at any time.

For more information
www.fickledragon.com
jamie@fickledragon.com

ACKNOWLEDGMENTS

To Diane Greenwood Muir for excellence in editing and word-smithery. My wife, Janet, for polishing myriad rough passages so they are readable and kindly fixing my poor grammatical habits. I cannot imagine working through these projects without you both.

To my beta readers: Carol Greenwood, Kelli Whyte, Barbara Simmons, Matt Strbjak and Nancy Higgins Quist for wonderful and thoughtful suggestions. It is a joy to work with this intelligent and considerate group of people. Also, to my advanced reading team, you're a zany, fun group who I look forward to bouncing ideas off.

Finally, to Elsa Mathern, cover artist extraordinaire.

ALSO BY JAMIE MCFARLANE

Henry Biggston Thrillers

Privateer Tales Series

Privateer Tales Universe

Made in the USA
Lexington, KY
14 September 2019